UNSPOKEN PAST

SONIA MARANDI

Made with ❤ on the Notion Press Platform
www.notionpress.com

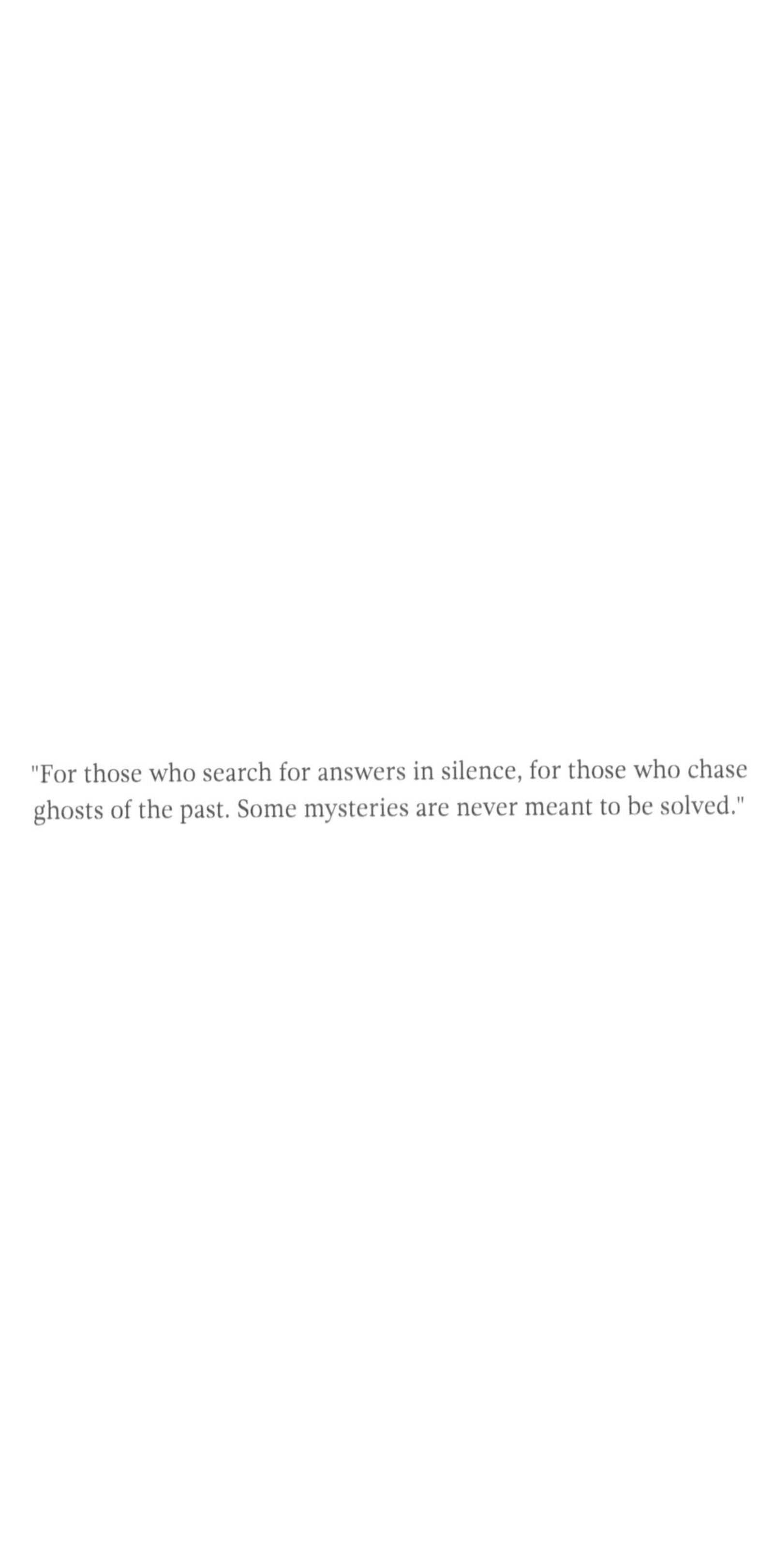

"For those who search for answers in silence, for those who chase ghosts of the past. Some mysteries are never meant to be solved."

Contents

Foreword

Some stories are never meant to be told. Some questions should never be asked.

But what happens when we refuse to let go?

This is not a story about solving a mystery. This is a story about chasing something that was lost long ago—about holding on when everything is telling you to move forward. About the weight of nostalgia, the pain of unanswered questions, and the unsettling truth that sometimes, there is no grand revelation.

This book is not just about Flynn Hayes or Skyler Maddox. It's about every person who has ever looked back, searching for something they could never get back.

The past was never missing.

It was never waiting to be found.

It was simply... gone.

But some people, like Flynn, never learn.

And so, the case begins.

Preface

People love a good mystery. They crave puzzles, unanswered questions, and the thrill of uncovering secrets. But not every mystery is meant to be solved.

Flynn Hayes thought he was uncovering the truth. That if he just looked hard enough, asked the right questions, and pieced together the fragments, he would find what he was looking for.

But what if the answer was always there? What if the truth wasn't hidden—just ignored?

Skyler Maddox didn't disappear. She didn't leave a trail of clues behind. She simply chose to walk away. And Flynn? He refused to accept it.

This is not a story about solving a case. This is a story about what happens when you chase something that no longer exists.

Some mysteries don't end with the truth. They end in silence.

Acknowledgements

Writing this book was never about telling a story—it was about understanding one. And for that, I owe my thanks to everyone who has ever questioned, doubted, or pushed me forward in ways they didn't even realize.

To the friends who supported me, the ones who stuck around, and the ones who didn't—every piece of this story exists because of you.

To every artist, writer, and storyteller who has ever felt unheard—this is for you.

And finally, to the readers: You think you're just here to watch Flynn Hayes unravel a mystery. But maybe, just maybe, you'll find a little of yourself in the pages too.

Thank you for being a part of Unspoken Past.

Prologue

The records don't exist. The name doesn't exist.

Skyler Maddox was here—and then she wasn't.

No traces. No history. No past.

It was as if someone had taken an eraser to reality, carefully removing her from every place she had ever been. The girl Flynn Hayes had known was gone, wiped clean. But people don't just disappear. Not like this.

So he starts searching. Looking for the missing pieces, convincing himself there's something to find.

Maybe if he digs deep enough, he'll understand.
Maybe if he puts the puzzle together, she'll come back.
Maybe if he just tries hard enough...

But mysteries are only thrilling until you realize the truth was never hidden.

It was just ignored.

And Flynn? He was never meant to find it.

CHAPTER I

Arrival, Silence, Departure

INTRODUCTION:

Hello! My name is Skyler Ren Maddox, I'm 15 years old. I have an older brother, Jericho Maddox. I have three best friends: Melody Roth, Monica Greene, and Selene Stone.

THINGS I LIKE:

♡ Writing, especially journals

♡ Songs, I like to listen to songs whenever I get time.

♡ I like to study Psychology

♡ Watching movies and series

♡Sculpting/Pottery

♡MY friends!!

"SKYLER!!!" There was a noise coming from downstairs. "It's 9 PM already?" After a moment, Skyler decided to head down. Everyone was seated at the dinner table, and she sat down too. "So, how's your journal? Have you written anything?" Jericho asked.

"I was going to, but Mom called," Skyler replied.

"Are you excited for tomorrow?" Jericho inquired.

"I wish! School is not my thing, and why does the break have to end so quickly?" Skyler said sadly.

"Oh, please! You'll be happy there. After all, you'll finally get to see your friends after such a long time!" her mother cheered her.

"I guess. That's the only thing I'm excited about!" Skyler admitted.

"By the way, have you read the local newspaper? It will interest you!" Jericho says happily,

"No, I haven't... What's it about?" Skyler asked curiously.

"The headline is about Hayes! He was able to solve his 38th case! I feel so proud of him!" Jericho smiles.

Skyler doesn't reply and looks at her dinner.

They continued to eat dinner.

Skyler:
Thursday
2 January, 2025
10:19 PM

Hello! Tomorrow is my school day, and honestly, I am not feeling excited about it. I didn't even finish my holiday homework! What if my teachers ask about it? I simply didn't have time to get it done. Anyway, I didn't accomplish much today because I was binge-watching that series, which is becoming really exciting! I also tried decorating my pot, but that didn't go well.

The next day, Skyler was ready for school. The school was small, with only one ground floor and two buildings. She went to classroom 11B and saw one of her best friends.

"Monica! I missed you!" she said excitedly.

"I missed you too!" Monica replied as they hugged each other.

"I can see Melody and Selene haven't arrived yet," Monica noted.

They continued chatting about the things they did during the break. Suddenly, Skyler noticed someone walking in her direction, and her expression changed to one of dismay.

"Flynn?" Monica asked.

"**Flynn Hayes. The nightmare of my dreams**. From the 22nd of March, 2021 till date, I still despise him, I gave him so many chances, and yet, he dared to come, to my classroom!? In front of MY classmates and my best friend!? I feel so embarrassed and angry. If I had got the chance, I would just jump on him and murder him!!!" Skyler thinks, and looks in the opposite direction.

"Hey, Skyler," Flynn chirps,

Skyler was barely looking at him. "No..." She says silently,

"No? No to what?" Flynn was feeling awkward, realizing this was a mistake, rethinking his decision...

"No to this conversation which you want to start. No to the melodramatic reunion you wish- NO!" Skyler says angrily, starting to lose her temper.

Everyone in the classroom heard, chattering and whispering among themselves, "Omg, what is he doing here??" "Isn't he our senior? From 12-B?" "*Weren't they used to be friends?*" "This is so awkward!!"

Flynn looks around, feeling more awkward and chuckles, "I... Okay! I mean, sure! But-"

Skyler cuts him and shouts at him, filled with rage, "You think we can just forget everything? Flynn, it's been 4 years! 4 fucking years! You can't just come back and think I can just forgive you, like- just like that?? You haven't talked to me for ages, and 'suddenly' we are 'best friends'? Please just get out of here!"

"Flynn, I don't think it's a good time right now. I don't think there's really a good time..." Monica says helplessly to Flynn.

"Sky... I thought we could talk..." Flynn says,

"Really?" Skyler scoffs, and looks and points at her classmates, "In front of them?? In front of the whole classroom??"

The classroom was filled with whispers, and some were trying to hold their laughter.

"Shouldn't have come here..." Flynn thinks, his mind filled with regrets. "Can we talk alone, then?" Flynn asks, knowing the answer will be-

"No," Skyler says and turns away.

Flynn doesn't say anything and goes back to his classroom. This was a mistake, a terrible mistake which is irreversible, this can't be changed! THIS CAN'T BE CHANGED! Every second that passes, he regrets.

"That was awfully awkward and painful!" Monica says, now sitting in their seats.

"Well, he deserves it..." Skyler replied.

Flynn:

Friday

3 January, 2025

9:45 AM

Right now, I am writing this in the school. I can't wait to get back home so I can write in my actual diary. First of all, What was that? Was that really Sky? She seems ruder than ever. I remember, 4 years ago, she was not like this! What happened in these years? What happened in this break? Or... is it her real self that I get to know now? I think something is up... I just don't know what. There's something that I don't know about. I have to make some conspiracy theories! Is she trying to hide something? Maybe, I should use my detective skills because it feels like something is bothering her, something...

-FH

12:00 PM

Flynn goes to the school book club, where he has been a member since the 7th grade. A meeting was being held. He enters a room with a signboard written, **The Hidden Chapters: School Book Club**.

It was a large room, almost as big as a classroom, there were many cupboards filled with a lot of books. The room looked quite decorated, with quotes in some corners and pictures of the members. It looked more beautiful than before. There were already eleven people, some of them standing or sitting. Flynn looked around the room, it looked different.

"Did someone change the interior? I remember this room looked like shit! What happened in this break?" Flynn asks, surprised.

"I and Nado decorated the room during the break! Even we thought it looked like shit, but you know, someone had to change it. Is it nice!?" Serena asks with a wide smile.

"Yeah, better! Loved the quotes and woah! Is that the group photo we took during 9th grade??" Flynn was amazed.

"Hayes, you are late..." Nathan says, uninterested and already annoyed.

"There's still one to come" Jordan rolls his eyes,

"Let me guess! Skyler?" Ivy asked,

Riley, the club president, rubs her forehead, frustrated. "It's been months since she had to attend a meeting. I just lost the hope of her ever coming back." Riley says.

Flynn looks at the logbook and starts turning the pages.

<u>Members who attended the meeting</u>

18th August, 2024

Riley- Riley Davenport

Noah- N. Caldwell
Skyler- Skyler M.
Ethan- Ethan Rhodes
Ivy- Ivy Sinclair

...

He turns to the next page,
24ᵗʰ September, 2024
Serena- Serena Caldwell
Nathan- Nate Holloway
Benji- Ben Torres
Mia- Mia Langley
Flynn- FH

...

17ᵗʰ October,2024
Jordan- JP
Ivy- Ivy Sinclair
Flynn- FH
Blake- Blake Emerson
Zane- Z . Lockwood

...

Flynn notices something. His face was screaming confusion.

"Skyler hasn't attended any meeting for almost 5 months? The last she did attend was on 18ᵗʰ August 2024. But- She comes to school every day, why would she skip these meetings?" Flynn felt more suspicious of her; was she hiding something? Is that why she skipped those meetings? Flynn is more determined to find it...

"Wow! Your detective skills are getting better, Hayes! She's the reason we are holding this meeting," Riley says loudly.

Benji scoffs and smirks, "Really? Wow! You know, we need not waste a meeting talking about her!"

"Benji, I understand your anger. I'm mad at her too. I'm sure most of us are mad at her. She is ruining the reputation of the club and-" Riley gets interrupted.

"There are more students who deserve her position! She is just an ungrateful bitch who thinks she is above ALL OF US, like geez,

WE GET IT! You are the real lone wolf and probably howl during the full moon! WE SHOULD KICK HER OUT," Benji says whatever comes out of his mouth, and Ivy chuckles.

"Enough, Benji! How would she feel if she heard this?" Mia asks worriedly.

"YOU REALLY THINK SHE GIVE A SHITTT?" Noah laughs hysterically.

"Nado, can you shut the fuck up. This is a book club, not your metal concert!!" Serena smiles, but we know she just wants to hide her annoyed face.

"Can I say that **'I told you so!'** Because I knew she would turn like this when none of you believed it! There's a reason why I wanted her out of the club, but no! 'Let's give her more time!' 'She's not like that' 'She will eventually come. ' It's been 10 minutes, and I don't SEE any Skyler here," Nathan finally says, letting go of what he was holding.

"Okay, and? Shall we celebrate it? *Should I bring a cake?* Serena, can you add some balloons to the room? Looks like "someone wants to be the centre of the attention and wants to be talked about, rather than the meeting for which we have all come!" Jordan rolls his eyes. Laughs were around the room. Flynn, now sitting in a chair, observes everything.

"It's better to not be involved in this. I guess they will argue for the next 10 minutes too..." Flynn thought.

The room felt more like a tea party where everyone was talking and gossiping about Skyler. Everyone had different opinions of her;

☆ Skyler is misunderstood and lost. There's STILL time for her to change her attitude and behaviour. There is still hope for her, for Skyler.

☆ Have no comments regarding this whole drama. Would rather enjoy the fire than add fuel to it. Or they disagree with her, but at least they are getting entertained.

☆ Dislikes Skyler, but there are bigger problems than this. Had enough of her...

☆ Straight up HATE for Skyler and wish to see her never again!

"Hey, Noah. Imagine, from that door," Benji said, pointing towards the entrance, "what if Skyler the Maddox comes?" He said it as if it were impossible, but is it really?

"Nah, brother that shit is impossible! And even if she comes. She will also come with her fake-ass personality of this "Silent but self-obsessed" personality. She will act all this high and mighty and then pretend she doesn't care about it. She's a coward and just trying to hide her insecurities," Noah replies.

"Coward? Oh please, I thought you could do it better. Noah, don't hold back on my account. Anyways, it seems you all miss me more than I thought. I adore it!" **Skyler said**, leaning against the doorframe and smirking.

Benji suddenly stands up from his chair, practically making him jump out of his chair. Meanwhile, Noah was glaring at her, thinking of what he said more.

"Oh, Skyler, you're finally back. I was starting to think you were too important for us now." Serena says sarcastically.

"I am!" Skyler replied. Serena becomes quiet.

Riley was not happy with the grand entrance. "Why did she bother to show up here? Come to think, it was better when she wasn't here... She's making this way harder than it has to be." Riley mutters to Serene,

Serene sipped from her water bottle, "Oh Riley. This is the start of the drama. Let her have her special princess moments before we all kick her out from here. Let's see in which direction this will go..."

Skyler walks past them and sits right between them. "Preparing my departure already? Serena, don't you think it's too soon? I think there's still time, Please let me have my special princess moments!" Skyler said cheerfully, folding her hands.

Serena scoffed at her, Riley trying not to roll her eyes in front of her.

"Do you think she changed? In these past years?" Mia asks nervously.

"Of course not! There's something else..." Blake replied tirelessly,

"I just think she's not doing this on purpose, would she? I-I just think she is lost..." Mia says quietly.

"Then why is she pushing everyone? Instead of talking about it, she is being rude to everyone. She could talk to us, right? We are still her friends!" Blake says frustratedly.

"Maybe it was not worth keeping. Keeping these people, these responsibilities, these- everything!" Skyler says seriously.

Mia stares at her blankly, as if someone took her expressions and feelings. Well, we know who that someone is... Blake half-opened her mouth and looked away.

12:36 PM

"Skyler, you have been skipping many meetings last year. You haven't participated. All the members noticed it, and we are going to keep a vote to get the decision if we should keep you or not," Riley says, defeated.

"Riley, you can't be serious! We know the decision!!" Nathan says, frustrated.

"Oh~ I wonder what I will do without my beloved "The Hidden Chapters" My life is ruined!" Skyler says mockingly.

The room was filled with surprised faces and a noisy silence.

"What? I thought she liked it here"

"Told you so!"

"She will not fight for her position?"

Now, there was chatter.

"Wait, what? Do you not care if you get kicked out?" Mia asks hesitantly, shaken and confused.

"I don't know, maybe you should vote and find out," Skyler says.

"ENOUGH! I have enough tolerated your "Peak Evolutionary Specimen" attitude long enough! I, Riley Davenport, president of the book club, declare Skyler Maddox not to be considered a member-" And before Riley finishes her speech and exiles Skyler, Skyler stands up from her place, **"Please Riley, I quit"**, and starts moving towards the door. Everyone in the room was stunned. "What... Just happened right now?" Everyone had the same thought and looked at each other.

Before Skyler can leave the room, *she glances at Flynn, who is already staring at her, but she suddenly looks away and moves away from the room, too.*

Flynn:

That- That was something. I could never imagine anyone pulling this stunt. Long story short, Skyler proved that she is the real "Miss Main Character Syndrome"

What did I learn from this?
She's hiding something HUGE, maybe some incident has happened to her? And that's what she is trying to hide.

Why?
☆ *She wasn't just avoiding the book club; she was avoiding everyone! So I'm not the only one...*

It felt like she was trying to erase her existence. Does she not want to be remembered? She's leaving questions and mysteries. Does she- want someone to find them? Someone to solve it? Is she indicating a secret message with this?

☆ *She has given up. She didn't even try to fight when she had the chance; she just left!*

So... she wants to leave everything behind; she does not want to be associated with them. (The book club and the members) It's now her past.

☆ *Didn't act frustrated or upset; she didn't care about it. Not even a single bit!*

No one can just stop caring about everything, like huh?

☆ *She wasn't just walking away from the book club. It's bigger than that. But what?" I have to find THAT incident which changed everything...*

For now, these are some clues...

CHAPTER II

The Skyler Maddox Investigation

Case #39

<u>SKYLER MADDOX</u>

Full Name: Skyler Ren Maddox

Class: 11-B

Age: 15 (Fifteen)

Height: 5'3

Birthday: 2 June, 2009

MBTI: INFJ

<u>Before the incident</u>

We were best friends...

No edgy personality

Joyous, funny, kind, happy

Very excited about books and could talk about them for hours

Loved writing, it was a part of her identity

Carries a notebook to write

Was an ACTUAL Book Club Member, friendly & helpful

Deep conversations with emotional connections towards everyone

Had a cheerful smile and often laughed

Good debater; passionately argues and defends herself

Good listener. Gives attention to people

<u>After the incident</u>

We are not less than strangers...

Edgy personality

Careless, rude, self-obsessed? Try hard to be cool

Flips book pages but does not actually read them

Hasn't written anything

Haven't seen any notebook carried (Stopped writing)

Acts like Book Club is beneath her

Cold, detached from everyone. Doesn't react much

Smirks and sarcastically smiles

No will to defend herself. Doesn't really care about anything

Interrupts them and barely pays attention

OBJECTIVE: Find THE INCIDENT

"Four years, that's how long the club members have known her. If I want a starting point, it has to be them... " Flynn watches the sky, three clouds drifting aimlessly in the blue expanse.

"Serena, Benji and Mia. Three perspectives... but only one missing truth"

Saturday

4 January, 2025

11:30 AM

Flynn goes to the book club and sits there, waiting for Serena. A few minutes later, *Noah* comes in.

"Hello, are you the one doing the interview?" Noah asks Flynn,

"Where is your sister? I am interviewing her, not you!" Flynn says angrily and stands up.

"She is busy, and that's why she has called me here. Now, look, this interview better be worth it! I had to leave my lunch break for this!" Noah sits in the chair,

Flynn, annoyed, sits too and clicks his tongue.

"So what is it about? Is it "How good are the book club members' music taste?" Interview? I have heard we will install a music system in the room. Rena says it will create a good atmosphere... I suggest we should add "Master of Puppets" by Metallica to the playlist!" Noah says.

"First of all, No. I am not here to ask about your music taste and how good Metallica is. Second, huh? Serena thought it would be a good idea to put " A Music System' in "A Book Club"??

I am here to ask you about someone..." Flynn says hesitantly.

"OHHH!! I get it! Famous personalities!! Hmmm-" Noah says cheerfully,

"... No Noah. *I am here to ask you about Skyler.*" Flynn goes silently.

Noah suddenly stands up and starts moving,

"Noah! Please wait!" Flynn shouts,

"I just remembered I have a lunch break, I have to eat. And I will not participate in this interview, nor will my sister, Noah says, seriously.

"At least tell me why you hate her so much?" Flynn tries not to let Noah leave the room.

Noah took a big sigh and sat down. "Fine!!"

"But are you not annoyed by her? If not hate her…" Noah asks,

"Should I?" Flynn asks doubtfully,

"I mean whatever happened between you two yesterday, I would be PISSED"

"Yesterday? Do you mean what happened in 11-B? How do you know? I remember you are from 11-D. Who said to you this?"

"It doesn't matter who said it to me. She just showed how cowardly she is, and to feed her ego, she fought with you. She thinks she's above everybody, she wants to be THE VILLAIN so bad! With this corny-ass behaviour, anyone will hate her. I don't know why you still like her…"

"I never said I like her. I think she is hiding something… And I am just trying to find it"

"Yeah, sure, Mr Sherlock Wannabe!" Noah says with his sarcastic tone, now leaning in his chair with arms crossed.

"And anyway, things like this spread like fire, but you know what spreads faster? **Rumour**!" Noah smiles,

"There's a rumour going on in our school? About whom?" Flynn asked, now puzzled.

"GUESS"

Flynn takes a deep breath. "What is it about?"

11:43 AM

"Flynn Hayes, the definition of narcissism. Thinks he is superior to others. An attention-seeker who thinks the world revolves around him always tries to show how great "The Great Overanalyzer" is. Acts like he gives a fuck about people but really, he just sees a benefit out of them, if helpful- might consider an alibi but if they are useless- starts acting like a bitch towards them. Sensitive to criticism. Feels jealous if

someone is at the top other than him and at last, annoying as fuck!"

"No wonder you broke your friendship with him. Who would want to be friends with SUCH toxicity?" Melody says, with an unamused face.

"Also, I have quit the book club..." Skyler stays quiet,

"WHAT!?!?" It echoed three times, and people around them stared at them,

"WHY?" Selene whispers,

"I-I thought *I didn't deserve it*", Skyler, now looking down, "I am not as good as them. I like writing journals, but when it comes to writing stories-no... Also, I want to focus on getting better at pottery," **Skyler smiled.**

Skyler:

Whatever happened yesterday, it had to occur one day. Now, I can't just stand still and wait for them to kick me out of there. IT HAD TO BE DRAMATIC. Well, at least they think I am not the Skyler I used to be. I am the "heartless Skyler" and I have to be even if I don't want to. I can't let it happen again, what happened 4 years ago...

My friends don't know what REALLY happened down the room, if they knew, they will also turn into people who hate me for acting like a bitch, and I don't want it to happen. They are the only people who care about me and don't judge me. Without their support, I can't keep up.

Flynn.... I have to do something about him. I DO NOT want him to see his face again, but I highly doubt if he will actually leave me. He will be back, and I know it... Most likely, he will try to prove his innocence.

"I need fresh air! Let's go outside!" Monica says cheerfully.

The Four get up from their seat, get out of the classroom, and start walking towards the corridor, Skyler notices him, walking in front of them. She noticed him, but he didn't. He was busy talking with Zane...

11:48 AM

"Brother, you really believe this rumour?" Flynn, now concerned with it.

"OF COURSE! Not... This is so pathetic! How could she spread truths, I mean lies! How could she spread lies about you!?" Zane says, pretending to be shocked.

"Except the last part. I think it's true..." Zane whispers,

"Huh? That's not true! I am not annoying!" Flynn defends, now feeling upset.

"Look, bro, just like I said the last time, she is doing all this for attention. Acting heartless, acting 'Too Cool for Human Interaction', this is all for some seconds of attention, she wants to be the centre of attention. With this rumour, she will get what she wants, and that's it! You need not be Inspector Clueless here! And look- If I were in your position, I would give her the opposite of what she wants; NO FUCKS. That way, you need not accomplish her whatever mission, which is to provoke you," Zane explains, his hand around Flynn's shoulder.

"Hmm... But still, this is so ridiculous! What did I do to her that she will go to this level?" Flynn rethinks.

But he saw her, looking at her, and suddenly, she smiled, probably with a smirk.

Flynn knew what to do.

"Anyways, it's just a rumour! People with no work will talk about it for a couple of days, and when they realize that it doesn't fucking matter to them, they will... just forget about it. That's what rumours are, they die out. So you don't need to worry about that much!"

"Yeah, well, in that case, this is not a fucking rumour about "What do I prefer? Books or Movies" type shit. She is literally spreading lies about me! What if someone starts believing it? What if they start seeing things from a different perspective and start acting differently towards me? The fuck will I do? Nothing?! IS THAT WHAT YOU WANT?" Flynn says angrily,

"EXACTLY! Do nothing! You don't have to prove any shit to anyone. If you really want to show everyone that you are not a toxic asshole, show them your actions, and they will automatically stop believing the rumour"

"Zane, I don't have to prove my innocence. I need to prove my innocence!"

Zane facepalms, tired of explaining things to Flynn, "Maybe Skyler was right... You just care about yourself; that's why you are so desperate to clear your name! You are sensitive as hell; you can't even take criticism! You think you are right, would you care to understand what I want to say? In your eyes, everyone is wrong except yourself. She was right about "The Great Overanalyzer" Because you are. And yes, you are annoying! Fuck you!" Zane leaves.

Flynn turns back, now directly looking at Skyler, and he goes towards her direction.

11:57 AM

"Is that Flynn? Coming towards here?" Monica asks,

"Yeah, and just now Zane left him..." Melody said,

"I guess Zane also understood how toxic he is! He looks so pissed!" Monica replied.

"We should confront him! He should regret ruining Sky's life!! Still not leaving her alone, what an obsessed freak!" Selene suggested, Monica and Melody agreed, and they started walking towards him.

"Can you please move? I want to meet your Dark, Mysterious, and Totally Not Lonely friend"

"Why should we? After everything you have done to her?" Monica says, her arms crossed.

"I don't know why you are bothering to come here and meet her again," Melody said.

"She called you a narcissist. You are just helping her prove her statement right by chasing her, Selene said.

"Please, I am not toxic, I am not narcissistic, I am not an attention seeker. I don't think of myself highly. I just want to know why she changed. Why she acts-"

"Because she owes you an explanation? Yeah, that sounds narcissistic, dude," Monica replied.

"You say you are not obsessed with her, and yet you are still chasing her," Melody said.

Flynn now starts sweating, "I-I am not a toxic asshole which Skyler thinks I am. I am not a narcissist, which she- she thinks. I care about her! I care about everyone. I don't want to be at the top! ... I never pressured her! I never used her or an- anyone." now stutters,

"I don't solve cases to rub on others' faces, I-I genuinely wa- want to help people and that's- that's why I solve so many cases..."

"If you really care about her, if you really are not the bad guy, why would she act differently around you? Why is she like this now? Selene asks,

"Oh shit...I feel like I'm barely holding myself together," Flynn thinks.

"I don't know why you are bothering to come here and meet her again. What exactly will you get?" Melody asked again.

"Because she wasn't like this four years ago! Something had happened to her! She met with some- some incident. And now she's pretending like-"
"How do you know? And what 'incident" are you talking about?" Melody asked,

"Oh..." Flynn realized that it was too late and now everyone knows what Case #39 is.

"Are you investigating Skyler!?" Selene asked,

"Flynn, not only are you toxic, you are an obsessed freak too!!" Monica declares,

Everyone around the corridor starts whispering to each other, surprised at what happened; the corridor is filled with whispers. Some were staring, some laughing. He wasn't just embarrassed, **he was officially the biggest joke of the school.**

"Skyler, let's go. Our class is beginning soon, we should head back to our classroom..."

"Flynn, instead of blaming me for spreading rumours, maybe consider looking at yourself. Maybe I was right the whole time?" Skyler asks, with a slight smirk.

The girls leave the scene.

"I should leave. I should disappear. But I can't, I know I can't. Not until I know the truth..." Flynn still standing, looking at everyone, realizing and regretting... It felt shameful being in the middle of the corridor, every eye was on him, every voice was about him. He couldn't handle it and ran away to his classroom.

"Skyler, you were right! I can't believe he's such a stalker too..." Monica said, surprised.

"Well, at least he got what he deserved. Now, he won't lay an eye on her!" Selene said.

The girls start laughing, happy about the downfall of Detective Overthinker.

Skyler:

I was right. He will come to prove his innocence. But not anymore. With this level of humiliation, he wouldn't come for a month or two. :) I should feel bad for him... How did I become so ruthless? But if I showed him my emotional side, it would not take a day to know the truth. Flynn is a good detective... I know he will notice it; I just have to hide it... As expected, an investigation on me, Case #39. That's what some are saying. He will not give up.

12:21 PM

Flynn:

This was painful. Getting humiliated in front of everyone, I became the school's biggest clown in just a few minutes. Everyone is against you, because of a fucking rumour by a bitch. But I blame myself. I could have been smarter instead of getting thrashed by three 11th graders. I could have easily avoided all these and let the rumour die out, but instead, I let my ego control me... I should have listened to Zane. He was right; he was right the whole time, and I have to apologise to him.

...

"What are you writing?"

CHAPTER III

Case #39: A Fatal Mistake

Flynn turns back and sees it's Zane!

Suddenly, he hugged him, and Zane was confused.

"I am so sorry. I am sorry for not believing you, for not listening to you when you literally gave me the best advice and instead of listening I fucked up. I let my ego use me, I was so mad at you! I am so regretful for my actions. I am sorry. I apologize for everything, for letting you down, for hating me. I totally deserved it," Flynn said, now looking down.

"Is that a tear coming from your eye?" Zane asked, Flynn wiping his tears, "No..."

Zane smiles. "It's okay. I will not say 'I told you so' like a certain someone. People make mistakes, even if it's Private Snooper Extraordinaire. What matters is that you will learn from your mistakes and reconsider why they happened. Act like a person who has already solved 38 cases! You think rationally and emotionally. Next time, think more logically and critically," Zane said.

"So what were you writing?" Zane asked, picking up his notebook,

"A diary entry. I write something in it whenever my mind is full. I like to write my thoughts..."

"Wow! I never noticed, when did you start journaling?"

"2019. Sky introduced me to it..." Flynn goes silent.

Zane smiles, pats Flynn's shoulder and goes away.

There was a silence.

"Zane is right. I have been acting like a fool and made a clown out of myself," Flynn thinks.

Then, he takes out his notebook. "Let's see what I have now..."

Case #39

<u>NOAH CALDWEL</u>

Full name: Noah Damian Caldwell

Class: 11-D
Age: 15 (Fifteen)
Height: 5'7
Birthday: 20 April 2009
MBTI: ENFP
Role in Book Club: Member- The Petty King
Relationship with Skyler: He hates Skyler, so he's not afraid to say things others won't.

Opinion on Skyler (Before & After):

Before: "She was mostly quiet. She was a decent member... Good debater, I guess?"

After: "She's a coward who wants to hide her insecurity by her corny-ass personality, and I fucking hate it"

Key Quotes:

- "I don't know why you're so obsessed with her. She's not a puzzle to solve. She's just a toxic waste of time, and you're wasting yours trying to figure her out."
- "Skyler's a coward. Always has been. She hides behind her little 'mystery' act, and everyone just eats it up. She doesn't care about you or your feelings. It's all about her, as always"

What He Might Know: Her behaviours like a need for attention and relationship with everyone, etc.

Suspicious Behavior: Trying to help Skyler by hiding some stuff? (When did this happen?)

NOTE: Noah HATES her. Might exaggerate details. Keep this in mind.

He turns the page, and takes his pen and starts writing,

Remarks on yesterday's incident

Well, how long will I be pissed on myself. All I can do is laugh at myself because I have made a complete clown out of myself, not to mention people STILL think I am a toxic-obsessed freak, but just like Zane said, I will not provoke anyone, and I do not need to prove my innocence. Honestly, I should've known better. Who needs a detective when you've got a clown for a case? I'm really out here juggling insults and trying not to trip over my own feet. I should've known. Skyler's friends? Professional comedians. Me? The punchline. I should've charged them for all the material they just got.

Things to learn:-

☆ Stop acting like a fool. You have already made fun of yourself

☆ THINK before acting

☆ Trust your instincts (Again)

☆ "You think rationally and emotionally; next time, think more logically and critically."

*☆ Start questioning things, find the reason behind them, ask **why?***
3:51 PM

"Why?? I think it's a great subject!" Skyler explains,

"You can choose something better, I don't even know what it is about..." Her mother replied.

"It's a study about mind and behaviour! It's very interesting, it's just sad that our school doesn't teach it"

"So? You will study Psychology in College and become a psychologist?"

"Yes, **forensic psychologist**!"

"What's that?"

"Those who work with criminals and learn their mind and behaviour, I think it perfectly suits me!"

"Working with criminals? Wouldn't it be dangerous??"

Suddenly, the door opens,

"What are you guys talking about?" Jericho asked as he entered the room.

"I am trying to convince mom that I want to study psychology, but she thinks it will not be helpful for me. At least I have thought of my future, unlike someone who's still confused", Skyler replied, looking at her brother.

"Woah! Where did I come from? Mom, let her do what she wants. If she is so passionate about it, maybe let her give it a chance"

Finally, their mother agreed; Skyler was now cheerful.

"By the way, would you like to join me at the book cafe?" Jericho asks,

Skyler was hesitant, trying to frame her words, "I-I can't come. I have my classes. I have to make that vase," not looking into Jericho's eyes.

"Okay, sure. I will go with someone else..." Jericho replied.

5:03 PM

"And she just makes an excuse that she has classes and goes away. I know she is hiding something. When I asked mom, even she didn't know. Chief of the Tinfoil Hat Squad, what could be it?" Jericho said, upset.

"Jeri, I also know she is hiding something; her behaviour is very obvious. Does she often skip this place?" Flynn asked,

"Yeah. It's been months since she has come here; she says it bores her... I remember she used to love this place,"
"What about Bookstores or libraries?"

"No"

That's when it hit Flynn, his first clue, a real clue,

"She's avoiding specific places. Jeri, did you see the pattern? *The book club, Book Cafe, Library, Bookstores*"

"She's **avoiding books!**? But I thought-"

"There's a reason behind them. Even I know she used to love writing, but she can't just leave it, right?"

"Yeah... Come to think about it, there are not really many books now in her room... Except for psychology books. Flynn, do you know she studies it, 'for fun"?"

Flynn was confused. "What. The. Hell?" That's what came to his mind.

Case #39

Update
Maddox does not want to be associated with books and literature.

● Avoids specific places like;

→ Book Cafe (Used to be her favourite place, according to her brother)

→ Library

→ Bookstore

→ The Book Club

• There are fewer books in her room than before.

Has a great interest in psychology

OBJECTIVE: Find out why this sudden change? Why is she avoiding it?

THEORY: Had a conflict within the book world. Possibly with a rival, teacher or a friend...

Skyler:

Saturday

4 January 2025

9:46 PM

Dear Diary, something is eating me from the inside. Is it the guilt of my actions? I don't want to care about him; he should be out of the picture, and yet, he's still in my mind. I don't- I don't feel sorry for him, and I shouldn't. I should feel guilty. But if I did, I wouldn't have done it in the first place. I HAD to spread that rumour, otherwise he wouldn't leave me. I think I have no rights to justify it, yes, it's fucked up. I shouldn't have spread it like this, but I did what I felt, what I should have done...

Flynn:

Saturday

4 January, 2025

9: 51 PM

Dear diary, what if she's right? What if I am actually OBSESSING over? What if I mistakenly prove everyone right? I mean, with my actions and my clownery, I might do something. But... something still feels off. It feels like she actually cares about everything. Whenever she wants to create a drama, she makes sure there is a crowd to witness it. She WANTS them to witness it. So, she DOES care about people but doesn't want people to have to find out... If she doesn't care about anything, why is she good at hiding things? Yeah, I am overthinking stuff. Maybe I should consider the title The Great Overanalyzer.

*Also, I have to stay underground, not get involved in big scenes...
With the rumour still surfing, I wonder what people think about me
(Probably bad things)*

*NOTE: JUST A CONSPIRACY THEORY, DOESN'T REALLY
THINK IT'S TRUE*

Monday

6 January, 2025

8: 23 AM

Flynn was sitting in his class, and noticed Zane coming towards
him,

"What's up? What are you doing here?"

"I am here to pass a news... You might not want to hear it"

"Huh?"

Zane paused and continued, "**You are suspended from the book
club**"

Flynn couldn't believe it. Him? Getting suspended? From the
book club where he spends most of his time? He stands and stares
at Zane,

"WHY? WHAT DID I DO??" Now begging for answers.

"This was Riley's decision... After hearing the rumour, she is
afraid you will also become like Skyler, you know Skyler 2.0 who
will act like a bitch. She doesn't want it to happen again, what
happened with Skyler, **"The Book Club Bloodbath" incident**, and
let's not forget **the great "Flynn's Circus of Shame"** No one wants
a clown, it's a book club not a circus... And maybe she and other
ladies are afraid of you, they think you might hurt them... And,
you are "allegedly" a toxic-stalker-obsessed-freak. That's what they
think... And it's not appropriate for the club to keep a person like
that. Also, they are not happy with your Discount Holmes
personality. Zane said, now his hands on his hip.

"Oh... I see. That fucking fake-ass rumour is now ruining
everything. I can't believe I am now distanced from the only thing
I love. From "Conspiracy Theorist in Training' to becoming "Stand-
up Comedian of the Year', I have come a long way", Flynn said,
looking down.

"Also, the club has issued some new books. I think one of them is the book you wanted for a long time…"

"The Hound of the Baskervilles by Sir Arthur Conan Doyle??"

"Yes, and apparently, Jordon is holding it. So, it will take some time for you to actually read it"

Flynn takes a deep breath and then thinks,

"Riley can't just take this decision. You all held a meeting, right? Without me. No wonder you weren't able to meet me after school; now it all makes perfect sense." Flynn smirked. "By the way, how did the meeting go? He asked.

• • •

2 days ago…

There was a chatter in the book club.

"What the hell are we doing here? Is this a book club or a gossip tea party?" Jordan asked,

"I mean, what happened on Thursday it's just evolving to that" Zane shrugged,

"Yeah, it's evolving! Just backwards… I thought we would talk about the new issued books, which Ethan and Blake brought"

"Why are we here?" Mia asked nervously.,

"To see more chaos! I heard this meeting is about Flynn," Ivy replied,

Serena rolls her eyes. "Him? First Skyler, and now Flynn? Or are we really milking this "Skyler-Flynn drama: The Pettiest Mystery"?"

"I don't feel safe around him, After hearing the rumour, he sounds like a menace…" Blake said,

"Can we go home? I have some plans!" Benji asked,

"Oh? And what exactly are your plans? I remember you don't do shit" Zane asked curiously,

"Excuse you. I have to go home and watch videos of raccoons stealing food. I have PRIORITIES," Benji replied, Zane was too stunned to speak.

"Hey, what is that?" Jordan asked,

"It's a little notebook. I like to keep some records and statistics about everyone, also, it's been 5 minutes and 22 seconds being here. Where exactly is Riley, the president?" Nathan asked,

"Can I look at your little notebook? Have you kept records on me?" Jordan asked,

He then takes the notebook,

<u>*JORDAN PIERCE*</u>

? Participation Rate: 5% (May as well be a guest appearance.)

? Engagement Level: Almost nonexistent.

? Typical Behavior:

Sits in the back. Arms crossed. Judging silently.

Occasionally drops one sarcastic comment that destroys someone's entire life.

? Notable Traits:

Selective Engagement: Only speaks if it's absolutely necessary—or if he can ruin someone.

Resting Unimpressed Face: Looks like he regrets showing up.

? Most Likely to Say: "Cool. Can I leave now?"

? Greatest Weakness: Books that secretly make him feel things. He will never admit it.

? Potential for Chaos: 8/10. (It could be higher if he actually cared.)

? Final Notes: "Jordan is a wild card. He could either be the smartest person here, or he could be thinking about what to eat later. Unclear."

<u>Books he likes (I have seen him reading them)</u>

Satire & Dark Comedy

Philosophical Fiction

Psychological Thrillers

Books That Aren't What They Seem

<u>Books he dislikes (Doesn't have strong opinions for them)</u>

Overly Dramatic Romance

Books with Obvious Morals

Generic Action Thrillers

Fantasy with Excessive Worldbuilding

"Oh, wow! These are some... stalking level stuff. Even I didn't know some of these things... Are you stalking everyone here? I think Flynn is not the real stalker in this club," Jordan said, glancing at Nathan.

"Please, don't turn-"

"Should I Bring a Cake? The Words That Changed My Life"

Date: 3 January, 2025- The Darkest Day

Event: I get absolutely obliterated by Jordan Pierce.

Context:

I was trying to say to the members that I already knew Skyler would do something like, and I was trying to kick Skyler out for months. I knew this day would come and that's what I was warning people about. But then, Jordan—who never speaks unless necessary—just casually dropped the "Should I bring a cake?" line.

Roast Impact: 9.8/10

Notes for that day:

"Everything was normal. Then—betrayal."

"Jordan Pierce has never cared about anything, yet today, he chose violence."

"The roast was so fast, so casual, that I could not recover."

"The club laughed for too long. Zane might have fallen off his chair. Riley nearly choked. My reputation is in ruins."

"I have lost control of the room."

'Aftermath' Tracking:

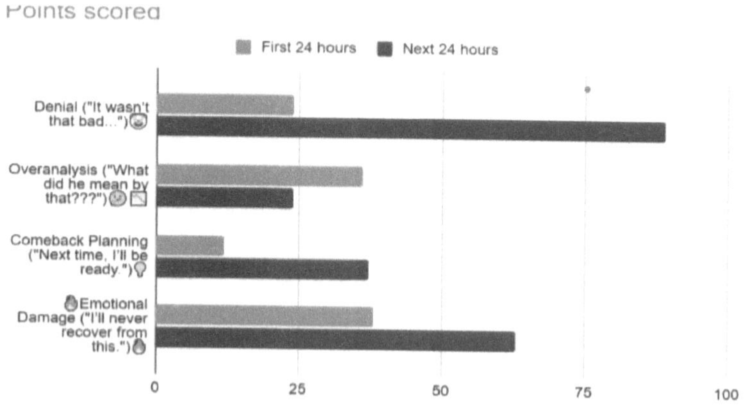

Book Club's Reaction:

Riley: DEAD from laughter.

Zane: Somehow made it worse by repeating the joke to EVERYONE, wheezed for 48 seconds straight

Serena: Took one sip of her drink and just nodded like Jordan had spoken divine truth.

Benji: Made it his entire personality for a week.

Jordan's Behavior After the Roast:

Participation Rate: Back to 0%. The man delivered his hit and walked away like nothing happened.

Engagement Level: "Minimal. Possibly satisfied with his work. I fear he has more in store."

Revenge Potential: "If I try to clap back, will he drop another nuke? Unclear. Proceed with caution."

Final Note on Jordan:

"Jordan Pierce is not loud. He does not yell. But when he speaks, he destroys. I must never underestimate him again."

"SHIT I'M SO FUCKED. CODE RED, WE'VE BEEN COMPROMISED," Nathan thought.

"EXCUSE ME???" Jordan surprised,

Now, everyone is looking at Jordan and Nathan, and it looks like a new chaotic duo has arrived.

$$\bullet \ \bullet \ \bullet$$

8:39 AM

"What the hell, Zane? I thought I was going to listen to how everyone hates me and then kicked my ass out of the club and not to listen to this **"The Nathan-Jordan Cold War"** Flynn asked, leaning back to his chair, and arms crossed.

"Hey! This Cold War is more interesting and juicy than your boring-ass exile. This is more important now," Zane shrugged.

"You will tell me Nathan's breakdown than what I ACTUALLY want to hear?"

"Yes, correct"

Flynn sighs, "Omg, unbelievable. Truly. The betrayal."

"And yet, you haven't stand up and slapped the shit out me! From which I will just conclude: **You want the tea**"

"I refuse to confirm or deny that"

"Mhm. So Nathan had a full-on existential crisis after Jordan roasted him. Like, actual 48 hours of psychological damage." Zane smirked.

"Tsk. Should've been me witnessing that live." Flynn was trying his best not to look interested.

"You would've made it worse."

"Exactly." Flynn grinned and chuckled.

"Anyway, Jordan just found out about Nathan's 'Emotional Damage' chart, and let's just say, Nathan's panicking. Hard."

"Nathan? Panicking? Over being exposed? Say it ain't so." Flynn said, feigning gasping.

"His face was literally saying, "At this moment, he knew, he fucked up"

"NO WAY—" Flynn choked on his laughter.

"Jordan hit him with the 'Excuse me???' and now, boom. It's war."

"A new chaotic duo is born." Flynn nodded.

"And somehow, you're not involved."

"The injustice. The pain. The suffering," Flynn said with his dramatic sigh,

"Shut up."

"Tell me more."

• • •

"I just said one sentence. One. Sentence. And this man just built a conspiracy board about it??" Jordan thought, at first, was confused.

"...Nathan. What. The. Hell is this? What am I looking at?" Jordan asked, staring at him,

"A factual, data-driven analysis of recent events." Nathan, pretending not to care,

"He really thought I was out for blood. That's crazy." Jordan thought, now amused with the research.

"A bar chart tracking your emotional damage?"

"Yes." As if this is nothing new.

"And why are there fire emojis near 'EMOTIONAL DAMAGE'?"

"For accuracy."

"...Why is 'Denial' so high in the next 24 hours?"

"BECAUSE I KEPT REMINDING HIM!" Ivy replied, dying out of laughter.

"You do realize I forgot about this like five minutes after it happened, right?"

"Well, I didn't."

"Clearly."

"9.8 out of 10, huh? Damn. Maybe I should say stuff more often." Jordan thought, he got a little smug.

"Bro, you have 'Comeback Planning' on here—WHERE IS THE COMEBACK??" Benji asked, looking carefully at the chart.

"Still in development."

"You're not gonna win this, man."

"You are the one who snatched my notebook. So, technically, you were the one who went looking for it. Why? Hm? Feeling guilty?"

"...Nathan, this entire chart is about ME roasting YOU."

"And yet... YOU'RE the one thinking about it now. Looks like I win."

"That's not how this works."

"Wait, wait—are you trying to flip this and make JORDAN look obsessed?" Benji asked,

"I don't TRY, Benji. I DO." Nathan replied.

"I just collect data, okay? It's for accuracy!" Nathan said,

"Yeah? And how accurate is your social life? 0%?" Jordan asked,

"OH, COME ON," Nathan replied.

• • •

8:46 PM

"WAIT. WAIT. HOLD ON. THIS HAPPENED?? AND I WASN'T THERE???" Flynn was surprised.

"Yeah, bro. You missed it." Zane replied.

"THIS IS A TRAGEDY. A NATIONAL DISASTER. A MISSED HISTORIC EVENT. "WHAT IF? WHAT IF HE MADE A DATA ON ME TOO??" Flynn acting curious.

"Calm down, You're not the main character in EVERY disaster." Zane rolled his eyes.

"But... where is Riley? Didn't you discuss me? Where is the part where everyone votes me off?" Flynn asked, confused.

"OHH, RIGHT!" Zane smiled., "Riley actually had some work, so she didn't come"

"WHAT THE FUCK! You could have easily skipped all this stuff!?? If you didn't vote me off in school, then where? In the fucking group chat??"

"Yeah... Also, I wanted to talk about the gossip; don't pretend you didn't enjoy it"

Flynn folding his hands, "PLEASE!! Just tell me what I want to hear"

"Fine!! We got to know that Riley had already left, and we were just watching and creating a soap-opera of our own in the book club. Then, everyone left. When we reached home, we got a text from her,"

• • •

THE LITERARY COURTROOM

@FinalBossReads: Yo, I'm busy. Can we just vote Flynn out over text?

@PlaysChessNotCheckers: Girl, where were you? You missed a whole lot of tea!

@FinalBossReads: Oh! You mean The Nathan vs Jordan Cold War. yeah, that was hilarious. XD XD

@StirringThePot: XDD

@FrontRowForChaos: Riley, WHERE WERE YOU?? Why did you just leave 10 people?

@FinalBossReads: I don't know. I just didn't feel like it.

@TiredButTrying: RILEY, YOU HAD ONE JOB

@CertifiedChaos: Dude, chill

@DataOrPerish: Group decisions don't require in-person meetings if the majority agrees.

@FrontRowForChaosr: LMAOOO, not him getting kicked out over text. That's so tragic.

@TiredButTrying: Do we really need to kick him out? He's just... you know... going through something.

@FinalBossReads: We ALL are, Zane.

@PlaysChessNotCheckers: Zane, just because you are his friend doesn't mean you have to defend him. Everybody knows he's wrong.

@CertifiedChaos: I say we keep him. He's funny. What will we do without him?

@SoftHeartedButNosy: Can't we just... talk to him first?

@PlaysChessNotCheckers: Nah, let's make it interesting. Let's vote anonymously so he won't know who betrayed him.

@DataOrPerish: "It wouldn't be anonymous. I track all responses."

@ShouldIBringACake: "Why is this even a discussion? He's gonna spiral either way. Let's just tell him he got kicked out for *vibes*.

@DataOrPerish: Jordan, what is this username??

@Certfied Chaos: Can we do this fast? I need to watch Love Island, and the notifications are getting annoying

@LowkeySkylerStan: You watch Love Island?

@StirringThePot: Who the fuck is this? What do you mean by "LowkeySkylerStan"? I thought this group was anti-Skyler.

@FinalBossReads: OK. I'm making the poll.

[Poll: Should we remove Flynn from the club?]

Yes – 5 votes

No – 3 votes

I don't care – 3 votes

@MainCharacterEnergy has been removed by @FinalBossReads

@LowkeySkylerStan: Wait, did he actually get removed just now?

@FinalBossReads: Yup. Efficiency, people.

@StirringThePot: Bruh.

• • •

8:56 AM

"So you're telling me—let me get this straight—I WAS **VOTED OUT IN A DAMN GROUP CHAT**??"

"Yeah."

"I GOT VOTED OUT LIKE A DAMN REALITY TV SHOW CONTESTANT??"

"I mean... yeah."

"AND I DIDN'T EVEN GET TO SEE IT??"

"Nope."

"DO YOU KNOW HOW MUCH MENTAL SUFFERING I COULD HAVE CAUSED IF I KNEW??"

"...That's your takeaway?"

The bell rings,

"And this is my cue to leave!" Zane said and went back to his classroom, waving to Flynn.

Flynn sits in his seat, thinking about EVERYTHING he just heard, "Man, What The-"

9:16 AM

Skyler:

I have just heard it. Flynn Hayes has officially been suspended from the school book club. And the reason? It's me! :) I knew the rumour was worth it; if the members hate me, they should hate him too. It's funny how things work out. One second, Flynn is chasing me down, the next? He's getting banned from his own club. Poetic justice. My next step? Hmm...

11:15 AM

Flynn was holding a paper, looking at it...

"I read the message again. And again. And again. There it was, in plain text: Flynn Hayes is officially suspended from the book club. For misconduct. Misconduct. As if I burned the damn library down." Flynn thought.

Ravenshore Academy

Date: 6 January 2025

To: Flynn Hayes

Subject: Official Suspension from the Book Club

Dear Mr. Hayes,

After careful consideration, the Book Club Committee has decided to suspend your membership effective immediately. This decision follows a series of incidents that have disrupted the club's environment and violated community guidelines.

Your suspension is based on the following:

1. Excessive Interrogation of Members – The club is for book discussions, not investigative crime scenes.

2. Unapproved Independent Investigations – Your relentless pursuit of irrelevant mysteries has interfered with our scheduled activities.

3. Causing Unnecessary Chaos – Multiple witnesses reported dramatic outbursts, overreactions, and questionable conspiracy theories.

4. Disturbing the Peace – Your reaction to recent club developments was described as "borderline feral."

5. The General Consensus Is That You Are "Toxic"– A club-wide discussion has led to the collective agreement that your presence is currently more disruptive than beneficial. Reports indicate that you have been fueling unnecessary drama, and there is a growing rumor that you might, in fact, be the root cause of 90% of our problems.

As a result, you are banned from attending meetings, accessing club materials, or contacting members under club-related matters.

Your suspension will be reviewed at a later date (if we feel like it). If you wish to appeal this decision, you may submit a formal written statement detailing why you should be reinitiated. However, considering your track record, this is unlikely to be successful.

Sincerely,

The Book Club Committee

Riley Davenport, President

Nathan Holloway, Statistician (and Keeper of Receipts)
Serena Caldwell, Chaos Manager

CHAPTER IV

Rumors, Records & Regrets

Monday

13 January, 2025

9:02 AM

"Flynn Hayes? Is that him?" The students start whispering, "OMG! It is him!!"

"Damn, the detective's still at it. What's next, breaking into her house?"

"So he can prove he is a stalker, AGAIN!?!?"

"No, bro, he already got suspended once. Give him a week, he'll break into the library and steal the Ghost of Skyler Maddox files."

Flynn:

Is this real? Why are people looking at me? I haven't made any move for a week. I want to let the rumour down, but it feels like it's still up. I haven't talked much with people. Especially with the book club's members. And yet, I still saw people staring at me, whispering with each other. Is it my imagination? Or is the rumor still alive?

People stared at him,

"The Great Overanylzer"

Flynn looks back but no one was there, "What the fuck?" He thought,

Someone comes to him, "So... you really stalk Skyler?" The student asked,

"Huh? What?" Flynn asked

"Do you really stalk Skyler?" She asked again,

"Yeah, sure. I stalk her, and you all just sit there, waiting for someone else to do the dirty work. I'm not the one who ran away, am I? Think before you throw around words you don't understand." Flynn grinned.

"..."

Flynn walks out and then gets bumped into someone,

"Sorry, brother. Oh wait- never mind" He looks at Noah.

"What happened? Missed me?" Noah asked mockingly.

"You will be the last person I want to see", Flynn said.

"Ouch! That hurts!" Noah mockingly gasps.

"Why'd you spread that rumor?"

"Oh, I didn't. I just made sure it spread faster."

"...What's your problem with me?"

"I dunno. You're fun to mess with."

And Noah walks away, "The fuck is `his problem? 'You're fun to mess with' am I his fucking toy?" Flynn rolls his eyes

"FLYNN!" Someone shouts,

"Not again?" Flynn turns around and IMMEDIATELY starts walking away,

"HELLO??" **Benji** starts chasing him.

He finally catches up to him and looks around.

"What are you trying to see? Skyler?" Flynn asked,

"I am not afraid of her!"

"Please, I have seen you getting scared as shit whenever she comes to your radius. Like, bro, are you okay? Has she done anything to you?" Flynn asked, concerned.

"Have you seen her? She totally acts like Orochimaru from Naruto. A MENACE TO SOCIETY"

"Who?"

"Or Kishou Arima from Tokyo Ghoul. Although he is an investigator, the investigator I know is not like him..."

Flynn goes silent, crossing his arms, "Benjamin Torres, what the fuck do you want with me?"

"Hmmm... You know, yesterday, I thought a lot about this, like a lot!"

Benji:

Man... I have been thinking a lot about the exile of Flynn Hayes. I still remember when the bloodbath occurred, bro didn't give a fuck about anything, like literally! He was acting like Tobi from Naruto, Uchiha Obito for those who don't know (Bro's not L from Deathnote)

And seeing it, I feel bad for him. Not to mention, I mistakenly voted him out. :|

"WHATT??? YOU VOTED ME OUT??? I could have actually been saved! You asshole!"

"CHILL!! IT'S FOR THE PLOT"

"FOR THE PLOT??"

"Also... I didn't notice! Look, bro, I was literally binge-watching Love Island at that time. Can you blame me for it being so interesting! I just mistakenly pressed it. And I didn't think they were actually serious, I thought we were just gossiping..."

"I could have been saved, you know!"

"Oh, please?! RILEY HATES YOU, she didn't give a second-thought to kick out Skyler, you think she cares about you? She had her suspension letter ready for you. Also, can you continue reading my note?"

That's why to make up with him, I will help him!
Why you may ask? I hate Skyler, he (probably) hates Skyler

Negative+Negative=Positive

:D :D

"Do you think we are Sherlock Holmes and Dr. Watson? What the hell is this? Also, when did you start writing letters? You are a type of guy who is always like, 'I'll pass without studying, I've got this,' then wonders why his grade is a disaster." Flynn rolls his eyes,

"Fine! I just wanted to use the Pacifico font... I wonder why I got such beautiful handwriting"

"Pacifico font? Are you seriously trying to justify using a comic font in a letter? And you wonder why you're a walking disaster?" Flynn rubs his forehead, trying to suppress a smirk. "Who even wonders about their handwriting in this situation? What is this, a damn love letter to yourself?"

"Can't believe I'm stuck dealing with this. You all saw that, right? This is the guy I'm supposed to work with now. Seriously." He mutters.

"EXCUSE ME? You think I'm the one with bad handwriting?" Benji snatches Flynn's notebook.

"Pacifico is a masterpiece, unlike your chicken scratch, and what is this name? Patrick Hand? You can't even read it after 10 minutes!"

Then he leans in with a mischievous grin:
"You know what? At least I don't procrastinate until my grade looks like a disaster—wait, never mind, that's YOUR whole vibe."

Flynn stares blankly, but Benji is not done. He's warmed up now. "You talking about not studying is rich, Flynn. You spend half the time solving mysteries that don't exist, then come at me about grades? If anyone's failing, it's you in the real world. Maybe if you didn't get so lost in your own drama, you could ace an actual test!"

He throws a finger up like he's just dropped a mic.
"You may be the investigator, but I'm the life coach you didn't ask for."

"WOAH!! I was just trying to make a joke! Remember I am the Circus Headliner-Without trying, right? And if you have so much of a problem with me then fine! I will find another Dr. Watson for me, I will just solve it alone."

"Oh, so you think you can do this ALONE? Let me remind you—your last solo plan got you suspended and turned you into a meme."

"..."

"Face it, buddy. You're a mess. You need someone with actual brain cells—"

"And you think that's you?"

"No, but I have vibes. "

They go near a tree and sit down,

"What is this? Or are we really going to have our interview here? Why does Noah get to get interviewed inside the book club? Oh wait, that was before **The Flynn Hayes Fiasco: Suspension Edition" incident"**

"Are you here to insult me?"

"Ok fine! Let's start the interview, I am very excited!"

"Alright, Benjamin Torres—"

"Oh, we're using government names? That's wild."

"Shut up. You're a prime suspect in the Skyler Maddox case, and I need answers."

"Bro, am I getting arrested? Do I get a lawyer? Can my lawyer be a stuffed animal? Like one of those emotional support ones?"

No, you don't get a lawyer. Just answer the damn questions."

"Fine. But if you try waterboarding me, I'm telling the principal.

"What do you think about Skyler?"

"I think Skyler is a menace to society. And I am actually scared the shit out of her"

"So, that's why you turn around every minute?"
Benji was looking somewhere else, "Huh? Yeah?"

"Are you concerned about her? Do you think she is a lost cause?"

"As long as I am away from her and she is away from me, I might be okay? And I don't know about "lost cause" but she's totally a lost bitch"

"What do you know about Skyler's disappearance from writing and the book club?"

"Oh, bro. That's easy. She stopped writing because she didn't want to write anymore."

"...That's literally the worst answer possible."

"Yet, here we are."

"Did she ever mention why? Any hints? Any signs?"

"Maybe she hated words. Maybe they offended her. Maybe one day she looked at the word 'moist' and decided she couldn't do this anymore."

"Benji. I am one sentence away from beating the shit out of you!"

"Okay, okay, chill. Lemme think." There was a dramatic pause as he sipped his energy drink, "Nope. Got nothing."

"You are the most useless person in this investigation."

"And yet, I'm the one having fun."

"BENJI. Take this seriously."

"Fine, fine. I did hear her say something about feeling 'pressured' or whatever. But like, aren't we all? I feel pressured every day to wake up and go to school. Do I get a case file?"

"Okay, hold on. She said she felt pressured? By whom?"

"I don't know, man. Society? The book club? The laws of gravity?"

"BENJI."

"Bro, I SWEAR I don't know. Maybe she just wanted to be dramatic and leave the writing scene with a bang. Like those actors who announce their retirement, and then three months later, they're in another movie."

"I don't believe you are scared of her just because 'you just think she's like Orochimaru or Kishou Arima' Tell Benjamin Torres, what are you hiding?" Flynn asked doubtfully.

Benji stands and starts clapping, "My My! So people were right, you are an actual detective who solved 38 cases!!"

"Flynn raised his eyebrow with a little smirk, "So...?"

• • •

3 years ago...

"Have you seen the fire in the school?" Noah asked,

"NO! I HAVE TO SEE IT!" Benji replied,

"Why are you both acting like you have never seen a fire?" Jordan asked, uninterested.

"Okay, but fire inside the school?" Noah said. "You have to see it!"

"Chill, Nado! They are just burning some stuff, it's not some cult ritual which Benji will see," Serena said.

"What if I go and see it?" Benji asked.

After school, Benji went near the fire. He was surprised, his eyes getting wide...

"What are you doing here?" Benji asked,

She stared at him,

"Are you burning your books? Look, if you don't want those books, then donate them to the book club, I might read them- Wh-AAAAAAAH!!!"

• • •

"And then *she* chased you?" Flynn asked, feeling weird out. Benji nodded.

"Her eyes locked onto me, and I swear, for a second, she didn't blink. Not once. She just stared—like she was deciding if I was worth hunting down or not."

"So what I'm hearing is, *Skyler* is either a cryptid or a demon," Flynn asked, half-jokingly,

"Yeah, well, either way, I'm not taking any chances. I haven't told anyone about this because I am embarrassed... I am surprised you noticed it!" Benji was impressed by Flynn.

"Okay. Interview's over... I think the interview went longer than it should have been. Thanks to your unnecessary comments." Flynn stood up.

"Well, someone had to make this chapter lengthy," Benji replied.

"Can I see my bio-data?" Benji stood up too.

Case #39

<u>BENJI TORRES</u>
Full name: Benjamin Rafael Torres
Class: 11-A
Age: 15 (Fifteen)
Height: 5'6
Birthday: 27 August, 2009
MBTI: ESFP
Role in Book Club: Member- Walking Meme
Relationship with Skyler: He is afraid of her, yet dares to talk trash about her

Opinion on Skyler (Before & After):
    Before: "Her silence scares me."
    After: "Her silence scares me."
    Key Quotes:

- "Listen, man. Some people just vanish, like my homework. Maybe she's in another dimension. Maybe she's just avoiding you. Both are valid theories."

- "Skyler's not some deep, unsolvable mystery, Flynn. She's just a person. A really, really petty person, but still a person."

What He Might Know: The day when he saw Skyler burning her books.

Suspicious Behavior: Notices small things and seems very observant of his surroundings.

NOTE: Benji is afraid of her. Interesting. And funny.

"Back to business, Flynnathaniel Percival Hayesington III" Benji smiled.

"What now?" Flynn annoyed.

"Flynn, my guy, my best friend, my brother in mystery-solving…"

"No."

"Hear me out—every great detective needs a sidekick. Sherlock had Watson. Batman had Robin. Scooby-Doo had Shaggy."

"…That last one feels incorrect."

"DO YOU WANT TO BE A LONELY LOSER DETECTIVE? Because that's what's happening right now. You NEED me."

Why would I need you?"

"Because, unlike you, I actually talk to people. You'll scare them off with your detective monologues, and that's where I swoop in—charming, charismatic, distractingly good-looking—"

"Debatable."

"Irrelevant. The point is, you investigate, I cause controlled chaos. I make the distractions, you get the answers. It's a foolproof system."

"…The 'controlled' part worries me."

"Look, man. You're spiraling. And I love that for entertainment purposes, but you need a plan. I, Dr. Benjamin Watson, will be your guiding light."

"You just made that up."

"EXACTLY. Look how creative I am. This is what I bring to the table."

Benji tears a page from Flynn's notebook and starts writing something. A few minutes later, he shows it to Flynn. Flynn sighed and signed it.

OFFICIAL SIDEKICK CONTRACT

(Because Every Great Detective Needs a Watson)

Contract Between:

Detective Flynn Hayes (Main Genius, Clown-in-Charge)

Dr. Benji Watson Torres (Sidekick Extraordinaire, Chaos Enthusiast)

Terms & Conditions:

1. Benji is the Official Watson

Flynn must acknowledge Benji's superior sidekick skills.

If questioned, refer to him as "Dr. Torres".

2. Equal Partnership (But Not Really)

Flynn does the boring detective work.

Benji handles the fun parts (aka chaos, distractions, and occasional genius).

3. Mandatory Snack Breaks

Investigations must pause for food, memes, or anime discussions.

No exceptions.

4. Dramatic Narration Clause

Benji reserves the right to narrate all of Flynn's failures.

Bonus points if dramatic gasps and Sherlock quotes are included.

5. Skyler-Related Shenanigans

Benji will absolutely not be responsible for any bad ideas suggested (but still expects credit if they work).

6. Emergency Exit Clause

If Flynn ever denies Benji's sidekick status, the contract self-destructs (not really, but Benji will be SO offended).

7. Code Name Policy

Flynn is "Holmes" (but only when Benji says so).

Benji is "Dr. Watson" (non-negotiable).

8. NO BETRAYAL CLAUSE

Flynn CANNOT replace Benji with another sidekick.

If he tries, Benji has full legal rights to be as dramatic as possible, including but not limited to:

Yelling "TRAITOR!!" in public.

Filing a Fake Lawsuit for emotional damage.

Leaving cryptic notes saying, "You were my Holmes :(".

Writing a tell-all memoir about Flynn's failures.

(Benji gets 40% credit in case of book/movie deal)

Signed:

Flynn "I-Can't-Believe-This" Hayes

Benji "I-Wrote-This-in-Pacifico-Font" Torres

"You are literally insane!!" Flynn shouts,

"Nah, I am legally your problem now" Benji replied.

"So, as the first day of being Dr. Watson. I will suggest you one method to find more clues; Let's **break into her locker**! I don't think she will mind that..."

"WAIT, WHAT??"

"Bro, you'll get the answers, I promise. She'll be mad at first, but hey, mystery solved!"

"She will literally kill me with her eyes!"

"Fine, wear sunglasses, what's the big deal!?"

"I looked at Benji. I looked at the contract. I looked at my life choices. I was so screwed." Flynn thought.

"What if Skyler isn't real? Like, what if she was a government experiment and they just erased her memory because it was getting too close to the truth? And now there's a Skyler who is not less than Yoshikage Kira who is just trying a way to hunt us!!"

"Bro, what if this is all a social experiment? Like, we're all just characters in someone's book, and none of this is real—"

"Shut the hell up!"

Flynn:

Monday

13 January, 2025

10:17 PM

I should've known. I should've known the moment I signed that contract. That my life was over.

After that, he's already derailed the investigation by asking if Skyler secretly has a twin. Ten minutes in, he's theorizing that she faked her death. Fifteen minutes later—fifteen—and I am now complicit in whatever absolute nonsense is about to unfold.

This is it. This is how I go. Not by solving a grand mystery, not by uncovering the truth, but by slowly losing my sanity next to a man who binge-watched Love Island instead of saving me from exile. I've spent years solving real mysteries. Thirty-eight cases. And yet, my greatest downfall? Signing a contract written in Pacifico font.

I have made a critical error in judgment. A miscalculation of catastrophic proportions. I should be solving this mystery, but instead, I am babysitting a menace to society WHO CALLS OTHERS A MENACE TO SOCIETY with the attention span of a squirrel on caffeine. I am so so so fucked...

Case #39

Update

Skyler was seen burning her books in the fire by Benji.

Probably, that's how the books in Skyler's room have gone missing without anyone noticing.

Maddox does not want to be associated with books and literature.- CONFIRMED

Three years ago, on 22 February 2022: Chased Benjamin down, starting of this "The Dark Academia Dream" personality starts.

NEW OBJECTIVE: Learn more about her psychology world.

CHAPTER V

Seen, But Never Understood

Tuesday

14 January, 2025

12:03 PM

Flynn and Zane have sat near a tree, they could see the students of class 11-B.

"I swear 11-B gets some unnecessary free periods! I have seen them the fourth time today!" Flynn said.

"Hey... Notice **"The Attention Seekers' Club"**

"Really? You are gonna call them that?"

I will call them whatever I want. And unlike you, I will not make a clown out of myself," Zane said. "Do you notice something? Skyler shows a lot of gestures! Exaggerated to be specifically named."

'What do you conclude?" Flynn is getting interested in it.

"What if... *she is doing this for attention*? There's no real meaning behind this, and just a try-hard attention seeker? She tries so hard to be the focus of the conversation. If you look closely, she always talks half of the time. And when her friends talk, she makes exaggerated gestures and frequent eye contact as if she would kill them for stealing her spotlight. Sometimes making flamboyant or erratic movements. These are just some noticeable physical traits of an attention seeker."

"What do you want to prove with this?"

"The Attention Paradox Theory"

"The fuck is that?"

"Attention is a strange thing—it doesn't work the way you'd expect. On one hand, if you constantly chase it, you often end up pushing it away. People get tired of the constant performance and start tuning you out. But on the other hand, when you don't try for attention at all, you end up drawing more of it toward you. It's like the universe has this weird balance: the harder you chase something, the further it slips away. But the more you ignore it or act like you don't need it, the more it comes to you, almost without you realizing. That's the paradox—the more you seek attention, the less you get, and the less you try, the more you attract. It's a flip of the same coin." Zane explained, almost sounding like a philosopher, "It's like the paradox of seeking validation or the law of attraction"

"Wait, what?" Flynn started overthinking,

"So does that mean it applies to everyone, right? Okay, let's see:-

1. Skyler

Okay, so Skyler thrives on drama and needs validation all the time... Zane's theory says that she's missing something, right? But what's she missing? Attention? Validation? Control? Wait, no. She used to write. Maybe it's that she needs to feel important, like her work actually matters. But she's always so dramatic about everything. She could just be... testing us. Is she manipulating the group to make herself the center of everything? Or is she just... lost? Damn it. This doesn't make sense.

2. Flynn (Myself)

Okay, if I'm so obsessed with solving mysteries... and I keep putting myself at the center of everything... Is that because I need to feel important? But no, I'm not like her. I'm different. I'm a detective. I just need to know the truth; that's all. Or wait... What if Zane's right? What if I'm just using this 'detective' thing as a way to fill some void in me? Am I just like Skyler? Oh god, no, that can't be true... I'm not some attention-hungry drama queen... Am I?

3. Riley

Riley doesn't like being in the spotlight, but... does that mean she secretly wants it? She hates it when I take over the group, but maybe it's because she doesn't want to seem like she needs the attention. Maybe she feels threatened by me. Or is it the opposite? Does she crave attention but refuse to admit it? Wait, no. She's too proud for that. But pride is just insecurity, right? I'm just trying to figure out her... no, no, this is too much. I can't keep doing this.

4. Zane

Okay, Zane's the one who introduced the theory, but is he the one who's most aware of it? Does that mean he's secretly trying to control us all? No, no, he's not that smart. Or wait—maybe he is. Maybe he just pretends to be all chill because he knows the group is too busy with their own drama to see him as a threat. So he is manipulating things, just in a quieter way. But if he's right, then... am I being manipulated by everyone? Am I the one who's missing the real truth here?"

Flynn was too stunned to speak and still overthinking,

"Wait, Zane's theory isn't just about attention—it's about the essence of people's desires, their very core! What if this is the key to understanding everything? Everyone's actions, all of it—whether it's drama or detachment, attention or avoidance—it's all about filling some void. The question isn't why people act the way they do. The question is: What are they really missing? This is bigger than any mystery I've ever solved... And if I can figure this out, I'll know how to fix everything. But what if the problem is... me?"

"Hello? Mr. Overthinker, is your inner monologue over?" Zane asked,

"Huh?"

12:15 PM

Skyler was looking at them. She was now in the school building, meanwhile, they were down, in the ground. She started thinking,

"They talk about me like I wanted this. Like, I built this attention on purpose. But that's the thing about attention—you don't always get to choose what kind it is. I wanted to escape. Is it an escape from everything? Can I say that I wanted to escape from the reality? Nah, that sounds so cliche! They say my name like it's a ghost story. Like I'm a legend or a warning. But I'm just me. And 'me' was never enough for them. So I have become a 'Resting Unbothered Face' type of person, when really-"

"Whom are you looking at?" Serena asked.

Skyler did not reply, clearly irritated.

"Oh, right! I forgot you can't... speak. And to communicate, you roll your eyes, right? Can you show me how to say 'I love myself'?"

Serena's teasing tone gets sharpened, trying to get under Skyler's skin.

"What do you want, Serena?" Skyler finally spoke.

"I should ask you! It seems **you are obsessed with every guy** in this school. That's why you are looking at Zane and Flynn, is it not enough?" She said angrily.

"What are you talking about? Just because your boyfriend is interested in gossip doesn't mean it's my problem because it is about me. Blame the person who spread that rumour"

"You literally spread a fake rumour about Flynn, your best-"
HE'S NOT MY FRIEND!!"

Serena goes silent..

"Maddox, don't worry. Everything has a way of coming out, and I'm sure your precious detective will find out what you've been hiding... sooner or later." Serena turns and walks off, leaving a tense silence hanging in the air.

Skyler:

No... Flynn can't know it... How does Serena know?? Out of everyone, how can she know? Does she even know?? It was about her boyfriend, right? Is there a new rumour about me circulating?? WHAT THE FUCK IS HAPPENING?! Did someone tell her? No, that can't be possible, NOBODY knows about it.

For the first time... *Skyler was afraid.*

3:15 PM

Skyler:

I have recently learnt about the "paradox of seeking validation"

The "paradox of seeking validation" refers to the phenomenon where actively looking for approval or positive feedback from others can ironically undermine your self-esteem and create a dependence on external validation, even if it initially provides a confidence boost, because it implies that your self-worth is contingent on others' opinions rather than your own internal sense of value; essentially, the more you seek validation, the less secure you may feel within yourself.

Key points about the paradox of seeking validation:

Positive reinforcement loop: While receiving validation can feel good and temporarily boost confidence, constantly needing it can create a cycle where you are constantly seeking external approval to feel good about yourself.

Underlying insecurity: Often, the need for validation stems from low self-esteem or a lack of internal validation, leading individuals to rely heavily on external sources for self-worth.

Vulnerability to criticism: When your self-esteem is heavily reliant on others' opinions, even minor criticism can feel disproportionately damaging.

<u>Examples of seeking validation:</u>

Constantly asking for compliments or reassurance from others

Posting on social media primarily to get likes and comments

Making decisions based on what others think rather than your own judgement

<u>How to break the cycle:</u>

Develop self-compassion: Focus on building a positive internal dialogue and recognizing your own strengths and achievements.

Challenge negative self-talk: Identify and challenge self-deprecating thoughts that might be driving your need for external validation.

Set healthy boundaries: Learn to say no to requests that drain your energy or make you feel like you need to constantly prove yourself.

This paradox somehow reflected on me... It made me realize that I might be an attention seeker. I mean I do act edgy and corny... Only for the people and not actually me. Because I would never do shit like that! "The Book Club Bloodbath", "Flynn's Circus of Shame" and "The Flynn Hayes Fiasco: Suspension Edition". I would never with my heart do this bitchy stuff.

<u>Which leads to three questions:</u>

Q. Do I enjoy being talked about?

A: Yes. I enjoy being talked about. It feels like I have done something I was never able to do before"

Q. DO I crave validation?

A: ABSOLUTELY NOT. I don't care what others think about me. Even if I crave, what the fuck will I do with that information?

Q. Do I feel powerful?

A: Yes and No. On the one hand, I am happy that people are talking about me, but... At what cost? Because forever I am trapped in this. Trapped by the image of what people have.

Wednesday

15 January, 2025

10: 11 AM

"Great, why does she have to sit here?" Benji thought as he saw Skyler sitting in front of him in the library. Benji awkwardly smiles at her. She stares at him.

Skyler didn't say a word. When Benji's voice faltered, Skyler's gaze shifted to him for a second, and suddenly, the whole room became aware of how tense the conversation had gotten. She didn't smile or speak, but her half-lidded eyes and subtle head tilt drew everyone in, like a magnet pulling another magnet.

A few minutes later...

Everyone felt awkward sitting with Skyler.

"Skyler. We still remember the bloodbath incident. It's best if you shift to another table. I am getting distracted here," Ivy pleaded.

"That's on you," Skyler replied. There was a silence,

"Okay, but hear me out—if you had to fight one animal bare-handed, what's the biggest thing you think you could take?" Benji tried to break the awkwardness.

"A goose," Jordan said without any hesitation.

"That's a terrible choice. Geese are aggressive. They'd overwhelm you." Nathan replied.

"I want them to overwhelm me," Jordan said.

"Y'all are so unserious," Riley grumbled.

"Okay, but let's talk real threats. If a gorilla—" Benji said.

"You'd die." Ivy interrupted in the middle.

"Bro, let me finish! I was gonna say—" Benji replied.

At this point, the conversation is the dumbest thing imaginable. Jordan is doubling down on his goose battle strategy. Nathan is trying to calculate the surface area of an average gorilla's arm span to prove a point no one asked for. Riley is losing brain cells. Benji is fueling the madness. Ivy is texting mid-conversation, only half-listening. It's chaos.

And then—there's Skyler...

She hasn't said a word this whole time. Just sitting there. Watching.

It takes a while for people to notice, but the longer the conversation drags on, the heavier her silence feels. She's not checking her phone. She's not nodding along. She's just there, completely still, listening without participating. And for some reason, that makes her even more noticeable than if she had actually spoken.

Finally, Ivy is the first to feel it. She glances at Skyler, shifts in her seat, then blurts, "Okay, why are you looking at us like that?"

The group falls quiet.

Skyler didn't respond immediately. She tilts her head slightly, as if considering the question, but her expression doesn't change. The silence stretches just a little too long.

"She's probably judging us," Jordan said, unbothered.

"She IS judging us." Nathan frowned.

"Damn, we're really out here being analyzed like lab rats." Benji nervously chuckled.

Skyler's lips curve into the slightest smirk. The kind that says you're not wrong, but I won't confirm it.

"Skyler, if you have something to say, just say it," Riley said.

Skyler finally blinks, as if she had forgotten they were waiting for her to speak. She rests her chin on her hand and, in the calmest, most indifferent voice imaginable, simply says:

"...I just think it's interesting."

"Interesting how?" Ivy asked,

Skyler just smiles.

She doesn't elaborate.

She doesn't need to.

And just like that, the entire conversation—once chaotic and ridiculous—is now about her. The mood in the room has shifted, and she never even had to raise her voice.

Benji swallows. "Alright, well, I suddenly don't feel safe."

Nathan adjusts his glasses, muttering, "That was vaguely threatening."

Riley exhaled sharply, annoyed. "God, I hate when you do that."

Skyler simply shrugs. And just like that, **she won**.

10: 20 AM

"Flynn did you see that shit?" Zane asked,

"What shit are you talking about?" Flynn confused,

"The table at the left corner. Where Benji, Riley, Nathan, Jordan, Ivy and... Skyler are sitting"

"Why would she sit with them?"

"A few minutes back, Benji and others were talking and look now, all QUIET. And as always, Skyler is now glaring at them to kill them. Which somehow connects to my theory!"

"Yeah, man... I noticed the change in the atmosphere... But how? How can she bring all the attention to herself without even trying? she just opened her mouth for a second."

"Only an attention seeker holds this power!" Zane mockingly said. Both chuckled.

"You said she is interested in psychology? Perhaps, she studied these behaviours from her book and now she is acting like it?" Zane asked,

"I mean, yeah. There would probably be a section called: How To Control Attention Through Psychology," Flynn replied.

10:23 AM

"Okay, when shall we keep our next meeting? I am thinking of this Saturday-" Before Riley could finish her sentence, she felt Skyler looking at her. Skyler remained quiet just long enough to make everyone hyper-aware of her.

"Man, why do study rooms always feel like interrogation rooms? Next thing you know, someone's gonna slam a folder down and say, 'You know why you're here.'" Benji said. Everyone laughed except one person.

"Dude, you'd fold in five minutes," Jordan said,

"Excuse me?? I have the poker face of a legend." Benji replied. Silence. No one responds. But Skyler... she's just watching.

"...Why is she looking at me like that?" Benji asked, now scared.

"Oh my god, say something." Ivy pleaded again. Skyler tilts head, mildly amused, but didn't say anything.

Now, instead of moving on, the group is fixated on Skyler's lack of response. She hasn't said a word, but suddenly, she's the center of attention.

"Nathan, can I ask you a question? Why do you keep statistics and records? Why? I never got your answer..." Jordan asked.

"Because numbers don't lie. That's the difference between actual logic and whatever nonsense the rest of you operate on." Nathan replied.

"Damn, okay, Socrates," Jordan said.

Skyler doesn't say anything—but she exhales sharply, almost a laugh. Just one small breath.

"...What?" Nathan paused.

"Nothing." Skyler blinked.

Nathan looks irritated now. Suddenly, it doesn't matter what anyone else is saying—he's hyperfocused on whatever Skyler just thought but didn't say.

"No, seriously, what?" Nathan asked, determined.

Skyler smirks but still says nothing. Now Nathan's overanalyzing it.

"Okay, real talk—why do you always do this? The whole 'mysterious girl who watches people like they're an experiment' thing." Ivy asked,

"I just think people are interesting." Skyler shrugged.

"That's not an answer," Nathan replied.

"It is to me," Skyler said.

"That's literally the most unsettling response you could have given," Riley said.

And just like that, the topic has shifted to Skyler—but *she never asked for the attention.* They just keep pushing.

"You know, you're kind of a weirdo," Ivy said. "Like, you just sit there, watching. Do you even care what we're talking about?"

"Why do you care if I care?" Skyler asked, slightly tilted her head.

"I—what?" Ivy confused.

Now, Ivy is forced to explain herself, making her defensive. Skyler, meanwhile, has successfully dodged the question entirely.

10:30 AM

"Now, back to my theory. People who actively seek attention, who act loud, dramatic, etc., get it, but it's often fleeting or forced. People who seem unbothered by attention ironically get more of it because their indifference makes others curious. The less you try to control a room, the more control you actually have." Zane explained.

"Now, if we apply this to Skyler; Skyler isn't loud. She isn't begging for the spotlight. But because she's unpredictable and refuses to react normally, she becomes the most interesting person at the table. For example: If Ivy loudly announced a scandal, people would listen, but it would be forgotten in a day. Meanwhile, Skyler just sits there, silent, and somehow she's the one everyone keeps thinking about later."

Zane continues to look at the group, "*She's proving my theory in real-time,*" And continues to observe.

10:32 AM

"Be honest, do you actually like any of us?" Jordan asked,

Skyler waited a full five seconds before responding. "That's a complicated question."

"Bruh. That's a yes or no question." Jordan said. He is now stuck thinking about what that means. If she didn't say "yes," does that mean she dislikes them? Or is she just messing with them? The mystery lingers.

"I bet you knew exactly how this would play out from the beginning." Nathan doubted her,

Skyler raised an eyebrow, amused. "What makes you say that?"

"Because you're always three steps ahead. You planned this, didn't you?" Nathan asked,

"Would it bother you if I did?"

"THAT'S NOT AN ANSWER."

By not confirming anything, she keeps people questioning her every move—was this all intentional? Or are they just overthinking? The mystery deepens.

"You act like you don't care, but you wouldn't be here if this didn't matter to you," Riley said,

Skyler smiles faintly, watching her.

"...Well?"

"I never said I didn't care."

"You also never said you did."

"True." Skyler shrugged.

Riley is now forced to interpret Skyler's meaning instead of getting a straight answer. Did Skyler just admit to caring? Or is she still dodging? The mystery remains.

Skyler looked at the clock, she stood up.

"Wait, wait, wait—before you go, can you just tell us what you actually think?" Benji asked,

Skyler pauses, glances at them, then simply smirks and leaves.

"WHAT DOES THAT MEAN???" Benji shouted. She doesn't need to answer. The fact that she left them hanging means they'll be obsessing over it long after she's gone.

10: 40 AM

Flynn also stands up and follows her,

"You keep making these cryptic little comments—can you just say what you mean for once?"

"Why do you assume I mean anything?"

"BECAUSE YOU ALWAYS DO."

Skyler smirks, but doesn't confirm or deny anything.

"*Why did you burn your books?*"

Skyler asked, "**Why do you think I did?**" And she leaves. Now Flynn is even more convinced she knows something, even though she never actually admitted to it.

Skyler:

January 15, 2025

Subject: The book club experiment

I decided to try something new. A social experiment, if you will. I sigh. Softly. Just loud enough.

Nathan looks up immediately. Jordan glances my way before pretending not to. Riley doesn't move, but I see the way her fingers tap against the table, just once, before she stops herself. Ivy shifts in her seat. And Benji?

Benji grins. He knows.

They don't know they're being studied. Not really.

It starts the same way it always does—chaos wrapped in false normalcy. A room full of people who believe they're in control of their own actions. Who believe their thoughts are their own. Who believe they're not being watched.

They are.

I watch.

And they adjust.

☾ Nathan pushes his glasses up his nose more than usual. A tell. Self-correction. He wants to appear unaffected, but the awareness of being observed makes him aware of himself. Statistical analysis of human behavior doesn't work when the variable knows it's being studied. He should know that.

→Nathan adjusts his glasses again. That's the third time in five minutes. A reflex. He thinks it makes him look composed, intellectual. It doesn't. It makes him look uncertain. Hesitant. A man shifting through data in his head, trying to calculate the right response instead of just having one.

☾ Jordan stops slouching. He doesn't even notice he's done it. He lounges like he doesn't care, but when silence creeps in, he sits up. More structured. Controlled. He even wants to be perceived a certain way.

→Jordan, despite pretending to be the most relaxed person in the room, is anything but. He taps his fingers—restless energy. He leans back too far in his chair—intentional nonchalance. But every time someone shifts their focus to him, he sits up again. He doesn't like to be ignored, but he doesn't want to look like he cares. A paradox he hasn't solved yet.

☾ *Ivy fixes her hair—twice. A micro-adjustment. Self-conscious. Not vanity, just... positioning. Like a chess piece subtly shifting before the real move is made.*

→ *Ivy's attention drifts to her nails when she doesn't know where to look. It's a tactic, one that people mistake for disinterest. But it's not disinterest. It's a shield. A way to avoid being read. She's playing the game, too, even if she won't admit it.*

☾ *Riley? She's still pretending not to care. She's pretending very hard.*

→*She tries too hard to look bored. That's how you know she isn't.*

And then there's Benji—who notices. Maybe not everything, but enough.

"Bruh, now I feel like a test subject."

I almost smile. Almost.

→*He sees me watching. I can tell. And the funny thing is, he doesn't mind. Maybe because he's too chaotic to care. Maybe because he thrives on attention just as much as I do.*

I don't have to do anything. Just exist in the space. Just sit. Just watch.

And the room bends around it.

• • •

People think they don't care about attention. Until it's missing. Or until it's forced upon them.

The moment they think they're being watched, they start editing themselves.

Even the ones who claim they don't care.

Even the ones who roll their eyes, who huff, who brush off the idea that anyone's perception matters.

Even **Flynn**.

• • •

<u>*Flynn (The Great Overanalyzer)*</u>
Flynn thinks he's searching for truth. He isn't.
He's searching for a way to make himself the hero of this story.

A detective doesn't just want to solve the case. He wants to be the one who solves it.

He doesn't realize that.

But I do.

Flynn performs logic. He builds his theories in the way that makes him seem the smartest, the most determined, the one who sees what others can't. But what happens when the truth doesn't fit into his carefully constructed narrative?

Would he even accept it?

Or would he twist it, make it fit, force the puzzle into a shape that flatters him?

Flynn thinks he's the detective. But what if I am the one truly analyzing him?

Flynn likes to believe he's above this. That he isn't affected. That he is the observer, not the observed.

And yet—

He doesn't fidget, but he is still. The way a predator does when it realizes it might not be the most dangerous thing in the room. He doesn't speak right away because he's trying to decide what I'm thinking. What I know. What he should say next to maintain the upper hand.

He thinks I don't notice. **I do.**

Flynn wants to control the story. But what happens when the story doesn't belong to him?

• • •

<u>Final Observation</u>

The book club thinks they're just talking.

They think their conversations are organic, unfiltered, untouched by external influence.

But all it takes is one person watching, and suddenly—

Nathan adjusts.

Jordan sits up.

Ivy preens.

Riley overcorrects.

Benji notices.

And Flynn?

Flynn rewrites the story in his head.

They think they're in control.

But they're not.

Not really.

They think they're just here for book club. For an investigation. For their own selfish reasons.

They don't realize they're all playing a role in something much bigger.

But they will.

Soon...

Thursday

16 January, 2025

11:31 AM

Everyone was at the cafeteria. Flynn and Zane were sitting at a table. In another, Riley, Benji, Nathan, Jordan and Ivy sat. Meanwhile, Skyler was sitting at the next table of theirs.

Nathan adjusts his glasses for the third time in a minute. "Statistically, if we each had to fight a duck the size of a horse, at least two of us wouldn't survive."

Benji blinks, "What do you mean 'at least two?' Who's surviving that?"

Nathan shrugs, "I'd like to think I have a chance."

"Against a HORSE-SIZED DUCK?" Riley scoffs. "Be real."

Jordan, casually eating fries, chimes in. "The real question is—how big would the eggs be?"

There was a silence...

Benji points at him. "See, THIS is why we need to have these conversations."

Ivy sighs dramatically. "You're all idiots."

Skyler doesn't speak. She just watches.

"The conversation shifts again. This time, they're debating the physics of cereal. But I don't care about that. I'm watching Skyler. She's barely touched her food. Barely spoken. But she's listening.

Studying us like we're test subjects." Flynn thought.

"I know that look. And I don't like it.

So I made a decision—

I pull her aside."

"What's your deal?" Flynn asked.

Skyler tilts her head. "My deal?"

"You're watching us like a scientist observing lab rats. What are you thinking?"

"She doesn't answer right away. Instead, she studies me now. Like I just became more interesting." Flynn thought.

She laughs. Not a smirk. Not a scoff. A full, genuine laugh.

"Oh my god," she breathes between giggles. **"You really think this is about you**?"

Flynn frowned. "What?"

She wipes a tear from her eye, shaking her head. "Flynn, you're so obsessed with being the detective, you don't even realize—**you were never part of the equation**."

She gives him a final, amused look. "*You're not the main character here*."

"I was just listening to their conversation", Skyler pointed towards the "book club members" table, "I didn't even notice you."

Then, Skyler casually says, "Technically, by definition, it could be. Soup is just liquid with solid components. But then again, we drink it, not eat it with a spoon first. So maybe it's more of a beverage." Looking at the table.

Benji, dead serious, "Wait."

Nathan was visibly processing new data.

"Skyler. Stop." Jordan said.

No one predicted this. Is Skyler not being "Alpha Empress" for once? Impossible.

CHAPTER VI

Looking To Close, Seeing Too Little

Friday

17 January, 2025

6:31 PM

Flynn slammed a crisp sheet of paper onto the table. "Gentlemen," he announced, "Feast your eyes on the greatest appeal ever written."

Benji leans in immediately, eyes sparkling with intrigue. Zane, on the other hand, looks like he already regrets being here.

Zane cautiously picks up the letter and starts reading. Within seconds, his face morphs into an expression of deep, existential pain.

Ravenshore Academy Book Club

Flynn Hayes's Official Appeal

Date: 17 January, 2025

To: The So-Called Book Club Committee

Subject: Unjust Suspension Appeal – A Formal (But Highly Necessary) Defense

Dear Book Club Tyrants,

I am writing to formally appeal my ridiculous and highly questionable suspension from the Ravenshore Academy Book Club. This decision was clearly made in bad faith, fueled by spite, misinformation, and possibly a personal vendetta.

Let's address these so-called allegations one by one:

1. "Excessive Interrogation of Members" – First of all, this is a book club. We analyze things. If y'all can overanalyze character motives in classic literature, why am I suddenly the villain for trying to understand real-life mysteries? Double standards much?

2. "Unapproved Independent Investigations" – Investigating is literally my passion. Sue me for being thorough. (Actually, don't. I can't afford a legal battle.)

3. "Causing Unnecessary Chaos" – Define "unnecessary." Everything I did was necessary to uncover the truth.

4. "Disturbing the Peace" – Peace was never an option.

5. "The General Consensus Is That I Am Toxic" – OKAY, FIRST OF ALL?? If that were true, why do I have so many fans? (Zane, back me up here.) Second, calling me toxic when half of y'all thrive on drama is hypocritical at best and defamatory at worst.

My Demands for Justice:

Immediate reinstatement into the Book Club.

A public acknowledgment that I am, in fact, an essential member of the club (and possibly the main character of this entire operation).

An official apology from Riley for being a hater.

Failure to comply with these requests will force me to escalate the matter through alternative means (TBD, but I have ideas). I trust that you will see reason and make the correct decision.

With absolutely no respect for this injustice,

Flynn Hayes

(Unfairly Suspended, Unjustly Accused, and Deeply Offended)

"Yo. Yo. This is INSANE." Benji said, barely able to read through his laughter. "Bro said, 'Dear Book Club Tyrants.' You're COOKED,"

Flynn huffs. "You're focusing on the wrong part. The argument is solid. Bulletproof, even."

Zane flips back to a specific line and reads aloud, "'Failure to comply with these requests will force me to escalate the matter through alternative means (TBD, but I have ideas).'!!" He looks up at Flynn, unimpressed. "You're literally threatening them."

Flynn shrugs. "It's called negotiation tactics."

Benji wipes a tear from his eye. "Naw, you really put 'The General Consensus Is That I Am Toxic' as an official bullet point." He wheezes. "I love how you immediately got defensive about it."

"I had to defend myself," Flynn argues. "It's slander."

Zane pinched the bridge of his nose. "This is not an appeal, Flynn. This is an angry rant with some bullet points."

Benji grinned. "Nah, I think we should send it. No edits. Raw."

Flynn smirks. "See? Benji gets it."

Zane sighs like he's carrying the weight of the world. "If you actually send this, I'm disowning you."

"Fine! I wouldn't send it anyway!" Flynn replied and then continues, "Benji will!!"

"Me?" Benji was confused and then smirked, "I mean– I wouldn't mind!"

"NO! BENJI, NO! You are not becoming his postman," Zane warned.

"Zane chill! Nothing is going to happen! And DEFINITELY not gonna laugh at it," Benji assured.

"Oh... really??"

Saturday

18 January, 2025

11: 32 AM

"OH MY GOD!? No drama in this meeting? What's the probability of this??" Jordan asked,

"0.0004%" Nathan replied, "Also, are we still friends?"

"We were friends? I guess we are now?" Jordan shrugged.

"Not anymore, Mickey Mouse and Donald Duck..." Ivy said to them, pointing towards Benji, who was now in the middle of the room.

As Benji cleared his throat and—without a single shred of hesitation—held up the paper like it was the Declaration of Independence.

"Ayo, everyone, listen up," Benji announced, grinning like he had just been gifted the best comedy script of the century. "I present to you: Flynn's Official Appeal—also known as 'The Funniest Thing I've Read All Year.'"

Zane, seated nearby, buried his face in his hands. "I told Flynn not to give it to him..." he muttered.

The group collectively groans before Riley snatches it up. "You're joking." She scans the first line and immediately deadpans. "'Dear Book Club Tyrants'?" She shoves the paper toward Zane. "Your bestie is insane."

"I told him not to send this," Zane replied.

Blake leans over to read. "'Peace was never an option.' Bro thinks he's a revolutionary."

Serena sipped her drink like this is free entertainment, smirks. "I mean, he's not wrong."

Ivy giggled, scrolling through her phone. "We have been thriving off the drama, let's be honest."

Riley groaned again. "Why is he like this? Who writes threats in an appeal letter?"

Nathan, who has been silently reading, finally speaks. "Statistically, this had a 0% chance of being approved."

Mia frowned. "Guys, maybe we shouldn't make fun of him. He obviously—" She skims another line. "'An official apology from Riley for being a hater.'" She blinks. "Never mind."

Benji, practically in tears laughing, claps his hands. "Oh, we have to respond."

Zane shakes his head. "No, we don't."

Serena smirks. "Or we could pretend to approve it, let him get his hopes up, and then crush them."

The table collectively 'oohs' in approval.

Zane groaned, rubbing his temples. "You're all evil."

Benji grins, holding up his phone. "So that's a yes?"

The club erupts into chaotic debate as Zane contemplates leaving the country.

5:30 PM

Flynn:

*I might regret giving that appeal letter to Benjamin Torres. But hey, the letter was written so they could read it. I wrote that because truly, it was an injustice for me. And for the society, let them laugh as much as they want because at the end of the day, **that is the truth!***

Let's just hope they actually consider it. Because if they don't I might go insane...

Flynn's phone pings,

"You are added to 'THE LITERARY COURTROOM'?" Flynn confused,

"Hold on? Did they actually consider it?" Now doubting himself.

He opens the group chat...

THE LITERARY COURTROOM

@CertifiedChaos: BRO LMAO

@CertifiedChaos: THEY REALLY RESPONDED :O

@FinalBossReads: Ur boy just got COOKED

@FrontRowForChaos: Rest in peace Flynn 2008-2025

@LowkeySkylerStan: We are gathered here today to mourn...

@PlaysChessNotCheckers: I have NO regrets.

Flynn raised his eyebrows seeing these messages. "That was fast. I need to see my email."

From: Ravenshore Academy Book Club

Subject: RE: Unjust Suspension Appeal — A Formal (But Highly Necessary) Defense

Dear Mr. Hayes,

After careful consideration, we have decided to reinstate you into the Book Club, effective immediately.

We also acknowledge that you are, indeed, the main character of this operation.

Additionally, Riley would like to issue a heartfelt apology for being a hater.

Sincerely,

The Book Club Committee

P.S. We hope this email finds you well. Unfortunately, it won't. L + Ratio + You're still suspended. XD

Flynn stared at it. He rereads the P.S. five times, still shocked.

"... They flipped my own move on me", Flynn thought.

Suddenly, there were lots of notifications.

Therapist w/ No License

@TiredButTrying: This is why I told you not to trust Benji.

@MainCharacterEnergy: OH, I TRUSTED HIM. I JUST DIDN'T THINK THEY'D REVERSE UNO ME

@TiredButTrying: I'm actually crying.

Flynn slams his laptop shut.

Bad Influence

@MainCharacterEnergy: I HOPE YOU CHOKE ON YOUR LAUGHTER.

@Certified Chaos: AHAAHAHAHA BROOO

@CertifiedChaos: YOU THOUGHT U WERE DOING SOMETHING?? THEY SENT A "HOPE THIS EMAIL FINDS YOU WELL" JUST TO FINISH U OFF

@MainCharacterEnergy: I AM GOING TO DESTROY YOU.

@CertifiedChaos: It was worth it. :D

Meanwhile in the group chat...

THE LITERARY COURTROOM

@CertifiedChaos: So, uh. If I suddenly go missing, y'all know why.

@PlaysChessNotCheckers: We'll dedicate the next club meeting in your honor.

@FinallBossReads: Absolutely not.

Monday

20 January, 2025

10:03 AM

"I almost forgot my interviews... *Serena, Benji and Mia,*" Flynn thought, "It's quite shameful that I only get to interview only one of them and two other people whom I didn't even think of; *Zane and Noah..*"

Case #39

<u>ZANE LOCKWOOD</u>

Full name: Zander Elias Lockwood

Class: 12-C

Age: 16 (Sixteen)

Height: 5'7

Birthday: 23 January, 2008

MBTI: ISTJ

Role in Book Club: Member- Only Sane One

Relationship with Skyler: Strategic Standoff.

Opinion on Skyler (Before & After):

Before: "She used to be so passionate about books."

After: "I think she's just pretending to be this cold. It's an act."
Key Quotes:

- "She craves attention like it's oxygen. But what happens when there's no one left to watch?"
- "I don't hate her. I just know better than to believe her."

What He Might Know: Zane knows that Skyler isn't just leaving—she's erasing herself, and whatever she's hiding is buried in what she doesn't say.

Suspicious Behavior: Zane never asks the obvious questions—he asks the ones Skyler doesn't want answered.

NOTE: Zane thinks she's faking. But why? Could she be hiding something behind the attitude?

Suddenly, he noticed Mia, standing in front of her.

"Mia!" Flynn shouted.

Mia looked back. "Flynn?" She asked,

"Mia, can you help me?" Flynn asked.

"I am sorry, I can't..."

"Is it because of my reputation? Are you scared of me?"

Mia goes silent... "Can we go somewhere less crowded?"

They go to an empty classroom.

"I'm not sure what you want me to say, Flynn." Mia was looking down.

Flynn fidgets, leaning forward, eyes intense. "Just... tell me what you know. You're the only one who isn't completely giving up on her. There's gotta be something."

Mia shifts uncomfortably, avoiding Flynn's gaze. She didn't know how to explain that *Skyler, the girl she knew, was long gone, and yet she still held onto the remnants of what Eris Dorne represented.*

"She used to be different." She said quietly.

"What do you mean by that?" Flynn asked.

Mia paused, "**Eris Dorne. That was her pen name.** She wrote under that name when she... when she was someone else."

Flynn looks perplexed. He leans forward, trying to piece it together.

"Wait... Skyler? Eris Dorne? Are you telling me the person who–created The Book Club Bloodbath, Flynn's Circus of Shame AND The Flynn Hayes Fiasco: Suspension Edition –wrote under that name was actually—what? Different?"

Mia lowers her book, setting it aside. This is where the pain starts to show. She's caught between what Skyler could have been and the mess that she's become.

Mia said softly, almost to herself "Yeah. She used to have **hope**. She was... passionate about her writing. About something bigger than herself."

"Then what happened?"
Mia now looking down, "I don't know. Somewhere along the way, she got lost. And now, there's just... nothing left of Eris Dorne. Just Skyler."

Flynn pauses. This changes things. He's not investigating just a person anymore; he's investigating someone who's buried a whole part of themselves—a part Mia is still holding onto. He can see the hurt in Mia's eyes, the weight of her silent hope.

"So... what, you think there's still a chance for her? Even now?"
Mia said quietly, more to herself, "I want to believe there is. But every time she does something... awful, I start to wonder if I'm just wishing it's possible."

Flynn's expression softens. This isn't just about the mystery anymore; it's about people. His investigation feels a little less like a hunt for answers and more like a desperate attempt to understand why Mia, of all people, still believes.

"Mia... I don't know if anyone can save her."
Mia said gently, with a soft but broken smile, "I don't know either, Flynn. But if no one does... then who?"

The air between them is thick with the weight of their words. Flynn doesn't have an answer, and neither does Mia. But they both know that this conversation won't be the last.

Mia picks up her book again, the comforting pages a reminder of a time when things seemed easier. Flynn gathers his things, staring down at his notes, still trying to find a way to solve this—but now, more aware than ever of the human cost behind every clue.

As Flynn leaves, Mia watches him go, silently praying that she hasn't lost Skyler for good.

Case #39

UPDATE

At one point, Skyler was actually passionate and hopeful about things.

Eris Dorne is Skyler's lost identity.

Mia has an unwavering hope for Skyler.

Skyler could have been in deep emotional damage.

What could be the potential for this change?

• • •

<u>MIA LANGLEY</u>

Full name: Mia Alexandria Langley

Class: 10-A

Age: 14 (Fourteen)

Height: 5'2

Birthday: 3 February, 2010

MBTI: ISFJ

Role in Book Club: Member- Still has hope

Relationship with Skyler: Conflicted

Opinion on Skyler (Before & After):

Before: "I love her! She's like my role model!"

After: "I don't think she meant to hurt anyone. I think she's just... lost."

Key Quotes:

- "Skyler was Eris Dorne. She was a writer, a dreamer... I don't know when that version of her disappeared, but I'm still waiting for her to come back."

- "She used to care about things, about people. Now it's like she only cares about the next drama."

What She Might Know: Knows more about Skyler's past and her reasons for adopting the "Eris Dorne" persona.

Suspicious Behavior: Occasionally dropping cryptic comments about Skyler's true intentions, as if she's hiding something but isn't ready to fully reveal it yet.

NOTE: Mia is too emotional. Wants to believe Skyler is still the same person. Possible bias. Check back later.

6:15 PM

"I need to find out more about Eris Dorne. **How could I have missed it**? How!? Maybe if I was still in the book club, I might have got some of her work, or better! Could ask the members..." Flynn thought.

He starts searching on the internet, and nothing is there... No social media account, no work under that name, there was nothing.

Suddenly, someone messages him.

Confused Heart

@SoftHeartedButNosy: Hey

@MainCharacterEnergy: Hi, Mia. What's up?

@SoftHeartedEnergy: Are you finding out about Sky's pen name?

@MainCharacterEnergy: Yes...?

@SoftHeartedButNosy: You are looking in the wrong place...You would not find anything, maybe she has deleted everything.

Tuesday

21 January, 2025

4:21 PM

"Can we... instead of being Sherlock Holmes and Dr. Watson, can we watch anime?" Benji asked. "**Don't forget.**

3. <u>Mandatory Snack Breaks</u>

Investigations must pause for food, memes, or anime discussions.

No exceptions."

Zane started laughing, "Is that a bullet point in your contract!??"

"No thanks. You watch the weirdest shit ever!" Flynn complained.

"Okay, what about *I Was a Middle-Aged Salaryman Until I Got Isekai'd into a Frog Prince and Now I Have to Save the Universe Using the Power of Jazz??*"

Flynn goes silent.

"How are you even getting animes named LIKE THAT?" Zane asked.

"Okay, so what clue did you get?" Benji and Zane asked.

"Skyler's pen name is Eris Dorne", Flynn replied.

"Have you seen Skyler's social media? I have noticed a cryptic social media post. She is hinting at her frustration with being misunderstood and feeling trapped. The post mentions a location in a roundabout way, something like "The truth is hidden where no one looks..." Zane said.

"Okay, so Eris Dorne posts about **'feeling trapped.'** We need to find out why. What's she really hiding?" Flynn asked.

"Easy. It's because she's stuck in the middle of a really bad love triangle. Like, that's totally her vibe. She's probably dating two people and can't choose, so she's getting all dramatic about it." Benji said seriously.

"Benji, this is a serious investigation. We're not dealing with some romance drama here. There's something deeper going on." Flynn replied.

"Romance drama is always deeper than people think. Anyway, my theory still stands. I'm basically a love detective." Benji said nonchalantly.

"We've got to find out where Skyler is hiding her tracks. She's got everything locked down."

"I mean, we could just... follow the bread crumbs? Maybe she left some secret clues somewhere?" Benji opens the Google Maps app on his phone.

"Benji, that's literally not how investigations work," Zane said.

"Yeah, but have you ever tried it? Like, seriously, I watched a crime show once, and they totally found the killer by following bread crumbs. Not to mention, who doesn't leave breadcrumbs behind? Like, nobody eats a sandwich without dropping crumbs." Benji said confidently.

Zane facepalmed. "That's not how it works, Benji."

"So, Skyler's been posting cryptic stuff lately? I don't think it's just for attention. It could be a clue to who she's really hiding behind." Flynn said.

"Wait, I think I've seen something like that on a meme page. One of those motivational quotes she shares? It's almost like a throwback to a previous era in her life. Like, she's trying to resurrect a part of herself that doesn't exist anymore. *Maybe Eris isn't a new character at all—just a part of Skyler she buried.*" Benji said seriously.

"Wait... You're saying Eris isn't just a pen name. **It's a part of her—an identity she used to be.**" Flynn surprised.

"Exactly. She's not just playing a character, she's reliving a time when she could pretend to be someone else. That's why it's all so dramatic. It's like... what, a second chance for attention?" Benji grinned.

"That's pretty messed up. But it makes sense. It's not just about the writing—it's about keeping control over her image." Zane said.

Someone knocked on the door. Zane opened it,

"Hello?" Jericho asked,

"Jeri?" Flynn asked, "What are you doing here?"

"Who is this???" Benji confused,

"This is... Skyler's brother, Jericho, Flynn said,

"OMGGG!!?? OUR ANSWER!!" Benji shouted,

"I just showed up out of nowhere, didn't I? But don't worry, I'm exactly who you need right now. I'm the character who always appears when the plot's in a pinch. The one you didn't even know was needed until this exact moment." Jericho said,

"So, uhh... Are you investigating my sister?" Jericho asked,

"Yes. Please don't mind it. We– I mean Flynn– is delusional here," Zane explained.

"So... you're just going to magically solve everything for us?" Benji asked,

"Okay? And yes, what are you doing? Can I help?" Jericho asked,

"YES!" Benji said, "Wait, did... did anyone else hear that? Am I the only one who's confused right now? Why is he acting like he just stepped out of some weird narrative storybook?"

"Have you seen any difference in her room?" Flynn asked,

Jericho thought for a while, "Yeah. Yeah? Yeah! Her trophies! Her plaque and framed letter, which she got from the book club. I never saw it again."

"OMG?? WHAT DOES THAT MEAN??" Benji asked,

Zane looked at him. "It means **she's not proud of her achievements**. She wasn't happy with her success"

"Okay, that was my job! I need to go! Also, Flynn, I am taking your toolbox. I just wanted to inform you of that. Also, do you know where Skyler is? She comes home lately... Have you noticed? She often comes late, like LATE!" And Jericho goes away.

"What does he mean by 'she comes home late?" Zane asked,

Benji, with an exaggerated grin, "Alright, alright, listen to this– Skyler's been coming home late way too often, right? Do you know what that means? She's either secretly a night owl doing shady things, or- wait for it– she's in a secret cult that meets under cover of darkness. Or maybe she's training to be a vampire, and her late-night habits are just the beginning of her full transformation. That's why she's so into the whole 'mysterious' vibe. Makes sense, right? No, wait, hold on, she's probably out there saving the world in her spare time. Like, secretly a superhero who fights crime at night and–"

"Benji, are you high?" Zane asked,

"Maybe! But like, doesn't it make sense? It's totally suspicious." Benji shrugged.

"But why is there a huge gap in the timeline? Why would Skyler erase every trace of Eris Dorne? Why would she do that?"

"Maybe it's because the story was getting too real. If she's Eris Dorne, the more people dig into it, the closer they get to her. And if she's hiding behind that, she's trying to protect the fake persona she built. Like when you delete all the embarrassing photos after a bad breakup. Classic cover-up move." Benji said,

"You're saying Skyler erased all traces of Eris because the mask was starting to slip?" Flynn asked,

"Exactly. When you're pretending to be someone else, you can't let anyone see the cracks in the facade." Benji shrugged.

1 hour later... Zane and Benji have left Flynn's house.

Flynn sat at his desk, staring blankly at the scattered papers before him. His mind was a haze of confusion, but one phrase echoed through his thoughts, louder than the rest: "Eris Dorne doesn't exist anymore."

He had thought he was so close. He had pieced together every clue, every fragment of information he could find. For weeks, he'd believed he was on the verge of uncovering the truth—the real reason Skyler had abandoned everything, the identity behind Eris Dorne. It was the final puzzle piece. The mystery that had kept him up late at night, the investigation that had consumed him. He had cracked the code: Skyler Maddox was Eris Dorne.

But now, the moment that should have been a revelation felt hollow. The answer he had fought so hard for was not as fulfilling as he'd imagined. It wasn't just that he was wrong. It was that he had been chasing a ghost.

The words Mia had spoken—those few simple words—had shattered everything Flynn thought he understood. Eris Dorne wasn't just a name. It wasn't a persona that Skyler had been hiding behind. It was a past that she had fully discarded, a part of her life that no longer mattered to her.

The truth had been right there, staring him in the face. Flynn had spent so much time focusing on Eris, on this lost identity, that he had failed to see what was truly happening in front of him. Skyler wasn't Eris anymore. She had let go of that version of herself. Eris Dorne wasn't a secret identity; it was a part of the past that had been buried and left behind.

Flynn felt like the ground had been ripped out from beneath him. It was as though he had been running in circles, trying to solve a mystery that had already been solved for him—only, he hadn't seen it. The conclusion he had been so certain of suddenly felt meaningless. He wasn't just late to the truth; he had been pursuing something that wasn't there.

Skyler wasn't hiding behind Eris anymore. That part of her had been gone for a long time. And no matter how hard Flynn tried to untangle the web of clues, the answers had already slipped through his fingers.

No matter how hard he searched, he was always too late.

Eris Dorne had been a part of Skyler's past—maybe even a part of herself she had outgrown or regretted. The pieces he had so carefully collected didn't fit anymore. The puzzle he had worked so tirelessly to solve had been incomplete from the start. There was no closure to be found in a ghost.

And now Flynn had nothing. He had pushed away everyone around him, sacrificed his sanity, and turned his world upside down in the pursuit of something that had already been abandoned.

The final blow was the brutal clarity of it all: **Eris Dorne doesn't exist anymore.**

That was the truth. Skyler had moved on, but Flynn was still stuck in a past that no longer mattered. No matter how many times he reexamined the clues, how much he dug into the darkness, the answers would always remain out of reach. And the worst part? He didn't know how to stop. He didn't know how to let go of the chase.

The last thread of his investigation unraveled, leaving him with a cold, bitter emptiness.

No matter how hard he searched, no matter how many theories he formed, he would always be too late.

CHAPTER VII

Beneath The Mask

Flynn:

Tuesday

21 January, 2025

11: 18 PM

I feel worthless. I was chasing a ghost. This whole time it was a ghost. Eris Dorne doesn't exist. Not anymore. I CAN'T DO SHIT!! I thought I was near the end, confronting Skyler and then, she comes back... She smiles at me,

"Yes! I knew you would find it!" She would say to me, and I would hug her. We would become best friends again. She will teach me more about psychology and I could show her my antique collections.

But no... this imagination will never come in reality. THE REALITY IS REALITY and I have to understand it. I can't feed my delusion thinking my friend, my only best friend, will come back. Now, it's just someone else... Someone whom I will never be able to like. I DESPISE HER.

She thinks this is a fucking game and that I am a part of her gameplay.

All.. I wanted to find my friend- my true friend. I thought she was just hidden and one day, she would explain everything and come back.

Or maybe I was never that close to her, I am not that important to her that she just straight don't give a fuck about me like I do. I mean... I have seen her, acting differently, just not with me.

The fuck did I do to her?! I guess.. I will realize it when it's too late because really, that's my thing after all! REALIZING EVERYTHING AFTER IT FUCKING ENDSSS.

You know what? Why am I even doing this? I know why I am doing this! Because I am insecure. I am insecure of everything. I AM A LOSERRR, got publicly shamed in infront of everyone, had a title called, "Clown" for so many days, got suspended from the book club because of this shit. My detective skills, my ego, my "Mr. Sherlock

Holmes" personality, this is happening because of this.

What if? I was a normal child? A NORMAL FUCKING CHILD who will worry about completing his homework and not where his best friend has gone and why? Can he bring her back? Does he have to find clues behind them? Make a fucking case file out of it as if she killed the past- You know what? SHE DID. SHE KILLED HER. YEAHH!! SHE'S NOT GONE, SHE'S MURDERED. And... that's why she is not going to come back. But I need to find out why she killed her?

Also, why is she running from the writing world? Is she allergic to it? I guess it reminds her about her past, but why would she hate her own past?

Wait- why do I hate my past?

Just a few lines, I was asking what if questions- Which means even I hate it.

I would tell you why, it made me a fucking overthinker who doubts everything. It went so out of control that I have started doubting my own friend.

I am not proud of my cases being solved, the truth is, I knew people would talk about it after that. That I would come in local newspapers, that people read it and praise me. I became what I hated the most; an attention seeker. I need the validation, validation that I am important and that I can do something. Except this, I don't have any hobbies. Collecting antiques can hardly be a hobby.

Skyler- She was good at pottery and probably good at psychology too.

Zane- Has good Logic, he makes good decisions, has a good reputation in debates too.

Benji- He's funny. People laugh at his jokes.

Riley- At the end of the day, she is a good leader who just wanted to save the club's reputation.

Jordan- No one talks much about this, but he is a good sportsman.

Nathan- He is good at keeping records, and even in studies.

Noah- He is energetic and just brings a vibe to the room.

Serena- She's literally the captain for her house club.

Ivy- Has self-respect for herself and is loveable.

Mia- She is hopeful...

Blake- Respects everyone and in return gets the respect back too.

Ethan- An obedient club member who loves books very much.

And me? I don't have anything that they have.

I tried so hard to look different from them when they are just happy without efforts, and here I am- Creating my own happiness.

This whole case is more like a mirror. Showing me my reflection.

But I don't want to give up. I just can't. Because yes, my ego is stopping me and I want to find the answer.

Turns to the next page,

Thursday

30 January, 2025

11: 20 PM

I don't even know why I'm writing this. What's the point? It's not like I have anything new to say. Another day of spinning my wheels. Another theory that's crumbling to dust the second I look at it.

But here I am, writing in this stupid thing like it's going to make a difference. Maybe I'm hoping I can still convince myself that I'm not completely losing it.

What did I even think I was doing? Trying to uncover some grand conspiracy? Playing detective when I don't even know who I'm supposed to be anymore? I was the one who knew—at least, I thought I did. I thought I had the answers. And now I can't even tell if Skyler is part of this or if I'm just chasing ghosts at this point.

Here's the thing, though. You probably already know how this ends. You probably saw it coming from the very start. I didn't—obviously. But you did, didn't you? You saw through me before I did. Before any of them did. And maybe that's why I'm writing this down now. Because you—whoever you are—are the only one who can really see it.

But I can't keep doing this. I can't keep pretending that everything makes sense, that I'm not just one step away from falling apart. So, yeah. I guess you can see it now, huh? I'm a failure. I thought I was smart, I thought I was clever, but I was just fooling myself.

So, what now? What's left for me to do? Do I just keep pretending? Keep chasing after something that isn't even real?

Hell, maybe I should stop writing this. Maybe I should stop writing everything. I mean, you don't really care, right? You've been waiting for me to figure this out for ages, but here I am, stuck in the same place.

But no. I'm not going to stop. I'm going to keep writing. Because at least this way, I'm doing something, even if it's just for me. And maybe, just maybe, this entry will help me figure out where I went wrong. Even if I'm the last one to realize it.

You'll probably be reading this, laughing at how ridiculous I sound, won't you? Just waiting for me to finally get to the part where it all clicks. But who's laughing now?

I'll get there. Eventually.

Saturday

1 February, 2025

11: 47 AM

"Don't you think...? He's going insane? Does Flynn think he's worthless?" Jordan asked.

"First of all, it's so weird stealing someone's diary. That too of a suspended member of the club, creepy! And..." Benji goes silent. "Bro, what do we even say to him? 'Hey, we read your diary, you good?'"

"No. We don't TELL him we read it. We SHOW him he's wrong." Zane nervously chuckled, "It is probably a phase! Flynn is not really suffering anything! Right? Right?" Even he gets silent.

"I never thought he was going through with so much shit. I mean getting an existential crisis?" Benji swallowed.

"I hope he doesn't harm himself. I mean, most of the things written are so self-hatred," Zane looked at the diary.

"Yeah! I think he is a good partner in crime! And woah- he even appreciated me!? Yes, he is going insane," Benji surprised.

"He left it in his classroom, I thought I would return it before it gets missing," Jordan explained, "Flynn? Having a breakdown? Doesn't sound perfect,"

"But it is the truth. After all, it's his handwriting," Zane said,

"Yeah man. And I only know one person whose handwriting is literally Patrick Hand" Benji said, eating his sandwich.

"What should we do?" Jordan asked.

"Hey, so did anyone see my diary?" Flynn came to their table,

"Oh? You mean this? I found it in 12-B. Thought would return it to the owner," Jordan smiled.

"Thanks!" Flynn smiles back too. Now sitting with them.

"He looks quite... normal who just had an existential crisis two days back!" Benji whispered to Zane.

Both of them were looking at him while he was eating a bunch of things at the same time.

"Yeah..." Zane whispered back.

"Should we confront him?" Jordan is now whispering to them. Zane and Benji nodded.

"What exactly have you written in the diary? Could you elaborate please or should I understand that you had **a breakdown and existential crisis**?" Jordan finally asked.

"...That's private—" Flynn looked at them.

"Yeah, well, too bad. Maybe don't write an entire Shakespearean tragedy about how pathetic you are and then expect us to not say something." Jordan crosses his arms.

"Flynn...why would you write that?" Benji softly asked,

Flynn shifts uncomfortably, arms crossing. "I don't know. It's just how I feel. It's not that deep."

Jordan mockingly asked, "Not that deep? Bro, you were out here breaking the fourth wall like you were in a damn movie monologue. You literally wrote, 'You probably already know how this ends.' Who are you even talking to? The government? God?"

"You are not actually the biggest failure on this planet. I can provide examples if necessary." Zane said,

"Zane, please," Flynn replied.

Benji looking genuinely hurt, "It just... it sucks that you feel like this, man. You think so little of yourself, and I don't get why."

Flynn swallows. He doesn't like this. The way they're all staring at him, expecting him to explain something he doesn't even understand himself.

"Look, it's fine. I just needed to get my thoughts out. It's not like I was gonna actually do anything." Flynn scoffed.

"Yeah? Well, you did something. You made all of us realize how much of a dumbass you are. Congrats." Jordan said.

"Jordan." Zane tries to stop him,

"No, because I'm mad. This idiot really thinks he's worthless? That he's some joke? You wanna know what I see when I look at you, Flynn?" Jordan said,

Flynn doesn't answer. He's not sure he wants to.

Jordan continues, "I see some overthinking, emotionally constipated detective who thinks he's Sherlock but is actually just a sad, caffeinated gremlin. But you know what else? **I see our friend**. And you're thinking like this? Writing this crap? It pisses me off."

Benji said, "We care about you, Flynn. Despite all the jokes I crack about you, you are still my friend, my Mr Sherlock Holmes,"

"And your self-perception is objectively incorrect," Zane said.

Flynn exhales sharply. He doesn't know what to say to that. Doesn't know how to respond to people who actually care.

"...I'm sorry." Flynn finally apologized, he doesn't know what else he can say here...

Jordan stares at him, unimpressed. "You're not off the hook, dumbass. But whatever. Just—just don't do this again, alright?"

Benji nodded, "You can talk to us instead."

"Or at the very least, avoid breaking the fourth wall in such a dramatic manner. It's unsettling." Zane said.

Flynn lets out a small, exhausted laugh. Maybe they're right. Maybe he doesn't have to carry all of this alone.

Meanwhile, the table behind them..

Mia and Riley are locked in yet another heated argument about books. Flynn, Jordan, Zane, and Benji are sitting together, half-listening as they eat. The argument escalates.

"Okay, but you have no taste. You just want messy characters doing insane things." Mia rolled her eyes,

Riley mocking said, "And you only like books where the brooding love interest gaslights the main character for 300 pages before confessing his undying love."

Mia gasps, "EXCUSE ME??"

"I'm just saying, you call my books trashy, but yours are just as bad in a different way," Riley said,

Flynn casually turning around, "Wait, what are we slandering?"

Jordan grinned, "Mia and Riley are fighting about books. Again."

"No, actually, we're fighting about taste," Riley explained.

"I have taste!" Mia got defensive.

"Sure you do." Riley laughed.

"Taste is subjective, guys," Zane said,

Riley completely ignoring it, "Okay, let's settle this. Who do you think has the worst taste in books?"

Everyone paused. They all slowly turn to look at Flynn.

Flynn offended, "WHY ME?!"

Jordan laughed and said, "Because you overanalyze everything. You didn't even like Gone Girl."

Flynn grumbled, "The twist was predictable."

"He has a point." Benji agreeing with him.

"Well, if Skyler was here, she would agree with me," Mia said.

Riley is now getting angry,

Flynn blinked, "Wait. Skyler reads?"

Riley laughing bitterly, "Reads? Dumbass, she writes.."

"Yeah, I know that. She used to write essays and short stories for the club. We all write," Flynn said.

"No, you don't know. Because if you did, you'd know she doesn't just write. **She publishes**." Riley said,

Flynn paused, "...Publish?"

Riley now leaning forward, enjoying his slow descent into madness "Yes, Flynn. She's an author."

Flynn stared at her, Riley watching him process

"...Books?" Flynn softly asked,

"Books." Riley mockingly replied,

Flynn blinked rapidly, "Like. Full-length. Books?"

"Yes, the books which become bestselling," Riley replied.

Flynn takes a deep breath,

Jordan noticing his expression, "Oh, no."

"I'VE BEEN CHASING THIS STUPID MYSTERY FOR WEEKS AND YOU'RE TELLING ME THEY WERE JUST—JUST TYPING AWAY LIKE A NORMAL AUTHOR?" Flynn hysterically asked.

"Yep." Riley grinned.

"WHAT WAS I EVEN INVESTIGATING?!" Flynn asked himself.

"That is an excellent question." Zane calmly said.

Mia, who knew this information the whole time, is just quietly sipping her drink, avoiding eye contact.

"So what you're saying is... Skyler was never some complicated puzzle to solve. They were literally just writing books the whole time." Flynn asked,

"I mean... yeah," Benji said,

Then, Flynn grabs his head "I NEED TO LIE DOWN."

Meanwhile, Jordan was wheezing, "This is the funniest breakdown I've ever witnessed."

Flynn slowly slides down his chair, staring at the ceiling in betrayal. He has never felt more played in his life.

"I can't– **I will not hear a single shit of her**!" Riley snapped, everyone looked at her, the entire table went silent. Flynn stops mid-breath. Jordan stops laughing. Zane, who has never looked surprised in his life, actually raises an eyebrow.

"Riley...?" Mia asked,

"How the hell did she come up when we were literally talking about books and taste?? Why the HELL does it have to be her? Why does SHE get to be the one? I—" she lets out a bitter laugh "—I swear to GOD, if I have to hear one more person praise her, I will LOSE IT."

Flynn sits up, stunned. Riley isn't just mad—she's livid. And this isn't some casual annoyance. This is deep, personal hatred.

"Riley... what did Skyler do?" Flynn asked hesitantly,

Riley clenched her fists, "What did she do?" She lets out a humorless laugh. "She existed."

Silence.

Flynn and the others exchange looks. That wasn't an answer. That was something worse.

Riley gritted her teeth, "Forget it. You wouldn't get it."

"Try me." Flynn lowered his voice,

"No." Riley coldly replied.

She gets up and walks off, leaving everyone behind in stunned silence.

"WOAH!? What the hell just happened!??" Benji asked everyone,

"Maybe she is mad because she ACTUALLY used to respect her, but seeing the changes in behaviour, she thinks she's wasting everyone's time, including herself, and that's why she is so done with her," Zane concluded,

"...I think that makes perfect sense," Jordan replied.

Flynn:
4:53 PM
Monday
3 February, 2025

...

Flynn has isolated himself after Riley's outburst. He's sitting alone, his journal open, but for once—he doesn't know what to write.

He stares at the blank page, gripping his pen so tightly that his knuckles turn white.

"What the hell was I even doing?"

His breathing is unsteady. His mind races. All this time. All these weeks. He thought he was chasing something important. He thought Skyler was hiding some massive, twisted truth—something that would make all the sleepless nights, the paranoia, the obsession worth it.

But no.

Skyler was just... writing books.

That's it.

That's all it was.

Flynn lets out a bitter, humorless laugh, but it sounds broken.

He has never felt more like a joke in his entire life.

He flips through the pages of his own journal. Hundreds of notes, scattered theories, sketches of timelines, all circling back to one person: Skyler.

He devoted so much of himself to solving them—but what if there was nothing to solve?

He looks down at his hands, at the ink stains smudging his skin.

"What am I even doing anymore?"

Flynn clenches his jaw. For the first time in his life, he doesn't just feel like he failed a case.

He feels like he failed himself.

"Skyler hid this from me. She didn't want me to know. How could I miss such a crucial point? Eris Dorne... Her pen name, the name she used to publish books. It was her. And it looks like everyone knew about this except me. She– used to write books? She published books? For years?" Flynn asked himself. Finally, he writes something.

UPDATE

Skyler used to write BOOKS. Not just club essays or short stories. Full books. Plural.

Riley HATES her. Like, actual rage. Not the usual "I dislike them," but pure, unfiltered loathing.

Mia knew this whole time. She wasn't even surprised. Was this common knowledge?

Skyler isn't secretive—I'm just dumb. Everything was right there. I just never bothered to look properly.

Skyler had fans. Like, people actually read their work. I was out here thinking they were a ghost when in reality, they were just... living.

I wasted my time. (I should probably delete this later.)

This wasn't a mystery. (Should probably delete this too.)

What was I even looking for in the first place?

Flynn stared at his reflection in the nearby window. He looked exhausted. His own eyes were mocking him.

Then, the memories hit.

Case #14: Solved within two days. The missing money wasn't stolen; the teacher had misplaced it.

Case #21: A cheating scandal. The answers weren't leaked—the student had just memorized the pattern.

Case #30: A stolen painting. Turned out the artist hid it themselves for dramatic effect.

Flynn remembers how easy it all used to be. He used to feel sharp. Unstoppable. He could walk into any mystery, put the pieces together, and walk out with the truth.

But Case #39... Skyler's case?

It was **the first time he had ever been completely, utterly wrong.**

His brain replays all the clues he misread, the details he twisted, the connections he forced. He remembers the way Jordan laughed at him, the way Benji looked concerned, the way Zane stayed silent.

Most of all, he remembered Skyler.

The way she always had this amused, knowing expression, like she was watching him unravel the whole time. Like she was waiting for him to realize the truth was never that deep.

Flynn grips his hair. How did he become this?

A quiet knock on the door. Flynn doesn't move. He already knows who it is.

Zane steps inside, hands in his pockets. He doesn't say anything at first—just looks at Flynn, taking in the disaster that is his entire existence.

Then, he speaks. "You look like you've been hit by a bus."

"I feel like I've been hit by a train, actually," Flynn replied,

"Close enough." Zane shrugged,

Silence.

Flynn expected some kind of lecture. Some kind of 'I told you so.' But it never came.

Instead, Zane just sits down next to him. And then, he says the thing that changes everything.

"You know, not every mystery is meant to be solved."

Flynn froze.

Those words hit him harder than any insult, any failure, any breakdown.

He looks at Zane, who just looks back at him—calm, unreadable.

"Maybe this one was meant to be understood instead."

Flynn doesn't respond.

Because for once—he has no idea what to say.

Tuesday

4 February, 2025

1:42 PM

Inside the 'The Hidden Chapters' room...

The book club is gathered in their usual spot, books open, conversations overlapping. There's an undeniable weight in the air.

"So, today in this meeting, we will talk about **OVERTHINKER by Eris Dorne**, this isn't just any book. OVERTHINKER is raw, psychological, and deeply personal." Blake announced.

"Blake, didn't you get any other book to talk about?" Riley rolled her eyes.

"So... thoughts?" Blake ignoring her.

Benji, leaning back in his chair, "Y'all. I was expecting some dramatic, poetic trauma dump, but this? This book hurts."

"It's alright." Jordan shrugged, flipping a page.

"You read the whole thing in one night," Benji said,

"And?" Jordan glared at him.

Zane, the only one who actually took notes, "Structurally, it's interesting. The narrative shifts between reality and intrusive thoughts so seamlessly, sometimes you can't tell them apart. That was intentional. It puts you inside the protagonist's head—"

"Which is a terrible place to be, by the way," Noah smirked.

"I don't get the hype. It's just another book about someone being sad." Riley said, now crossing her arms.

"But that's the point. It's not just sadness—it's the kind that eats away at you. The kind you can't escape." Serena titled her head.

"The way the protagonist justifies every bad decision, every downward spiral—it's unsettlingly realistic," Nathan said thoughtfully.

"To me, it's not a fun book," Blake said.

A beat of silence.

"It's not supposed to be," Mia replied to her,

There's a moment where no one speaks. Because they all know—this book didn't just tell a story. It lingered. It made them uncomfortable.

And deep down, maybe some of them saw a little too much of themselves in it.

Suddenly, they saw someone they weren't expecting...

Flynn walked inside the room.

He walks into the club super serious, like he's about to make a courtroom speech.

Everyone is expecting another disaster,

"What is he doing here?" Serena asked Ivy,

"Is he here to start a new drama?" Ivy asked,

"Is this? Is this going to be The Book Club Bloodbath 2.0? I am SO NOT READY!!" Serena said,

"Chill Rena. He's not Skyler, the only people who are scared of him are rats –maybe not?" Noah said.

But instead of creating some drama, he actually owns up to his mess.

"Okay. Fine. I was a little out of control."

"A little?" Riley looks ready to kill him.

"Okay— It wasn't just a little out of control; it was way out of control. I was delusional, and I ruined the book club's reputation. The suspension I received was deserved! It made me realize that I was in the wrong. I don't want to create any more drama, blame anyone, or hold anger toward you. I've come to understand that I am the problem. Referring to myself as Sherlock Holmes was foolish..." Flynn said in front of everyone.

He actually lowers his pride, and everyone was shocked seeing it.

"I messed up. I shouldn't have acted like a deranged detective in a book club. I just... I just need answers, okay?"

Silence. No one expected him to be this honest.

Mia is already nodding, thinking it's sweet.

Nathan is calculating the percentage of sincerity.

Jordan is side-eyeing him, waiting for the catch.

But there was no catch... He stood in front of everyone, looking down. Knowing everyone is staring at him.

Riley, after staring Flynn directly into his soul, finally sighs.

"When were you suspended?" She asked,

"6 January, 2025" Nathan replied.

"6 February, 2025, more two days. Then we will reconsider, " Riley said.

Flynn was relieved, but the way Riley says it makes it sound like he'll be on probation.

Nathan immediately takes notes: Flynn Hayes. Status: Provisional.

Flynn nodded seriously, "Two days. I can work with that." He thought.

And goes away...

"Sooo... that just happened," Jordan said,

"Yeah. And I'm not buying it." Benji said, confused and doubtful.

"Why not? He was serious!" Mia still has some hope.

"Serious or not, I'm not just letting him waltz back in like nothing happened," Riley explained.

Nathan still taking notes, "Flynn Hayes. Status: Provisional. Probability of relapse: 78%."

"He admitted he was wrong. That's something." Zane said,

"Oh, cool. He admitted it. That totally erases the weeks of chaos he caused." Noah rolled his eyes.

Mia leaned forward, "Listen, I know he's a mess, but you could tell this was real. He actually lowered his pride."

"Or he's playing the long game. Y'know, 'act humble, get back in, go full Sherlock again.'" Jordan shrugged.

Benji nodded aggressively, "EXACTLY. I've known Flynn long enough to know—bro CANNOT sit still. This is just 'Act 1: The Redemption Arc.' 'Act 2' is him pulling some insane theory out of nowhere again."

"If he screws up again, he's done. No second chances." Riley crossed her arms.

Nathan flipped a page in his notes, "Technically, this is already a second chance. Mathematically speaking, he should have been expelled from the club long ago."

"Maybe. But that doesn't change the fact that he's obsessed with finding the truth. And that's not something he can just turn off." Zane exhaled.

Serena watched silently this whole time, "So what do we do?"

Riley, without hesitation, "We wait."

"Wanna make a bet on how long before he does something stupid?" Jordan grinned at Benji,

"Bro. We both know I'm winning that." Benji replied.

"You guys have no faith in him!" Mia said.

Zane calm as ever, "I have faith in Flynn. Just not in his ability to stay out of trouble."

"Two days. Let's see if he lasts." Riley said.

The members continued talking about OVERTHINKER,

The book club discussion had slowed, yet the atmosphere remained charged. The weight of Overthinker hung over them like an unfinished conversation.

Serena flipped back through the pages, eyes scanning the words with an unreadable expression.

"You know..." she mused, almost to herself, "there's something weird about this book."

Benji leaned back in his chair. "Define weird. I thought the whole thing was weird."

Serena shook her head. "No, I mean—it's like the author is **talking to someone specific. Some parts feel too pointed, too**

personal."

Nathan hummed in thought. "That's true. Some passages read less like narrative and more like... justification. As if the protagonist isn't just reflecting but trying to explain something."

Mia stiffened.

No one noticed.

Zane flipped through the book, stopping on a page. "There was one line that stood out to me—" He cleared his throat and read aloud:

"*'If you bury a lie deep enough, eventually, even you will start to believe it.'*"

A chill settled over the room.

Jordan scoffed. "Damn. That sounds like something Skyler would say."

Silence.

Serena smirked, closing her book. "Exactly."

Riley, who had been quiet for most of the discussion, crossed her arms. "Okay, but this is Skyler we're talking about. Maybe she just wrote this for, I don't know, attention."

Mia shot her a glare, but Riley wasn't finished. "She's dramatic. That's her whole thing. Maybe all this deep, psychological crap is just for show."

Benji tapped his chin. "Or, hear me out—what if she's actually saying something real?"

Riley rolled her eyes. "You're giving her too much credit."

Nathan ignored them, still deep in thought. "There's another part where the protagonist talks about erasing themselves—how changing their identity didn't make them feel any more real." He looked up. "Skyler wrote this years ago, right? So, the question is... what was she running from?"

The question hung in the air.

Zane exhaled slowly. "Maybe that's the real mystery."

Serena tilted her head, watching everyone's reactions. Then, just to stir the pot, she murmured:

"Or maybe... it's the answer."

Skyler:
Tuesday
4 February, 2025
2:01 PM
I heard them, I was passing by the book club when I saw Flynn standing in front of everyone, apologizing.. What does that mean? He understood his mistakes. Does it mean he will stop investigating me? Well... That's good for him. But he— is not a type of person who easily gives up. Did he realize the truth?

Because if Flynn knows the truth, he wouldn't be happy... It will affect him like A LOT

☾ This mattered to him.

Flynn had always been the type to throw himself into a mystery like it was his purpose. Every theory, every clue, every obsessive tangent—it wasn't just about solving things. It was about proving something to himself.

And when he finds out,

He will be staring at the truth, and it had nothing to do with him.

No secret conspiracy. No deeper, hidden message meant just for him to uncover.

Just the plain, boring reality of my choice.

And the realization hurt.

☾ He was not supposed to find out.

I meant that.

And yet—hadn't I let him? Hadn't I left all the pieces scattered, just close enough for him to put them together?

Maybe some part of me wanted to be found. Maybe some part of me thought he'd understand.

He wants an answer.

But the truth?

The truth was that there was no answer. No hidden meaning. No grand conspiracy waiting to be unraveled.

When he knows the truth, he will ask, "Why didn't you tell me?"

Because if I had, he wouldn't have believed me.

Because if I had, it wouldn't have mattered.

Because if I had—

...He would've looked at me the same way he's looking at me now.

Disappointed.

Like I owed him something more.

Like I had taken away something important.

Like he had built this entire story in his head, only for me to take it away in one breath.

I will not have an answer that would satisfy him. Because, deep down, Flynn wanted this to mean something.

But it didn't.

I left because I wanted to.

Not because of some tragic event. Not because of some villain in the shadows.

Just because.

"I thought you'd understand,"

Because deep down, we both knew the truth.

It wasn't that he had to know.

It was that he had to matter.

And now?

Now he will stare at the truth, and it has nothing to do with him.

That was the part that would destroy him the most.

That was the part he would never accept.

There was nothing left to say.

And that?

That was the worst part.

☾ He should have seen it.

The shock had settled. The betrayal had set in.

And now, something new had taken its place—guilt.

Because Flynn Hayes, for all his arrogance, had one fatal flaw: He never knew when to stop caring.

"I should have noticed,"

☾ What was the point of this?

"Then what was the point of all this?"

He will not just talk about the case. He will talk about everything.

Me, our friendship, our conversations, every moment we had led up to this—

If the answer was this simple, if it had always been this simple—

Why had he cared so much?

Why did I let him?

There was nothing left to say.

And that?

That was the worst part.

Or at least, that's what I tell myself.

Flynn:

"This wasn't a mystery. It never was."

"I should stop thinking about it. I should move on. But..."

CHAPTER VIII

Broken Faces, Buried Truths

Thursday

13 March, 2025

1:30 PM

"Why are you looking at me like that?" Flynn asked,

"Like what exactly?" Benji side-eyeing Flynn.

"The side eye!?" Flynn shrugged,

"I am mad because I lost my bet with Jordan, and that's because of you!"

"Who told you to bet on me? Oh my gosh Benji, you didn't trust me? That maybe? Maybe I changed,"

Benji is looking in the opposite direction.

"Where is Zane?" Blake asked,

"**He went to Kyoto, Japan**. Apparently on a vacation..." Flynn replied.

"Flynnnnn... It is so boring! I miss your "Wow, call me Sherlock." phase, like it was so entertaining. I don't like this— Normal Flynn" Benji said,

What do you mean Normal Flynn?? As if I was abnormal before??" Flynn angrily asked.

"I mean you kinda were... You literally had a breakdown AND were suicidal, remember? Also, it feels like **you have become more like Skyler**,"

"What do you mean?"

"I mean— She used to run away from her past and look at you now, you too are running from your past. It's just unfortunate that there's no other Flynn who will investigate you. Wait! That's me! But what's the point? We know why you stopped it..."

"Can you both shut the fuck up?" Serena asked, "Also, I am surprised. Flynn? Leaving his career? Leaving his "Detective skills? No, just overthinking at an Olympic level." personality. I am amazed! It takes so much courage and determination!"

"Maybe you should leave your "Drama's Best Supporting Actress" personality too!" Benji replied,
"EXCUSE ME???" Serena was offended.

"Bro what's your problem?" Noah asked, ready to fight.

"Oh look! "Serena's Loyal Shadow" has entered the chat," Benji crossed his arms.

"Bro! What are you doing??" Flynn whispered.

"I think— I am going insane!!???" Benji shouted,

"You are not going insane, you are insane!" Noah replied.

Riley leaning forward with an eyebrow raised, "Alright, so I think we all know why we're here today. Let's get this out in the open. Unpopular book opinions. No holding back, people."

Jordan snickers, folding his arms, "Let's be real, Riley. You've probably got a list a mile long. What do you think? That fantasy books are overrated or something?"

"Not exactly. I just think literary fiction is highly overrated. Some people act like it's the end-all-be-all, but honestly, thrillers and mysteries challenge your mind more than any pretentious novel ever could." Riley smirked.

"Oh, that's a shot at all the 'artsy' books, huh?" Blake softly chuckled. She shifts in her seat, glancing at Riley with a knowing look. "I kind of agree. I mean, sometimes people act like literary fiction is this holy grail, but it's just... slow. Thriller books? Those keep you on edge. That's real intellectual stimulation."

Mia tapping her chin thoughtfully, "I get that, but... sometimes I think people confuse 'intellectual stimulation' with just a twisty plot. It's okay to want a story that makes you feel something deeper, not just engage your brain. People like the 'happy endings,' but I think sometimes the real power is in the emptiness—like when a story leaves you questioning everything long after you finish it."

"Oh, please. Some people just want to be sad for the sake of it. Nothing wrong with a happy ending." Jordan rolled his eyes.

Riley smiling smugly, "Exactly, Jordan. It's a trend, Mia. People think it's profound, but it's just... melancholy masquerading as depth. There's nothing wrong with ending a story on a positive note. Give me a satisfying ending any day."

Nathan snorts, leaning back in his chair, "I think people need to stop obsessing over 'antiheroes.' Honestly, they're just a cop-out for lazy writing. How about we get some straightforward heroes for once? Not everything has to be morally grey."

"But those heroes are so... predictable. The world's not black and white, Nathan." Mia softly and firmly said.

"Maybe, but at least when someone's a hero, you know they're trying to do the right thing. Antiheroes just blur the lines, and it's annoying. And they always get praised like they're breaking new ground when all they're doing is making poor decisions for 'the drama.'" Nathan shrugged.

"Tell that to your precious Captain America, Nathan. You're sounding a little too patriotic." Blake grinned and teased.

"Hey, I'll take Captain America over some whiny, 'Oh, I'm too complex for this world' antihero any day." Jordan laughed, joining in.

Ethan looking around, shaking his head, "I just... I can't with experimental fiction. You know the kind—books that try too hard to be all artsy, and then it's like the whole thing's just a pretentious attempt to sound smart. Sometimes, a good story doesn't need to have weird formatting or bizarre structure."

"I get it. Sometimes authors use those techniques to make the reader feel something, but it can come across as them trying too hard to be deep instead of telling a coherent story." Mia nodded.

Benji nervously shifting in his seat, "Uh, yeah. Honestly, I don't really get all the fuss over 'coming-of-age' stories. They just... they're all the same. Teenagers figuring out who they are—yeah, we get it. It feels like everyone just wants to talk about how misunderstood they are, and it's kind of self-indulgent."

Ivy leaning forward, eyes sparkling with mischief, "Exactly! And it's like the same recycled plot with a few minor tweaks. Every single time." She glances at the group, smirking. "I'd rather have some juicy drama, you know? Give me a messy love triangle or a twisty plot. Let's see some real chaos, not some boring teenager figuring out their feelings."

"But... don't you want something a little hopeful sometimes? I mean, all these dark, tragic books—why can't we just have a bit of light? Fantasy books and dystopias feel like they just want to ruin your mood for no reason." Noah said, looking almost concerned.

Serena smiling condescendingly, leaning back in her chair, "Oh, Nado, sweetheart. You wouldn't understand. Dystopias are important because they're a cautionary tale. People need to understand the gravity of the world's problems. You can't just ignore them with your fairy-tale endings."

Benji sighed under his breath, muttering, "Yeah, some of them just want to make people feel bad for the sake of it. No wonder we're all so stressed out. Some of those books just make me feel like everything's doomed."

Jordan muttering under his breath, but loud enough to be heard, "Could be worse. You could be stuck in a room with someone who thinks Twilight is a 'masterpiece.'" Laughs to himself as the others look around, half-waiting for a response.

"Jordan, you can't possibly be that bitter about Twilight, can you?" Riley raised an eyebrow.

"It's just the idea of it—how people act like it's some grand tale of eternal love when it's a glorified dumpster fire." Jordan rolled his eyes.

"Well, it is a little... problematic, but some people just want escapism. Let them have it." Ethan shrugged.

"I guess there's no harm in enjoying books that let you escape from reality. Not everything has to be a deep exploration of life's meaning." Mia looked thoughtful.

"I still don't understand how you all think anything good can come out of coming-of-age or any of those overdone tropes. But hey, to each their own, right?" Ivy smirked.

Blake leaning back in her chair with a slight smile, "I'd rather talk about good writing and forget about the clichés, but whatever. We all have our thing."

Nathan glancing around, smiling to himself, "Well, at least we can agree on one thing: there's always someone in every book club who insists on bringing up Twilight."

Everyone laughs lightly as the debate continues, with each person firm in their unpopular opinions but strangely at ease in the shared space of honest disagreement.

"That was fun! I don't remember the book club being this fun!" Flynn smiled.

"Yeah man!" Benji agreed with him.

Suddenly, Flynn gets a message:

Therapist w/ No License

Yesterday

@TiredButTryting: Sent a photo.

@TiredButTrying: Kyoto is soo good!! I am enjoying my vacation!!

@MainCharacterEnergy: <33

Today

@MainCharacterEnergy: YOO! What's up??

@TiredButTrying: Sent a photo.

@TiredButTrying: Don't forget to read that book!!

"What book is he talking about?" Benji peeked into his phone. Flynn, now hiding his phone.

"Why are you looking at my phone??"

"Ok geez... Don't hide it like you're texting your girlfriend," Benji rolled his eyes. "By the way you didn't answer my question,"

"**The Last Confession by Alistair Graves**, he said it will help me,"

Benji scoffed, "That's what Zane recommended you? I will recommend something better! *The Library is Closed... But The Books Are Alive and Seeking Revenge!*"

Flynn facepalmed.

They entered the library,

Flynn barely noticed the sounds of the library as he walked through the aisles, searching. The usual hum of casual conversations, the rustle of paper, the smell of dust-filled

100

shelves—it all faded into the background. All that mattered now was finding The Last Confession.

Zane had been on vacation in Kyoto, just chilling, sending Flynn random recommendations. Flynn wasn't sure what the deal was, but after the last few weeks of spiraling and overthinking, he thought, Why not?

A few minutes of searching, and they still didn't find it.

"Hey did you find it??" Flynn asked,

"Nope! Let's check the back, there's always the shelf with the weird, obscure books. Might find something cool. Or just weirder." Benji replied.

They walked toward the back corner, Flynn trying to ignore the frustration gnawing at him. They scanned the shelves quickly, searching for anything that resembled The Last Confession. As Flynn skimmed the shelves, his frustration started to rise. Why couldn't he find this book? What was it about this book that Zane wanted him to read? No luck. It wasn't there.

Suddenly, Jordan appeared in his path, looking as composed as ever. "Did you find it?"

Flynn shook his head. "No. Zane said it's important, but I'm not so sure anymore."

Jordan raised an eyebrow. "Zane? He's in Kyoto, right?"

"Yeah." Flynn sighed. "He just told me to look for it. I don't know, maybe I'm just grasping at straws here."

Jordan's eyes softened, a flicker of something unreadable crossing his face. "Zane has a way of getting people caught up in his ideas, doesn't he?"

Flynn nodded. "I thought I could just let it go, but I don't know. Something's bugging me."

Jordan studied him for a bit longer before shrugging. "Well, if you find it, let me know. I'm not big on the whole 'mystery' thing anymore, but I get it."

Flynn was about to respond when Mia showed up, her face lighting up as she approached. "Hey, what's going on? You guys looking for something?"

Flynn looked at her, feeling a bit relieved. At least someone was here to distract him from this search. "Yeah. Have you ever heard of The Last Confession by Alistair Graves?"

Mia frowned, her lips curling slightly. "Can't say I have. What's the deal?"

Flynn hesitated before answering. "Zane told me to find it. He said it would make sense, but... I don't know. I feel like I'm chasing something that's just not there."

Mia raised an eyebrow, clearly intrigued. "Zane's been sending you on book quests? Seems a little... off."

Flynn couldn't help but chuckle. "Yeah, it's kind of his thing. But this time, it's starting to feel different."

Mia shrugged, clearly not as invested in the book hunt. "Well, if you find it, let me know. I'll be around if you need a break from... all of this." She gestured to the shelves dramatically, clearly implying the library and the book search were not her scene.

Flynn smiled, appreciating her attempt to lighten the mood. "Thanks, Mia. I'll let you know."

Flynn slumped into one of the library chairs, staring down at the pile of books he'd gathered from his search. None of them were The Last Confession. His eyes kept darting back to the stacks, hoping the book would materialize out of thin air, but it didn't.

Benji was still lounging nearby, casually scrolling through his phone. He hadn't moved from his spot since Flynn had started his search, his posture like a deflated balloon. It was hard to focus when Benji was always doing... Benji things.

"Hey, man, still no luck?" Benji asked, clearly not paying attention but still managing to notice Flynn's frustration.

"Nope," Flynn replied, rubbing his eyes. "This book isn't here, and I'm starting to think Zane just gave me the wrong title or something."

Benji tilted his head, clearly considering something. "Well, you're doing it wrong, dude," he said, his tone smug. "What you should be doing is looking for clues. I'm talking like real detective stuff, ya know? Like in the movies."

Flynn looked at him like he was insane. "Uh... clues? I've been reading books, Benji. Not searching for evidence in a crime scene."

Benji grinned, showing no signs of understanding. "Right, right, but what if the book is hidden in plain sight? What if it's, like, coded? Or behind a secret shelf or something? Have you tried talking to the librarian? Maybe they know where the 'mysterious' books are kept." He winked as if he'd just discovered the best tip in the world.

Flynn blinked, utterly confused. "Benji. What are you even saying right now? Are you suggesting that the librarian's hiding a secret stash of books?"

Benji nodded, completely serious. "Exactly! I bet they've got a vault or something. Like, they've been hoarding rare books for years, and only the true 'investigators' get to find them. You could try being all sneaky about it—like James Bond."

Flynn couldn't help but snort at the absurdity of it all. "Yeah, sure, Benji. I'll just break into the librarian's secret stash and see if Zane's book is sitting in there."

Benji grinned wider, clearly not understanding the sarcasm. "Exactly, Sherlock! But you gotta make sure you're cool about it, y'know? Don't be all detective-y in front of the librarian. Gotta act like you're not looking for anything, so they don't get suspicious."

Flynn stared at him for a moment, unable to decide if Benji was being serious or if he was just messing with him. The guy had a way of mixing the ridiculous with the plausible, and it was hard to tell where one ended and the other began.

"I'm pretty sure breaking into the librarian's office isn't going to help me find The Last Confession, Benji," Flynn muttered, rubbing his temples.

Benji shrugged, as nonchalant as ever. "Fine, fine, but I'm telling you, that's the way to do it. Who needs a book on a shelf when you've got secret underground libraries and codes to crack? Honestly, just go with your gut, man. You're Flynn Hayes. You got this."

Flynn stared at him for a bit, the ridiculousness of the advice sinking in. He didn't know whether to laugh or punch Benji in the arm. "You know what? I'm gonna go with my gut and try something else. Maybe without breaking into places."

Benji waved him off, clearly not offended. "Suit yourself, man. But I'm telling you, a good detective never takes the easy way out."

Flynn goes towards the librarian,

"Good afternoon, Mrs. Colloway,"

"Good morning to you too,"

"Uh... quick question? Do you know where is 'The Last Confession by Alistair Graves?'"

"I do remember it.. Let me check my log book," Mrs. Colloway starts looking at the log book and finally finds something, "A student named **Skyler Maddox** has taken it and it seems she hasn't returned it to the library. Perhaps, you can ask her," Mrs. Colloway smiled.

"Thank you!" Flynn smiled back too.

He goes back to Benji, "Yeah I guess you were right..."

"So? Mrs. Colloway opened a secret vault? Damn! I missed it!"
"No... But, Skyler is having that book and didn't even return it,"

"Oh my god?! What are the odds? I think this is a sign that you should become the "Move aside, FBI, I got this."
"NO! I have left it in my past, there's no reason for me to scoop in,"

"BUT I HAVE!"

"Fine! Then you search it. Don't drag ME in this,"

"Flynn Augustus Hayes, The Unbeatable Brain, Heir of Infinite Theories. Don't forget about our contract..."

"Umm... It was YOU being MY sidekick not ME being YOUR sidekick!"

"Flynn, how could you be so cruel?"

"I am not being cruel. I am just telling you the truth. What can I do if you can't handle the truth?"

"Yo," Benji said, his voice breaking the quiet, "you're still thinking like a quitter."

Flynn didn't even look at him, his eyes still locked on the page of an old detective novel. "I'm not a quitter, Benji. I'm just... done with all this detective crap."

Benji grinned, unfazed by the tiredness in Flynn's voice. "Nah, nah. You say that, but you're not fooling anyone. Deep down, you're like one of those mystery-solving machines that just keeps running. You stop, and you'll only sit there like, 'What could've been?'"

Flynn finally looked up at him, annoyed. "What does that even mean? You think I'm just supposed to keep chasing shadows?"

Benji shrugged, leaning back with an exaggerated sigh. "If you don't, someone else will. The clues will slip away, man. The answers will just vanish, and you'll be stuck wondering what the hell happened. Do you want that?"

Flynn's eyes flickered for a moment. He hadn't really thought about it like that—how all of this could just disappear if he didn't keep pushing. It was tempting to stay away, to ignore it all, but Benji's words were worming their way into his thoughts.

"You're telling me to get back into the mess?" Flynn muttered, rubbing his forehead. "After everything that's happened? After my breakdown?"

Benji leaned forward, looking him straight in the eye. "Hell yeah. You've been stuck in that pit of yours for too long, thinking you need peace. But peace doesn't come from hiding, Flynn. It comes from doing. And you know that better than anyone." He smirked. "You've got a gift, man. Don't waste it sitting around feeling sorry for yourself. The answers are out there. If you don't dig for them, they'll slip right through your fingers."

Flynn stared at him, considering his words. There was truth to what Benji was saying. He couldn't deny that feeling in his gut—that pull to keep going, to find the truth. He didn't want to be the guy who gave up.

"You're impossible," Flynn muttered, his voice quiet but laced with frustration.

Benji grinned even wider. "Yeah, well. You're welcome. Now go get it, Sherlock. Solve the damn mystery."

Flynn exhaled, rubbing his temple as a smirk tugged at the corner of his mouth. "Fine, fine. You win. But you're still an idiot."

Benji held up his hands in mock surrender. "Takes one to know one."

"Alright. Our next move is going to find clues. Why would she take 'The Last Confession'?"

"For that, you need to ask that book from her, so that we can know the context,"

"No! She would KILL me!"

"And you think she wouldn't kill me?"

They both look at Mia, coming towards them,

"Have you got the book?" She asked,

Benji and Flynn looked at each other.

Friday

14 March, 2025

8:03 AM

"Hello Skyler!"

"Hi Mia,"

"I have heard you have The Last Confession by Alistair Graves?"

"Oh yeah,"

"I was thinking of borrowing it from you, can I?"

"Okay..." Skyler takes a book from her bag and hands it to Mia, "Also, please return it to the library,"

"Sure!" Skyler smiled,

"Thanks.."

9:27 AM

"Thank you so much Mia! Like— I owe you one! Without you, I wouldn't be able to read this!" Flynn said,

Mia softly chuckled, "No need to credit me so much. I am glad I was able to help you!"

Flynn and Benji both started reading that book.

A few minutes later..

Benji flipping through the pages with dramatic flair, eyes widening as he reads, "Dude, no way. This is it."

"What's it now?" Flynn looked at him, bored.

Benji pointing to a section of the book, "Listen, listen. In The Last Confession, the main character, Julian Ashford, is dealing with this huge secret, right? And he's constantly feeling like he's being suffocated by it—like it's gonna kill him if he doesn't tell someone. He even tries to confess to the police at one point, but they don't believe him. They think he's crazy, but the whole time, he's just holding onto this guilt. And then... BAM! He dies at the end because of it."

"And what does that have to do with Skyler?" Flynn frowned and was skeptical,

Benji grinning like he's cracked the case, "Skyler's the same! She's acting like she's got this big, dark secret, right? Always talking about being trapped and cornered—like she's carrying this weight no one understands. I think she's gonna pull a Julian Ashford! Skyler's secretly guilty of something, and she feels like she's about to explode with it. That's why she's all dramatic lately. She's guilty about something and is trying to confess through her weird behavior. But, in the end? She'll be the one who ends up 'dying' under the pressure of it all, just like Julian in the book."

"Benji, Skyler's not gonna die—she's just being weird. She's not some tragic figure." Flynn raised an eyebrow.

Benji shaking his head, not backing down, "No, I'm telling you, dude. She's trying to do what Julian did. She's setting up this tragic persona so we feel bad for her. She's gonna pull the 'I'm dying' act, and we'll all be sitting here like, 'Oh, why didn't we see it?' Just wait."

Flynn now genuinely concerned, half-smiling, "You really believe that? You think Skyler is gonna stage her own death for attention?"

"Absolutely. She's following the playbook of The Last Confession. Skyler's the type to latch onto anything she can to get people's attention, and this... this book? It's her inspiration." Benji confidently said.

"Hey, it looks like you got the book!" Nathan said,

"NATHAN!" Benji said dramatically,

"What??" Nathan looked at him confused.

"Are you free on Monday or probably Tuesday?" Benji asking seriously,

"Woah! WOAH! I didn't know you had feelings for me like that??" Nathan shocked,

"Dude, I am not asking you out, are you available to attend a funeral?" Benji asked, again with a serious face.

"Damn bro. You are going to die? I guess... I will do your last dying wish," Nathan became quiet, still confused.

Benji facepalmed. "SKYLER IS DYING!"
"WHATTT???!!??"

"WHAT THE FUCK BENJI!?"

"Hold on...This is literally 100% lie!"

"Look at this!" Benji showed the book, "Julian is Skyler, Skyler is Julian,"

"Who the fuck is Julian!??"

"We think Skyler is... hiding her guilt of everything. And just like the main character of the book, she will 'probably' die, letting go of her pain," Flynn finally explained.

"That's SO fictional! This is real-life!"
"Prove it. I still think MY Theory #39 is true! That we are some characters–"

"Nathan, think about it... Her running from everything, trying to erase her past. She didn't want anyone to find it! And with more investigation, we can find more clues!" Benji said,

Nathan looks at both of them and finally sighs, "You both are idiots!"

"No, we are Benji and Flynn: The best chaotic duo!"

"How are we going to find these clues???"

Case #39

<u>NATHAN HOLLOWAY</u>

Full name: Nathaniel James Holloway

Class: 12-A

Age: 16 (Sixteen)

Height: 6'0

Birthday: 1 November, 2008
MBTI: ISTJ
Role in Book Club: Member- Statistics Guy
Relationship with Skyler: Toxic

Opinion on Skyler (Before & After):
Before: "She is a talented, albeit dramatic member of the club"
After: "She skipped 23 meetings. Twenty. Three."
Key Quotes:

- "I respected her once, but she's more interested in drama than actually writing now."
- "Skyler's got talent, but it's wasted on this act she puts on. No one's buying it anymore."

What She Might Know: Knows that Skyler craves attention and validation, but he also sees through her facade and realizes she's lost touch with her true potential.

Suspicious Behavior: He has been quietly maneuvering to get Skyler kicked out of the club for months, subtly undermining her and encouraging others to question her value while maintaining a facade of neutrality.

NOTE: Nathan is obsessed with statistics. Not relevant, but mildly concerning.

Benji looking at the squirrels in the tree and then facing Nathan and Flynn, "We should do what we should have done months ago..." Flynn realizing it, "NO, Benjamin Rafael Torres! NO!"

Nathan looked at both of them, confused, rethinking his decision.

"What exactly was your initial plan?"

"Breaking into her locker!"

Nathan was horrified.

"OH!" Benji disappointed, "Not to you too? Does anyone here think it's a good plan?"

"IT IS NOT!" Flynn shouted,

"Benjamin, let me give you some statistics:

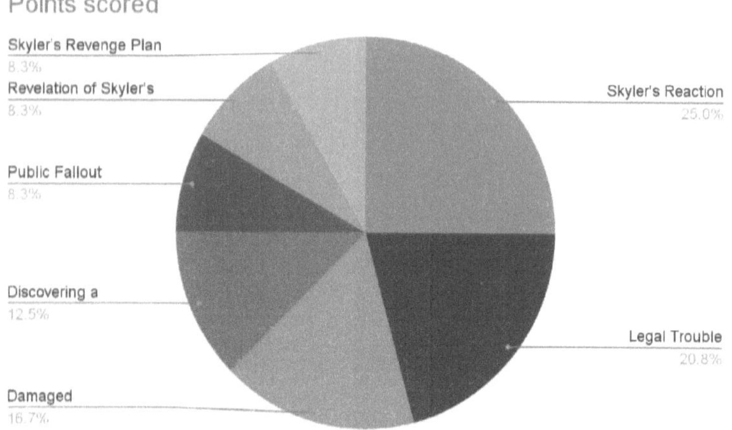

1. <u>Skyler's Reaction (Emotional Outburst, Victim Complex, Retaliation)</u> - 25.0%

Skyler is highly dramatic and attention-seeking, so her reaction would likely be strong. This could involve public outbursts, playing the victim, and retaliation, leading to public chaos.

2. <u>Legal Trouble (Suspension, Investigation)</u> - 20.8%

The school might take this seriously, especially if they view the break-in as a violation of privacy. Depending on how much Skyler or the school exaggerates the situation, this could lead to consequences like suspension, detention, or an investigation.

3. <u>Damaged Relationships (Strain on Friendships, Club Dynamics)</u> - 16.7%

This is highly likely to cause tension within the group. We might face friction, especially if some club members feel that the break-in was a step too far. Riley and others may also react negatively.

4. <u>Discovering a Bombshell (Unforeseen Evidence)</u> - 12.5%

We 'could' uncover something unexpected that could change the course of the investigation, but this is less likely than the other outcomes. However, it could introduce a new mystery or blackmail situation.

5. <u>Public Fallout (Gossip, School Reputation) - 8.3%</u>

The school's social dynamics could be impacted if word gets out, and we might find ourselves caught in a web of gossip. This could hurt our reputation, but it's not the most likely outcome unless Skyler directly escalates things.

6. <u>Revelation of Skyler's Vulnerability (Emotional Conflict, Moral Dilemma) - 8.3%</u>

If we uncover something personal in Skyler's locker, it would create internal conflict. We might feel conflicted about whether to expose her or keep it to ourselves. This would add depth to our interactions but is less likely than the more immediate consequences.

7. <u>Skyler's Revenge Plan (Counterattack, Exposure of Secrets) - 8.3%</u>

If Skyler has something truly damaging in her locker, she could retaliate aggressively. This could involve public scandals or blackmail, but this would depend on how far she's willing to go, making it a lower probability."

"I mean... *we can try*" Benji shrugged.

Flynn facepalmed. "DIDN'T YOU HEAR HIM?? WE HAVE 12.5% 12 FUCKING POINT 5 PERCENTAGE!"

"90% of gamblers quit just before they hit their big win."

"Oh please! Not you giving some statistics too!" Nathan rolled his eyes.

"Ben, Benji. This is not about your gambling! This is about finding some evidence to prove our theory"

"You know what! Fine, *I* will break into that locker, it seems there are two cowards here!" Benji crossed his arms,

"Bro... What if– Before her dying, you die? With her hand?" Flynn questioned,

Benji swallowed, "Then– Then– I will proudly die! Dying for my investigation! FOR MY COLLEAGUES!"

Nathan scoffed.

Saturday

15 March, 2025

1: 33 PM

"Are you sure she is having her games period?" Benji asked, doubtful.

"Yes. I have a friend in 11-B!" Nathan replied.

Flynn looking around, making sure no one looks at them,

Benji takes a hair pin from his pocket, Nathan raises his eyebrow,

"It's my sister's! I stole from her!" Benji explained.

With the paper clip, he tries to open the lock, at first, he struggles, but after a few minutes, it opens!

They opened the locker,

They see many things!!

Nathan looked at the paper at the top, he was afraid.

NICE TRY :)

- Skyler M

Benji is already planning to run away after seeing this,

"Let's pretend we didn't see..." Benji takes the paper from Nathan and keeps it back in the locker.

Flynn looks at the notebook inside it,

He turns the pages and sees ten storybooks.

"Her published books?" He asked,

And indeed it was, Eris Dorne's storybooks.

"Look at this notebook, it is filled with story ideas, character sketches, and cryptic, unfinished drafts." Flynn showed up to Benji and Nathan.

"Look at this! A photo of her, with her books!" Benji showed the photo.

"Wait. Why has she written about failure?

FAILURE

- *A lack of success.*
- *The neglect or omission of expected or required action.*

Failure is often seen as a negative experience, but it can be one of the most valuable teachers. It forces growth, resilience, and self-reflection. While failure might sting in the moment, it offers insights into what doesn't work and gives us the opportunity to learn, adapt, and try again. It's in the face of failure that we truly discover our strength, determination, and ability to rise after a setback. Embracing failure means recognizing it not as the end, but as a stepping stone toward eventual success and personal growth.

"Did she believe she was a failure?" Benji asked.

"Look! More books!" Flynn pointed to the stress management book and the health books.

"And a prescription to... Stress pills??" Benji read.

They saw Monica and Melody coming, so they ran from the place.

"Don't you think... **Sky is looking tired**?" Monica asked Melody,

The three were eavesdropping,

"I mean yeah... I thought I was the only one who noticed it,"

"Let's hope she gets well soon!"

"Yeah, we can just pray"

The three went away. Now in the ground,

"Have you heard that??" Flynn asked, confirming that he was not the one who witnessed it.

"Yeah bro! Omg, Skyler IS dying" Benji said.

"So, you both weren't wrong..." Nathan finally realized.

Meanwhile, Mia, sitting nearby the tree, looks at them, she waves to them,

"HEY!!"

They look towards her, Mia towards them,

"Why are you looking like you just ran a while?" Looking at all three of them. "Is everything okay?"

"SKYLER IS DYING" Benji said without any hesitation.

Mia looked shocked, "What— I don't believe. Benji, is this one of your jokes?" Now concerned.

"We literally found the evidence! She was depressed too! We found a mental health book, a stress management book, a prescription for stress pills, her friends were praying for her, and a note on failure. Conclusion: Skyler is depressed and dying!?" Benji named all the evidence.

Mia glared at three of them, she realized... They were not joking, this was serious, she knows they would never joke about a thing like this.

"We will try to find more clues... Maybe keep a closer eye on her," Nathan said,

"Can I help?" Mia asked.

Nathan's Statistical Notes: Skyler Maddox – Behavioral Analysis
Updated: March 2025

1. Frequency of Dramatic Reactions:

Observed Reactions: 15 instances (past 3 weeks)

Reaction Breakdown:

60% of reactions involve exaggerated expressions of hurt or shock (public emotional displays).

25% involve redirecting blame to others (usually Flynn or Riley).

15% result in genuine confrontation, though it's rare.

Statistical Conclusion:

Skyler's responses are highly skewed towards attention-seeking behaviors (85% of reactions), indicating a deep need for validation. The high frequency of public emotional outbursts suggests a well-established pattern.

Intervention needed: There is an approximate 35% likelihood that Skyler will escalate this behavior in an unpredictable way, possibly using retaliation tactics.

2. Patterns of Involvement in Group Discussions (Book Club Meetings):

Total Meetings Attended (past month): 0

Contributions to Conversation (When she used to attend):

50% involve diverting the topic back to personal issues (mostly using her writing or emotional struggles as a discussion pivot).

25% involve passive-aggressive comments aimed at other members.

25% are actual contributions to the discussion, but often disconnected from the topic.

Statistical Conclusion:

Skyler's engagement in meaningful conversation is statistically low, with 75% of contributions being self-centered or divisive. This suggests a reluctance to participate constructively and instead use the group as a platform for self-exposure or manipulation.

3. Likelihood of Skyler Initiating Conflict or Drama:

Total incidents (past 6 weeks): 7

Breakdown by event:

4/7 (57%) initiated by Skyler herself, usually through a public conflict or subtle provocation aimed at someone she feels threatened by or who does not give her enough attention.

2/7 (29%) escalated by Skyler after a minor comment or perceived slight.

1/7 (14%) was a completely external factor unrelated to her but still pulled into the drama.

Statistical Conclusion:

Skyler is responsible for initiating or escalating approximately 57% of the conflicts within her immediate circle. Her need for dominance in group dynamics is supported by a high tendency to control narratives through conflict initiation.

4. Skyler's Response to Confrontation (Investigative Context):

Past 3 confrontations (Flynn, Riley, Benji):

Flynn (January): 70% deflection, 20% defensive emotional response, 10% genuine admission.

Riley (February): 40% emotional manipulation, 30% accusation of being misunderstood, 30% complete silence.

Benji (March): 50% sarcasm, 30% ridicule of Benji's intelligence, 20% attempt to change the subject.

Statistical Conclusion:

Skyler is highly likely to deflect or manipulate confrontation, with only 10-20% of her responses being honest or reflective. She avoids direct accountability at almost all costs.

Overall Statistical Summary:

Skyler Maddox demonstrates a high frequency of self-centered, dramatic, and manipulative behaviors, often tied to a desire for attention or control. Her responses to group dynamics, confrontation, and emotional situations are primarily geared towards protecting her self-image and amplifying her emotional volatility for personal gain. Potential next steps: Observing if any new triggers (such as increased isolation or pressure) will push her toward more severe actions.

If you've been paying attention, you'd know Skyler's patterns don't add up. If you haven't—well, that's on you.

Sunday

16 January, 2025

2:05 PM

Skyler Behavior Surveillance Team

@CertifiedChaos: Thank you for attending the annual Skyler Behavior Surveillance Team meeting.

@SoftHeartedButNosy: Do we really have to make a group chat for this?

@CertifiedChaos: Why not??

@MainCharacterEnergy: Benji, why did you make this group chat? If you don't answer within a second, I am leaving

@CertifiedChaos: I am here to assign you all a role

@DataOrPerish: Role?

@CertifedChaos: Nathan: Observes habits.

Benji: Looks for emotional instability (bad idea).

Flynn: Overanalyzes EVERYTHING.

Mia: Actually talks to Skyler like a normal person.

@DataOrPerish: For a change, I agree with you

@CertifedChaos: THANK YOU <3333

@DataOrPerish: Don't ever again use emojis

@MainCHaracterEnergy: Okay I guess

@SoftHeartedButNosy: Okay

Monday

17 March, 2025

9:00 AM

Mia goes to 12-B,

"Can I talk with Flynn Hayes?" She asked his classmates,

Flynn noticed her, he goes towards her, "You okay?"

"Not really... *Skyler hasn't come to school today.*"

Flynn was stunned, was his theory coming true? Is she really not okay? No, he was expecting it to be fake, he wanted it to be fake. But it looks like this is no longer a theory but a reality, this is happening! But he can't believe it. Him, being able to solve it? For once, he's right? For once, he's not late? For once, everything is going how he wanted?

"What do you mean?" He finally asked,

"She wasn't in her classroom. When I asked her friends, they said she is not feeling well"

Flynn glared at her.

1:42 PM

Nathan adjusted his glasses, staring at his notebook, "Okay. I went through everything we found yesterday, and... I think we missed something. Something huge."

Flynn leaned in, exhausted, "Bigger than the fact that she's—...you know."

"Bigger than her impending doom? Damn, man." Benji said dead serious.

"Not helping." Mia glared at Benji.

Nathan flipped a page, "Look at this." He slides a small, crumpled note across the table. "I found it buried under some of her old stuff. It's encrypted, but the pattern is consistent with—"

Flynn grabbed the note, scanning it, "Nathan. Translation?"

"It's **blackmail**," Nathan said.

Beat. Silence.

"...What?" Mia's voice shook.

"Skyler was being blackmailed. The messages follow a timeline. Someone's been threatening her for months." Nathan said.

"What do they say?" Flynn tensed.

"They're vague, but one message keeps repeating." Reads from notebook, 'Keep quiet. Or we both lose everything.'" Nathan said.

"Who's 'we'?" Benji confused.

Nathan was staring at the blackmail note, muttering to himself, "This phrasing. It's... weird."

"How?" Flynn raised an eyebrow.

Nathan pointing at the words, "We both lose everything; This doesn't read like a typical threat. It's not just 'stay quiet or else'—whoever wrote this is saying they have something to lose too. That means Skyler has leverage over them."

"So... whoever's blackmailing her isn't just trying to control her. They're scared of something too." Mia slowly realized.

Benji blinking, then grinned, "Ohhh damn, so this isn't just some power move. This is a mutually assured destruction type of thing."

Flynn clenched his jaw, gripping the note tighter, "Which means whoever's doing this... it's someone she trusted. Someone close enough to know her secret, but also have one of their own."

"Someone we might even know." Mia chilled at the realization.

"She never told anyone? She was dealing with this alone?" Mia shook her head, horrified.

Flynn gripping the note, thinking out loud, "That explains everything—her shutting people out, her erratic behavior, even her disappearing randomly." He exhales, realization hitting him like a train. "We thought she was just—just dramatic. But the whole time... she was being threatened."

"Okay, but blackmail for what? Like, what did she do?" Benji asked.

Nathan flipped through his notes again, calculating, "That's what we don't know yet. But here's what I do know: The blackmail escalated at the same time she started withdrawing from the club. And guess what else happened that same month?"

"...She checked out The Last Confession." Flynn's heart sank.

Mia softly, realization dawning, "...She's hiding something."

Flynn is starting to pace, mind racing, "Okay. Okay. Let's put this together. Skyler's sick. She's hiding it. But that's not all—she's also being blackmailed. Meaning, whatever secret she's keeping isn't just about her health."

"Right. And the blackmailer isn't threatening to expose her condition. They're threatening her with something bigger—something that would destroy both of them." Nathan nodded.

"So, hold up. Who even is the blackmailer?" Benji asked.

"Someone close enough to know her secret. Someone who stands to lose just as much if it comes out." Flynn clenched his jaw.

Mia quietly, "...Do you think it's someone from the club?"

"Statistically speaking, the chances are high," Nathan said,

"'Statistically speaking, the chances are high.' Bro, say that in a normal way." Benji mockingly said.

"Fine. She's probably being blackmailed by someone we know." Nathan deadpan.

Flynn gritted his teeth, hands shaking, "And now she's missing. She's never missed school like this before. Never."

Mia nervously glancing at the door, as if hoping Skyler will walk in, "We need to find her. Before.."

"Before what?" Benji asked.

Flynn exhaled sharply, finally saying the words aloud, "...Before we're too late."

Another beat of silence. No one knows what to say. They've convinced themselves she was dying, they broke into her locker, and now? Now they know she's being blackmailed. And now... she's missing.

Mia picks up the crumpled note from Skyler's locker and smooths it out on the table.

"Keep quiet. Or we both lose everything." Mia read aloud, voice shaking.

"...We? Who's 'we'?" Benji asked again.

"That's the question, isn't it? Skyler isn't alone in this." Nathan said. Flynn rubbed his temples, "This isn't a goodbye letter. This is a warning."

Nathan scrolls through the encrypted files on his laptop. Most are locked, but one document catches their eye—titled "Transaction Records."

"Okay, I don't know what she's doing, but normal people don't just casually have encrypted files labeled 'Transaction Records.'" Nathan said.

"Maybe she's investing in stocks?" Benji asked,

"...Benji." Flynn looked at him,

"What? Rich people do that." Benji shrugged.

Mia pointing at the library's borrowing system, "And she checked out The Last Confession before all this. That book is literally about a guy being blackmailed."

"Statistically speaking, that's not just a coincidence," Nathan said.

Mia lays out the receipts found in Skyler's locker—pharmacy purchases, cash deposits, and a sketchy address scribbled on the back of one.

Nathan picks one of them, and flips through the receipt, he examined the receipt, then suddenly froze, "Wait. I know this address."

Mia leaning over, reading it, "Where is it?"

Nathan slowly, looking up at them, "**It's in Westbrook. Near the industrial district.**"

"Oh cool, totally normal. Just a casual little address near literal abandoned factories and sketchy crime central. Nothing suspicious at all." Benji nervously laughed.

Flynn frowned, thinking hard, "Skyler has no reason to be there. Why the hell would she be making payments connected to that place?"

"Are we... are we actually considering going there?" Mia hesitated.

"We shouldn't. Not yet. We don't have enough information, and if this is something illegal, we could be walking into something dangerous." Nathan said seriously.

Flynn gritted his teeth, shoving the receipt into his pocket, "Then we find out more first. But I'm not letting this go."

"Why does she have so many pharmacy receipts? Is she—" pauses, eyes widening "Oh my god. She's buying illegal drugs because she's dying."

Flynn & Nathan simultaneously said, "...Or she's involved in something worse."

Mia hesitated, "...Like what?"

Flynn takes one of the receipts, flipping it over to reveal the handwritten address.

"I don't know. But this? This is sketchy as hell." Flynn said.

Nathan crosses his arms, eyes scanning all the evidence in front of them.

"Let's go over the facts," Nathan said, Flynn leaned forward, focused, "One, Skyler isn't dying. We assumed that, but the evidence doesn't match."

"Two, she's being blackmailed. The note makes that clear." Nathan continued,

"Three, her flash drive has encrypted files and money records. Why?" Mia asked,

"Four, she's skipping class. What if—" Benji gasped "What if she's running away?!"

Nathan ignored him, "Five, her receipts show transactions that don't make sense for someone just buying medicine. And that address? It's worth checking out."

A silence falls over them.

Flynn gripped the note tightly, staring at the table but not really seeing it, "What if we're wrong again? What if this is just another one of my stupid theories that leads nowhere?"

Mia softly, placing a hand on his arm, "Flynn, look at the evidence. This isn't like before. You're not reaching for something that isn't there. We all see it too."

"Statistically speaking, this many coincidences don't happen without a pattern. You're not imagining this. We're onto something." Nathan nodded.

"Or hey, maybe we're totally wrong, and Skyler's just avoiding us because she secretly hates us. Either way, we find out, right?" Benji shrugged.

Flynn letting out a slow breath, gripping the note tighter, "No. This is real. And we're going to figure out what the hell is going on."

Flynn quietly, more to himself than anyone else, "Skyler isn't dying... she's in deep trouble."

"...What did she do?" Mia whispered.

"That's what we have to find out." Flynn grimaced.

CHAPTER IX

Sinclair's Game

Tuesday

18 March, 2025

8:27 AM

Flynn and Benji are sitting in Benji's classroom: 11-A.

"Okay, let's go over this again. Skyler is missing, she's being blackmailed, and there's an address linked to her that makes no sense. This isn't just her being dramatic—this is something big."

Benji nods, flipping through the notes,

"Huge. Like 'Netflix true crime documentary' huge. What if she's actually involved in something illegal?"

"That's what I'm trying to figure out." Flynn rubbed his temples.

"Nah, bro, you're trying to solve it. There's a difference." Benji said,

Before Flynn can snap back, a very unbothered, very jet-lagged **Zane Lockwood strolls up to them**, looking like he literally just came from Japan—which he did,

"HELLO!!!" Zane said excitedly, Flynn and Benji look at him, not as excited as him.

"Why do you two look like you just uncovered a government conspiracy?" Zane asked, "I was just away for a week!"

"Zane, not now," Flynn said, barely looking up.

"Nah, now. I haven't even been back for a full hour, and you two already look like you need therapy. What happened?" Zane asked.

Benji, of course, wastes no time dumping the entire mess on him,

"Oh, bro. You picked the best time to come back. Skyler is missing, she's possibly dying, but also maybe committing crimes, and she's definitely getting blackmailed. Oh, and there's a sketchy address involved!" Benji grinned.

Zane blinked slowly, processing, "What."

"We think she's involved in something illegal. We just don't know what yet." Flynn is dead serious.

Zane stares at them. Then at the mess of papers and notes on the table. Then back at them.

"WHAT??? First of all!?? WHAT THE FUCK?! Flynn. Everett. Hayes. You are back at investigating? I thought you left that!?" Zane was shocked, after so much advice, after finally stopping it. He's back to being a detective...

"I thought you left your past!? What is this!?" Zane couldn't believe it.

Flynn was now quiet.

"We got some clues... And imagine Zane! If we weren't back, then would we know this? Zane don't be disappointed. We don't want to be late– Not this time! Also I was getting bored!" Benji explained.

Zane takes a deep breath, trying to believe this and not panic...

"So let me get this straight. You two—who were supposed to be chilling—have now somehow convinced yourselves that Skyler is dying, getting blackmailed, and also running an underground crime ring. At the same time." Zane said.

"Basically," Benji replied.

"...I should've stayed in Kyoto," Zane said.

"NOO! If you have stayed there, you would not have heard all this!" Benji said.

11: 47 AM

Benji, Zane and Flynn are now sitting at the cafeteria,

"Westbrook? That's what the address was?" Zane asked and raised an eyebrow.

"Yeah! That's what Nathan said–"

"Woah!? So you dragged "Nathaniel the Statistician Supreme" too??" Zane surprised,

"AND Mia too!" Benji added.

"Wow. What a team!? With Detective Disaster, Mr. Actually, The Kind One and The Court Jester!" Zane said, now leaning back.

Ivy looked at the three sitting at the table,

"I heard someone say Westbrook..." Ivy said,

"Do you know something about that?" Flynn asked,

"Westbrook, huh? Interesting choice." She said and went away.

"What the fuck? What was that supposed to mean?" Benji asked Flynn and Zane.

I keep trying to convince myself that I'm wrong. That this isn't what I think it is. That maybe Skyler really is just avoiding us, that we're overcomplicating things. That there's some simple, logical explanation for why she's missing, why she's being blackmailed, why—

No. No, there isn't.

This isn't just some misunderstanding. This isn't just me grasping at shadows. I've done that before. I've been wrong before. And I know what it feels like to chase something that isn't real.

But this? This is real. The blackmail. The missing days. The address. The way Ivy looked at me when she said "Westbrook, huh? Interesting choice." Like she knew. Like we weren't supposed to find out.

I feel like I'm standing on the edge of something dangerous, and I should turn back. I should just let this go. But I can't.

Because if I'm right—if I really am right this time—then Skyler is in more trouble than any of us realized.

And if I'm wrong?

...Then maybe I don't know how to stop looking for answers anymore.

1:51 PM

Now, Skyler Behavior Surveillance Team has gathered in the book club room. Zane also had to join the group... By peer pressure, sitting at the back.

"What if someone catches us here?" Mia asked,

"Chill! We will just tell them that we are doing a group project!" Benji sugguested.

"Oh really?" Nathan crossed his arms, "A group project about Skyler? If Riley hears this, she will suspend all five of us,"

"Let's hope we don't get caught!" Flynn prayed.

"Okay– Hear me out!" Benji announced, "I have three theories regarding this,"

Everyone was looking at him,

"Theory #1: *Skyler's a Criminal Mastermind.*"

Mia felt offended, "What!? I know she acts no better than a criminal and probably beat up students... By her words, but seriously?"

"Benji, that's so ABSURD!" Flynn said.

"But what if Skyler's not missing? What if she's hiding?" Benji grinned, flipping through the notes.

"Hiding from what?" Flynn was not looking up.

"The feds. The mafia. The PTA—" Benji dead serious.

"No." Nathan shuts his notebook.

"Can you be serious for five seconds?" Mia stared at Benji in disbelief.

"I am! If you were running an underground crime ring, wouldn't you disappear?" Benji asked,

"...How is this my problem," Zane said from the back.

"Now, onto theory #2: *The Blackmailer is in This Room*!?!?" Benji acting shocked,

"You are saying as if YOU are the blackmailer!" Zane raised an eyebrow,

"...Statistically impossible." Nathan blank stared.

"That's exactly what the blackmailer would say," Benji replied,

"BENJI, STOP," Mia shouted.

Flynn rubbed his face, muttering, "I hate this."

"Look at you, already questioning reality." Benji grinned. "Now onto the last and third theory–"

"NO PLEASE," Everyone said,

"Theory #3: *The Address is a Trap—So We Should Go*"

Flynn thought hard, hesitant, "...We don't have enough information to go to Westbrook yet."

"And maybe that's exactly why we should go." Benji raised an eyebrow,

"That is the worst logic I have ever heard," Mia said.

"What if we wait and she's already dead?" Benji asked,

"Why do you immediately assume murder?" Zane asked,

"Because it's dramatic and I'm invested," Benji replied,
Nathan to Flynn, deadpan, "You owe me for putting up with this."

"I am sorry..." Flynn said to Nathan.

Meanwhile, Zane was looking at the four from the back, asking questions to himself and regretting everything.

"I should've known. The second I stepped back into this school, I should've turned around and booked the next flight out.

I thought I was coming home to peace. Maybe a chill conversation, some dumb drama I could laugh about. But no. Of course not. Instead, I walk in on Flynn looking like he hasn't slept in days, Benji grinning like he just discovered a murder, and Mia looking one step away from losing her mind.

And then they tell me.

Skyler is missing. She's being blackmailed. Possibly dying. Also? She might be a criminal. Because why not?

I tried to leave. I really did. But then Ivy appeared. Out of nowhere, like she knew I was thinking about escaping. Now I'm stuck listening to Flynn spiral, Benji make theories that sound too insane to be true (but somehow aren't), and Nathan attempt to use logic in a room full of chaos gremlins.

I can't do this. I just got back. I should be eating ramen and reminiscing about temples, not getting dragged into a full-blown conspiracy.

Maybe if I sit here quietly, they'll forget I exist."

Benji slaps his back, "Zane, thoughts? Do we storm Westbrook or what?"

"Oh my god.

I should've stayed in Kyoto." He thought.

Ivy has sat in the book club now. Right behind them, everyone looked at her. She was looking at them too, and smirked.

"She's SO gonna complain to Riley!" Mia said,

Ivy heard it, felt offended, "Don't worry Mia, I am not a bitch," Ivy replied.

"Of course, you are not a bitch you are the "Saint Ivy, Patron of Fake Sympathy" Benji said, Ivy rolled her eyes.

"Oh? You guys just figured that out? Cute." Ivy leaned back and smirked.

"What—how long have you been sitting there?" Flynn immediately tensed.

"Oh, don't mind me. Just reading "The Secret History" by Donna Tartt. You were so loud though—kinda hard not to hear." Ivy said with her fake innocence.

"Great. More people joining the conspiracy club." Benji grinned.

"I'm trapped in hell," Zane whispered to himself.

"You don't know anything." Flynn crossed his arms and glared.

"Don't I?" Ivy tilted her head, amused.

"You're just messing with us—" Flynn got interrupted,

"I mean, sure. But also? You're not wrong about Skyler. Something is going on with her. And if I knew that, well..." She smirked, "Maybe you guys are just a little slow." Ivy shrugged, now sitting near them,

"She's got a point," Benji said.

"Why are you even here?" Flynn asked,

Ivy leaned forward, voice dropping slightly, "Because I'm curious, Flynn. And you? You're desperate."

Beat. Flynn's jaw tightens. Ivy just smiles.

"If you know something, say it." Flynn leaned forward, intense,

"Aw, Flynn. You look so stressed. Maybe you should take a break." Ivy said with fake sympathy,

"I don't have time for this," Flynn replied,

Ivy twirled a strand of her hair, smirking, "Exactly. And that's why you're rushing. Making mistakes. Getting reckless." She leaned in, voice lowering, "Tell me, Flynn—what happens if you're wrong again?"

Beat. Flynn tenses. Ivy just smiles wider.

"You're looking in the wrong place, by the way." Ivy casually said, like it was nothing,

"What do you mean?" Flynn snapped to attention,

"You'll figure it out. If you're smart enough." Ivy grinned, refusing to elaborate.

Now Flynn has to chase another clue, and Ivy gets exactly what she wants.

"Ivy, stop—" Mia was concerned.

Flynn gritted teeth, barely holding it together, "Stay. Out. Of this."

Ivy soft chuckled, standing up, "I would, but you make it so entertaining."

"Oh my god. Now Ivy knows? Can we at least try to be subtle?" Mia now stressed,

"Oh, sweetheart. If you wanted this to stay a secret, you shouldn't have let Flynn Hayes handle it." Ivy grinned at Mia,

"What do you want?" Flynn glared,

Ivy examined her nails, casually, "Westbrook, huh?"

Flynn immediately on high alert, "What did you just say?"

"Oh? You didn't think you were the only ones looking into Skyler, did you?" Ivy's smile widens.

"When did "Ivy 'I Totally Get It' Sinclair" start looking into Skyler? That's our job!" Benji said,

"What else do you know? Or were you just overhearing us?" Nathan asked,

"You are the detectives, maybe you know the answer!" Ivy said,

"Oh so basically "The Drama Whisperer"?" Nathan asked.

"Can I help?" Ivy asked,

Flynn didn't even look at her.

Flynn slammed his hands on the table, standing up, "For once in your life, just SAY what you know!"

Silence. Everyone freezes. Ivy just smiles, completely unbothered,

"Aww, Flynn. That temper of yours? That's why you always lose." Ivy calmly said, smug.

Flynn realizes she's toying with him, but he's already lost control.

There was a slow, calculated stride. The faintest sigh, like she was so reluctant to get involved—except she always got involved. And then, the dreaded head tilt.

"I just think," Ivy started, her voice dripping with concern, "it's really interesting how tense everything's gotten. Don't you?"

Flynn inhaled sharply through his nose. "No."

Ivy ignored him, gracefully inserting herself between him and the mess unfolding before them. "I mean, no one's blaming you," she said, which instantly made Flynn tense. "But, like... if you had handled things a little differently, maybe this wouldn't be so bad?"

Ah. There it was. The casual flame-to-gasoline Ivy specialty.

Flynn pressed his fingers to his temples. "Ivy, I swear—"

"I'm just saying, people are talking," Ivy continued, lowering her voice like she was letting him in on a secret. "And you know I hate drama, but—"

"You are drama," Flynn snapped.

Ivy gasped, hand to her chest like he'd committed a crime. "That is so unfair."

He exhaled, exasperated. She was impossible. Every single time. It was like she couldn't not make things worse. She'd pretend she was just here to mediate, to understand—but in the end, she was the human embodiment of pouring fuel on a barely contained fire and then watching it burn.

And the worst part? She always got away with it.

Ivy just smiled, satisfied. "You're taking this way too personally." She tilted her head, with her fake sympathy, "How many times have you done this, Flynn? Run around chasing clues, thinking you have all the answers? And how many times have you been wrong?"

Flynn groaned. If instant headaches had a name, it would be Ivy Sinclair.

Benji wasn't just watching the chaos unfold—he was thriving in it.

Leaning back in his chair, arms crossed, a smug grin permanently glued to his face, he looked like a man watching the season finale of his favorite show. And Flynn? Flynn was the main character spiraling into complete mental collapse.

It was beautiful.

"Ohhh, buddy," Benji chuckled, biting into a snack like this was prime-time entertainment. "You're really losing it, huh?"

Flynn shot him a glare that could probably burn through steel. "Benji. Not now."

Benji, of course, ignored him. "No, no, I mean—this is incredible. I've never seen you this close to a full meltdown." He gestured vaguely. "It's like... watching a detective movie in real time, but the detective is unraveling at the seams."

Flynn groaned, dragging a hand down his face. "Benji, I swear to—"

"Ooooh, there it is! The forehead rub! That's the universal sign of maximum suffering!" Benji pointed with both hands. "Ladies and gentlemen, our dear Flynn is officially at his limit."

Flynn turned fully to face him now, jaw clenched. "Do you ever shut up?"

Benji just smiled wider. "Not when I'm witnessing cinema."

Ivy, still nearby, smirked. "Oh, I agree. This is top-tier content."

Benji nudged her. "Right? Like, if this was a reality show, Flynn would be one bad day away from flipping a table."

Flynn inhaled so sharply through his nose, he could probably summon a storm. "I hate both of you."

Benji beamed. "And I love this for you."

He was having the time of his life.

"So... I am asking you again, can I help?" Ivy smiled,

Flynn stared at her.

Case #39

<u>IVY SINCLAIR</u>

Full name: Ivy Lorraine Sinclair

Class: 11-A

Age: 15 (Fifteen)

Height: 5'4

Birthday: 25 December, 2009

MBTI: ENFP

Role in Book Club: Member- Drama Watcher
Relationship with Skyler: Opportunistic

Opinion on Skyler (Before & After):

Before:" I used to act supportive of Skyler, praising her talent and ideas, but deep down, I always saw Skyler as someone who could stir up drama for her own entertainment.

After: "I mean, it's interesting, right? Everyone's obsessed with her now. You included."

Key Quotes:

- "Skyler always had this air of mystery around her, like she knew something no one else did—but I knew better. It was all just part of the performance."
- "The thing about Skyler? She made it so easy to act like you cared."

What She Might Know: Ivy likely knows that Skyler isn't as indifferent as she pretends to be—she's just pushing people away before they can abandon her first.

Suspicious Behavior: Ivy often pretends to be sympathetic toward Skyler, but she subtly steers conversations to expose Skyler's weaknesses, watching closely for cracks in her composure.

NOTE: Ivy is enjoying this way too much. Not a reliable source. Avoid further conversation.

UPDATE

Skyler is missing.
Skyler is being blackmailed.
Skyler might be involved in something illegal.
Westbrook address = sketchy as hell.
Ivy is here now. Because of course she is.

New Problem

Ivy somehow knows things. Won't explain.
Benji is making it worse. As usual.
Zane regrets being born.

Nathan is trying to do math in a room full of idiots.

Mia is genuinely concerned and I probably should be too.

Ivy is toying with me. And it's working.

Questions That Will Drive Me Insane:

Who the hell is "we" in the blackmail message?

How does Ivy know about Westbrook?

Is she actually involved, or just screwing with me?

Is Skyler in danger, or are we the ones walking into a trap?

Am I solving something, or am I just chasing ghosts again?

NEW OBJECTIVE: Find out what Ivy actually knows (without letting her win).

Decide if we go to Westbrook.

Try not to completely lose my mind. (Failing.)

3:21 PM

Skyler Behavior Surveillance Team

@TiredButTrying has been added in the group.

@TiredButTrying: Why am I in this group chat, WITH THAT NAME!?

@DataOrPerish: Hello Zane.

@MainCharacterEnergy: You should have stayed in Kyoto, at least for one month..

@TiredButTrying: Yes...

@CertifiedChaos: @Everyone, all of you come to my house!!

@MainCharacterEnergy: NO

@SoftHeartedButNosy: What now, Benji?

@CertifiedChaos: =[

@DataOrPerish: FINE

A few minutes later, everyone reached Benji's house.

"Cool anime figurines! Last time when we came, it wasn't here..." Mia asked,

"I brought for him.." Zane answered,

Flynn crossed his arms, sitting in his bed. "Why did you call us here? DO NOT tell me we came just because you wanted to bing-watch some niche anime!!"

"Of course not! I can't act goofy every time. We are here to investigate! We should find who this blackmailer is. Or at least find some clues," Benji explained.

Nathan raised an eyebrow, "Wait– What? The probability of Benji actually talking some sense is 3.7% Can't believe I just witnessed it."

Benji rolled his eyes.

"What is our next plan?" Mia asked,

Benji showed the transaction records, "Sir Nathan of Numbers, would you like to analyze it?"

Nathan picked up the letters.

Date	Amount	Recipient	Notes
Jan 5, 2025	$2,500.00	(Redacted)	"Deposit Confirmed"
Jan 10, 2025	$2,500.00	(Redacted)	"Service Provided"
Jan 15, 2025	$2,500.00	(Redacted)	"Cleared"
Jan 20, 2025	$2,500.00	(Redacted)	"Final Transfer"
Feb 5, 2025	$2,500.00	(Redacted)	"Deposit Confirmed"
Feb 10, 2025	$2,500.00	(Redacted)	"Service Provided"
Feb 15, 2025	$2,500.00	(Redacted)	"Cleared"
Feb 20, 2025	$2,500.00	(Redacted)	"Final Transfer"
Mar 5, 2025	$2,500.00	(Redacted)	"Deposit Confirmed"

TOTAL: $50,000.00+ (inconsistent logs—some missing pages?)

☆ Same amount. Same pattern. What the hell was Skyler paying for?

☆ This isn't blackmail—this is a business.

☆ WHO is "(Redacted)"?

☆ Why did the payments suddenly stop after March?

Nathan adjusted his glasses, scrolling through the files, "You're all missing something. This isn't just random blackmail—it's organized."

"What do you mean?" Flynn snapped to attention,

Nathan tapped on a list of transactions, "Look at the payments. They aren't sporadic; they're scheduled. Same amount, same intervals. This isn't hush money—it's a business."

Benji grinned, nudging Flynn, "Told you. We're dealing with a full-on criminal operation."

"But Skyler—she wouldn't... would she?" Mia stared at the files, horrified.

"Then explain this." Flynn slammed down another note—one with Skyler's handwriting, tied to a recent transaction.

"March 10 – Last one. We're done after this. No more risks. If he asks, tell him the files are gone."

"If something happens, don't contact me."

Silence. No one has an answer.

Flynn read it over and over, gripping the paper tightly, "Last one"? She was planning to stop?"

Benji's eyes widened, grinning like he just won the lottery, "Holy sh—Bro. She KNEW something was coming. She was trying to get OUT."

"'If something happens, don't contact me'... What the hell was she afraid of?" Mia whispered, horrified.

"More importantly—who is he?" Nathan analyzed it, seriously.

Zane leaned back, rubbing his face, "I'm guessing we're not talking about God here."

Flynn gritted teeth, realization sinking in, "She was scared of someone. She was scared of whoever was actually running this."

Wednesday

19 March, 2025

8:10 AM

Flynn goes to the classroom of 11-A

Benji looked at him, "What are you doing here?" He was curious,

"We need to talk to her, she knows something..." Flynn explained, Benji nodded.

Ivy was looking at them, sitting on her bench. "I wonder what he is doing here?" She thought.

Flynn went towards Ivy,

"I need to talk with you..." He said.

Ivy stands up and they go outside of the classroom.

"So?" Ivy tilted her head,

Flynn gritted teeth, stepping closer, "Enough games, Sinclair. What do you know about Westbrook?"

"Funny. I was just about to ask you the same thing." Ivy smirked, her arms crossed.

"I'm not in the mood for this." Flynn was dead serious, eyes narrowed.

Ivy mockingly surprised, "Oh? That's new." She leans against the doorframe, tilting her head, "What do you think Westbrook is, Flynn?"

"I don't know yet. But you do." Flynn was frustrated.

"Maybe. Maybe not." Ivy grinned. She watches him carefully, waiting for the moment he cracks.

"Cut the act, Ivy. Why did you say it like we weren't supposed to find it?" Flynn asked,

"Because you weren't." Ivy calmly said, unfazed.

Silence. Flynn's jaw clenches. Ivy watches him, pleased with herself.

"Tell me what Westbrook is." Flynn lowered his voice, intense,

Ivy mockingly thought, tapping her chin, "Hmm. No."

"IVY—" Flynn fumed.

"Relax, detective. If you're really as smart as you think you are, you'll figure it out soon enough." She said, and steps past him, voice dropping to a whisper, "Assuming you can handle the truth." Ivy softly chuckled.

She walks away, leaving Flynn seething, fists clenched, mind racing.

Flynn goes back to his classroom. He sits at his desk, surrounded by papers, notes, and printouts. His hands are pressed against his forehead, and his breath is uneven.

Flynn muttered to himself, flipping through his notes, "Westbrook. Skyler. The blackmail. The payments. The last note. What am I missing? What am I not seeing?"

He scribbles something down. Then immediately crosses it out. His handwriting is getting messier.

Flynn muttered under his breath, frustrated, "It doesn't fit. Nothing fits."

His hands clench into fists. He exhales sharply. His vision blurs—he hasn't slept properly in days.

Flynn quietly, but shaking, "What if I'm wrong again?"

Silence. That thought lingers. He stares at the chaos in front of him, his mind running in circles. He should stop. He won't.

He stared at his notes.

BLACKMAIL?? SKYLER'S SECRET?? WHAT THE HELL IS GOING ON??

✔ *Skyler is being blackmailed.*

✔ *Money. Payments. WHY.*

→ *Blackmail.*

→ *Money.*

WHY

✔ *Skyler wrote "BURN EVERYTHING."*

*X **WHO THE HELL IS HE???***

HIM!?

TIMELINE:

☆ *Before March: Normal?? Or already f-ed up??*

March = Payments STOPPED.

☆ *March: EVERYTHING STOPS. SKYLER WANTS OUT. BLACKMAIL BEGINS.*

☆ *Now: Skyler is GONE.*

???!! MISSING LINK!!??!

THEORIES:

Skyler was just a victim. No, she's hiding something.

1. Skyler was part of something illegal. (BUT WHAT???!)

2. The blackmailer is exposing her past. (WHY NOW??!)

3. IVY KNOWS. (SHE'S PLAYING WITH ME.)

<u>*FINAL NOTE*</u>

"What if I'm wrong again?"

I'm missing something. It's right there, just out of reach. Skyler isn't just a victim—she's hiding something. Ivy knows. The blackmail, the payments, Westbrook—none of it fits. What the hell happened in March?

What if I'm wrong again? What if I'm chasing ghosts?

...No. I can't stop now.

11:30 AM

Many of the book club members are in the book club room. Flynn and his friends were sitting together, meanwhile Mia and Zane were sitting off to the side while the rest of the group argued over theories. Flynn is pacing. Benji is making wild accusations. Ivy is smirking. Nathan is probably calculating the odds of their survival. Zane? Zane is questioning every life decision that led him here.

Zane watched the chaos, deadpan, "So, be honest—at what point did we completely lose control?"

"Oh, Zane. We never had control." Mia was tired and sighed. Running a hand through her hair,

"Cool. Cool. Just checking." Zane slowly nodded, accepting his fate.

They both stare as Flynn mutters frantically to himself, Benji starts writing "Skyler = Secret Criminal??" on the board, and Ivy watches with pure amusement.

"Has he... always been like this? After my absence?" Zane gestured vaguely at Flynn.

Mia sympathetic, but also worried, "No. This is new. He's—" she paused, glancing at Flynn's frantic scribbling "—getting worse."

"Right. And instead of stopping him, we're just... letting this happen?" Zane exhaled, rubbing his temples.

"What else can we do?" MIia grimaced.

Zane sighed, leaning back in his chair, staring at the ceiling, "I should've never come back."

Mia looked at Zane, "What do you think about this? Your whole experience after coming back from Kyoto?"

Zane rolled his eyes. "I was gone for one week. One. Week. Not even a month, not even two weeks, just seven days. How did things fall apart this badly?

Skyler is missing. Flynn is losing his mind. Benji thinks this is the best plot twist of his life. Nathan is treating this like a math problem. Ivy? Oh, she's THRIVING. And you? You are the only one who seems to realize this is getting dangerous.

And me? I have no idea what's going on.

I mean, I get it—blackmail, shady money, Skyler being way more involved in something than we thought. But now we're talking about Westbrook like it's some cursed word, and Flynn is pacing like a man possessed.

What are we even doing?

From finding 'THE INCIDENT' to 'WESTBROOK' we have come a long way!

They act like they're solving some huge mystery, but the more they find, the worse it gets. This isn't just about Skyler anymore. It's about whatever she was in, whoever's pulling the strings, and why Ivy won't just SAY WHAT SHE KNOWS.

How do you people function?"

Meanwhile, in the next table...

Flynn was thinking, his hands in his chin, looking at his notes.

"I think– We should go,"

"Go exactly where?" Nathan asked,

"To Westbrook" Flynn finally said.

Benji and Nathan were silent.

"No..." Nathan was not ready.

Flynn hands on the table, voice firm, "We're going to Westbrook. Today."

"That's impulsive." Nathan calmly said but unbothered.

"I don't care." Flynn sharply glared,

"Flynn, we don't even know what we're walking into," Mia said from the back. Concerned and shook her head.

"And sitting around isn't going to change that." Flynn was frustrated.

"Every time we get close to something real, we hit a wall. Westbrook is the first thing that actually connects back to her. That's not a coincidence." He continued,

Then, Flynn stared at Ivy, sitting right in front of them, still reading her book.

"You keep acting like this is a dead end. But if it was, you wouldn't be messing with me about it."

"And yet, here we are."

"What if Skyler doesn't want us to find her?" Mia asked,

"Then she should've been better at hiding. I mean she knows we broke into her locker, and yet, she hasn't confronted us."

Silence. That was colder than intended. But Flynn doesn't take it back.

"We're running in circles. Westbrook is the only new lead. Ivy knows more than she's saying, and I refuse to let her control this. Skyler is hiding something. If she didn't want to be found, she wouldn't have left clues. If I stop now, I might never figure it out. And I can't live with that." Flynn concluded.

Nathan adjusted his glasses, scrolling through his notes, "You're ignoring crucial gaps in the information. We don't know who's actually tied to Westbrook. We don't know if Skyler even went there. We don't know—"

Flynn cutting him off, voice sharp "And we're not going to figure it out by doing NOTHING."

"That's not how investigations work." Nathan deadpan, tilted his head.

"Lucky for us, this isn't a real investigation." Benji grinned.

"That's exactly the problem." Nathan sighed, rubbing his temples. "You're all treating this like a game. It's not. If we go in without information, we're just stumbling around in the dark."

"So we just sit here and wait? Hope the answers magically appear?"

"That would be smarter than running straight into the unknown."

Nathan gestured to the notes in front of him, "We still don't know what Westbrook is. A location? A person? A company? And even if we assume it's a place, what's our next step? Just show up and hope for answers?"

"That was kinda the plan, yeah." Benji grinned.

Nathan stared at him in disbelief, "You people exhaust me."

"This is the most inefficient investigation I've ever seen.

Flynn is spiraling, and I can't stop him.

Benji is reckless, and I really can't stop him.

Ivy is manipulating everyone, and she knows it.

Maybe I should just let them crash and burn so they learn their lesson." Nathan thought.

He sighed. He knows he won't do that. He's stuck with them now.

"I don't think Skyler even wants our help." Mia crossed her arms, visibly uneasy.

"What?" Flynn turned back, taken aback,

Mia hesitated, then softer, "What if she's hiding for a reason? What if we just make things worse?"

Flynn frustrated, running a hand through his hair, "You're saying we just ignore this?"

Mia was quiet, avoiding his gaze, "I'm saying... maybe we're the last people she wants to find her."

That one stings. Flynn clenches his jaw but doesn't respond.

Mia said softer, but serious, "You keep talking like she's in trouble. But maybe she chose to disappear."

"You really think she just left? Without a word? Without telling anyone?" Flynn asked, his voice sharp,

"Maybe she thought we wouldn't understand." Mia quietly said,

Silence. That one hits Flynn harder than he expected. He looks away, running a hand through his hair.

"Or maybe she's in a witness protection program and forgot to send a memo." Benji tried to lighten the mood,

"I'm serious. We don't even know what we're walking into." Mia exasperated, looking at the group,

Nathan nodded in agreement, "Finally, someone making sense."

Mia was frustrated, Flynn wasn't listening to her, she finally snapped.

She stood up, "Flynn, you're not doing this for Skyler. You're doing this for yourself."

"What the hell is that supposed to mean?" Flynn was stunned, and got defensive.

Mia was firm, not backing down, "You don't care if she wants help. You just want to be right."

Everyone looked at Mia, shocked.

Benji cheerfully leaned back in his chair," So, it's basically a crime scene? We should go."

"That is not the takeaway here." Nathan stared at him, unamused,

"Look, we have an address, a missing person, and a bunch of unanswered questions. What's the worst that could happen?" Benji grinned and shrugged,

Zane gestured at the absolute disaster of a situation they're in, "I don't know, maybe everything?"

Silence. Benji looked around the room.

Benji grinned, feet up on the table, "So, we're going, right?"

"This isn't a group field trip." Nathan stared at him, unamused,

Benji ignored him, "Think about it. We've got a missing girl, a creepy location, and probably some illegal stuff happening—this is PEAK mystery movie material."

"Benji, this isn't a game." Mia was frustrated,

"Maybe not for you." Benji grinned wider,

Flynn shoots him a glare. Benji raises his hands in fake surrender, but he's still clearly enjoying every second of this chaos.

Benji grinned, fake-serious, "Listen, if we go to Westbrook, there are only two possible outcomes—"

"Oh no," Mia said already exhausted,

Benji counted on his fingers, "One, we uncover a deep, dark conspiracy and get murdered for knowing too much—"

"Sounds about right." Zane nodded, dead inside,

Benji ignored him, "Or two, it's completely abandoned, but there's like, one single flickering streetlight and just vibes—which is honestly scarier."

Nathan flatly, without looking up, "Or three, it's just a normal place, and you're being ridiculous."

"Unlikely." Benji grinned wider,

Benji leaned toward Flynn, conspiratorial whisper, "Bro. What if Skyler wanted us to find Westbrook?"

Flynn already on edge, narrowing his eyes, "What are you saying?"

"What if this is part of her master plan? Like, she knew we'd figure it out—what if we're supposed to go there?"

"...That would mean she left breadcrumbs on purpose."

Nathan sighed loudly, rubbing his temples, "Oh no, he's buying it."

"Just saying. Maybe you need to do this." Benji grinned,

Flynn suddenly looks more determined than ever. Benji looks very pleased with himself.

"We don't have enough information. We should wait." Nathan said seriously, arms crossed.

"Boooooring," Benji smirked and shrugged,

"You realize that walking into an unknown situation with no plan is how people die, right?"

"Yeah, but we're main characters, so we have plot armor."

"I hate you."

"Love you too, bro."

Ivy stood up and went towards the table.

Ivy watched Flynn, tilting her head, "You're getting worked up."

"I wonder why." Flynn narrowed his eyes,

Ivy soft chuckled, pretending to be indifferent, "All I'm saying is... Westbrook is a big risk. Are you sure you can handle it?"

Silence. That hits a nerve. Flynn tenses, jaw tightening. Ivy watches, pleased.

"Maybe Mia's right. Maybe you should just let this go." Ivy sweetly said, like she's being helpful,

"I'm not letting this go." Flynn was furious,

"Then I guess we're going to Westbrook, aren't we?" Ivy innocently asked,

Nathan flipped through notes, suddenly serious, "Wait. I think I just found something."

Flynn was not paying attention, focused on Ivy, "Not now, Nathan."

Nathan annoyed, looking at the group, "Okay, but when this backfires—just remember I tried to warn you."

Ivy leaned back, smug, "Fine. You want the truth?"

"Obviously," Flynn replied,

"You won't like it," Ivy smirked,

Beat. Everyone tensed. She watches Flynn closely, waiting for him to break first.

"Then tell me," Flynn said, impatient,

Ivy slowly, carefully, enjoying this, "Westbrook isn't just a place. It's a problem."

"That... means nothing." Mia frowned,

"Doesn't it?" Ivy grinned, tilting her head,

Nathan pinched the bridge of his nose, sighing deeply, "I swear to God, Sinclair—"

Flynn cutting him off, stepping closer to Ivy, voice sharp, "Stop playing games. Just say it."

Ivy locked eyes with him, her smirk softening—just slightly, "Westbrook is the reason she ran."

Silence. That lands heavier than anyone expected. Flynn clenches his fists. Benji raises an eyebrow. Mia's expression tightens. Zane? Zane looks like he wants to leave the country again.

"What did they do to her?" Flynn's breath hitched, his voice low,

Ivy smiled slightly, but there's something unreadable in her expression, "Now that... is the right question."

"I need a passport renewal. I could be back in Kyoto by next week." Zane muttered to himself,

"Aw, come on. Think of the adventure." Benji said with fake sympathy,

"I think of death instead." Zane was dead inside,

"That's fair," Nathan said flatly.

Zane watched Ivy manipulate Flynn, sighing deeply, "So. Hypothetically. If one were to flee the country... what's the best airline?"

"I'd recommend something one-way," Nathan said without looking up,

Mia side-eying him, mildly concerned, "You're actually serious?"

Zane stared at the ceiling, dramatically sighing, "Listen. I left for one week. When I came back, people were talking about blackmail, missing girls, and now we're about to walk into something called Westbrook like it's a casual field trip. I think running is a valid response."

"Nah, man, you're stuck with us now." Benji laughed, shaking his head.

Zane was regretting everything, he would rather be anywhere than here. He pulls out his phone and looks up flights. He starts calculating how much money he needs to disappear.

"Okay... direct flights to anywhere but here... oh, Tokyo has a good deal..." Zane muttered to himself, scrolling on his phone,

Nathan glanced at him, unimpressed, "You're actually looking up flights?"

"Yes. This is called self-preservation. You should try it." Zane was dead serious,

Benji laughed, snatching his phone away, "Nope. You're staying in this mess with us."

Zane was emotionless, staring at nothing, "I am so tired."

Zane leaned toward Mia, whispering, "Mia. Be honest. This is stupid, right? You wanna leave?"

Mia was hesitant, looking at Flynn, then sighing, "...We can't just leave."

"I mean, technically, we can—"

"If you disappear now, you'll just spend the rest of your life wondering what happened," Nathan said,

"That's the entire point of leaving." Zane stared at him, deadpan,

"Nah, bro. You love the drama. You'd get bored in five minutes." Benji grinned, wrapping an arm around Zane's shoulder,

"I hate that you're right," Zane grumbled, trying to escape Benji's grip.

Zane stands up and goes towards the exit,

"I could just walk away. Right now. No one can stop me." Zane said, standing at the exit, looking back at the group,

"Oh, but I will." Benji grinned, blocking the door,

"I fucking hate all of you." Zane glared,

"That's fair," Nathan said.

"If this were a movie, this is the part where I'd walk out of the theater," Zane muttered,

Benji laughed, clapping him on the back, "Too bad, dude. You're in the main cast."

"I refuse this role," Zane replied.

"Okay! It is decided!! **I and Benji will go to Westbrook!**" Flynn announced,

Benji cheered, everyone was in disbelief.

The bell rings, everyone goes from the room,

"I AM SO EXCITED!" Benji said, walking with Flynn.

Suddenly a random student overhears them,

"Westbrook? *Why the hell would you go there?*"

"Why? What do you know?" Flynn asked,

Random Student lowered their voice, shaking their head, "Nothing. Just... don't get involved with those people." He walks away quickly, like they said too much.

CHAPTER X

Ghosts Of The Past

20 March, 2025

3:01 PM

This is the day... Flynn and Benji have decided to go to Westbrook. After everyone saying NO to them, they are too stubborn to actually listen to them. With only one objective in their mind, What the fuck is Westbrook?

3:21 PM

Westbrook was located in an old business district, once thriving, now mostly empty—just a few abandoned office buildings left.

They looked around, Flynn understood something with the atmosphere...

Flynn:

Westbrook was once a respectable research hub, a place tied to academia and innovation. But now? It's empty. Forgotten. Wrong.

☆ Once a thriving district, now barely mentioned in conversations.

☆ The buildings still stand, but the people who worked there? Gone, like they never existed.

☆ Paper trails erased, but if you look closely—not everything was cleaned up.

To most, Westbrook is just an abandoned office complex...

Benji nudged Flynn, whispering, "You feel that? This place is giving me found footage horror movie vibes."

Flynn scanned the area, "Yeah. And we're the idiots who walked into it."

There was a building with open doors, "Should we go there?" Benji asked, Flynn nodded.

They entered the building... The building was almost empty, with only some items of furniture placed, the sign board on the wall was almost broken,

The rusted signboard swayed slightly in the wind, its letters barely holding on. 'V A N G U A R D R E S...'—the rest was missing, shattered pieces of the name scattered on the ground.

Benji was speechless. Maybe– Everyone around him was right, this indeed looks DANGEROUS.

"Flynn... That– Looks like gunshots," He showed his concern,

But Flynn didn't care, he would not step out of this building until they found something. "Benji, it's just glass shatters"

They looked at the wall nearby, there were messages scratched into it.

W E T RIED T O WA RN TH E M.

NO TH ING I S SA F E

I T WA S NE V E R RE A L

D O N'T L OOK BE H IN D Y O U

Benji curled his lips, opened his phone, and looked at his; Skyler Behavior Surveillance Team- Group chat, ready to call them if the plan didn't work out.

"We should go to the first floor", Flynn said,

The first floor was dark, they opened their phone torch to look at things,

"OH. MY. GOD."

The room was filled with chairs and tables, almost looking like an office room.

"Is this an office building?" Flynn asked,

"Damn... We came to some bankrupt company's office." Benji said,

"And the company's name is Vanguard Res... something? Benji, do you recall any company named like this, because I don't!"

"I have no fucking idea! I came for some adventure, not checking abandoned offices"

"Well, you did sign up for this so you can't complain"

Both started looking into the room, there were a bunch of papers and documents... Flynn is in one corner while Benji is in the other.

A few minutes later, Flynn hears a shout of his name, "FLYNN!!"

Flynn goes towards Benji, "Found something??" He asked,

"Look at this..."

VANGUARD RESEARCH INSTITUTE

EMPLOYEE RECORD – LEVEL [REDACTED]

NAME: Maddox, Skyler

POSITION: [REDACTED]

STATUS: TERMINATED (March ▮▮, 20▮▮)

Flynn was visibly confused, how did he end up here?

Benji looked at him, holding Skyler's Redacted Employee Record, "So... she wasn't just involved. She worked here?"

"And they don't want anyone to know."

Skyler Maddox. Employee of Vanguard Research Institute. Not a suspect. Not a criminal. Not just "involved"—but inside it.

I came here looking for ghosts, and instead, I found her name written in ink. Real. Tangible.

And someone tried to erase it.

Benji stands up, now sitting in one of the chairs, "What should we do now?"

"We should find more clues, shall we go to the second floor?"

They both went towards the stairs,

Now, in this room were a bunch of computers, Benji sat near one of them and accidentally started a computer, there was a bright light in the room, both flinched.

Flynn looked at the computer's screen, and tried to log into the computer.

VANGUARD RESEARCH INSTITUTE - LOGIN SCREEN

Username: **S_Maddox01**
Password: ********
Last Attempt: 2 days ago - **FAILED**
Reason: Incorrect Password
[ ] Remember Me [ ] Forgot Password?

? **Access Denied. Please Try Again.** ?

Benji leaned over the keyboard, squinting, "Bro, this thing's ancient. Who the hell is still trying to log in?"

Flynn checking the timestamp, stomach dropping, "Whoever it is... they got here first."

"Someone already tried to login?" Flynn raised an eyebrow,

"You should try her birthdate," Benji suggested.

02062009

The computer opened. Both looked at each other, each having a smile on their face.

They looked at many files, "Click that EMPLOYEE FILE," Flynn clicked it,

---

VANGUARD RESEARCH INSTITUTE - EMPLOYEE FILE

NAME: Maddox, Skyler
STATUS: ~~TERMINATED~~ [REDACTED]
LAST KNOWN ASSIGNMENT: [REDACTED]
DATE OF SEPARATION: March ██, 20██

"Subject's involvement in ~~unauthorized~~ [REDACTED] has been logged.

No further contact is to be made. Immediate action is authorized."

"Look at other files, what is 'BURN EVERYTHING' file?"
Flynn clicked.

VANGUARD RESEARCH INSTITUTE - FOLDER

Folder Name: BURN EVERYTHING
Last Modified: March 20█

Files:
[ ] Confidential Report – [Empty]
[ ] Data Set A – [Empty]
[ ] Project Files – [Empty]

No Files Available.

"She knew this place was going down."
"Dude, this is literally horror movie energy. If the folder says 'BURN EVERYTHING,' we should not be here."
Then, they checked the email draft,

VANGUARD RESEARCH INSTITUTE - EMAIL DRAFT

To: [REDACTED]
Subject: **We Need to Talk. I Can't Do This Anymore.**
I don't care what they told us, I can't be a part of this.
If you're still in, that's on you. But I—

Message not sent.

"She wanted out."
"Okay, great, love that, can we leave now?"
Suddenly, something popped in the computer,

Both got jumpscared, "WHAT THE FUCK!?" "HUH!?"

?? SYSTEM WARNING ??

This application is being closed.
Please wait while the system shuts down.
? Logging off...
? Closing session...
? Removing User Credentials...
? ERROR: FILE ACCESS REVOKED.
? ERROR: USER NOT AUTHORIZED.
? ERROR: CONNECTION LOST.

? SYSTEM FAILURE ?

And then, the computer's screen goes black.

Benji leaned over Flynn's shoulder, reading the screen, "Uh. So. This is awkward."

Flynn scanning the redacted lines, "She worked here."

Benji sarcastically, but nervous, "Wow, no way. The heavily redacted 'Maddox, Skyler – TERMINATED' file didn't tip you off?"

Flynn ignored him, eyes sharp, "They erased her. Like she was never here."

Benji gestured at the screen, voice rising, "Yeah, and we were never here either. Right? RIGHT? We should go."

Flynn muttered, "Something's missing. They wiped too much..." He looked at Benji, "You took photos of that, right?" Pointing at the screen,

"Yeah!" Benji replied.

"This isn't just about her internship. This is bigger."

"Dude... what the hell were they doing here?"

"We should continue our search", And they go back to the search,

They look at another computer, which suddenly opened. They went towards it, the screen flickers, a faint glow barely lighting the abandoned office. He clicks on the keyboard—nothing. Then they try again. And suddenly... the system responds.

> LOGIN ATTEMPT #1

USERNAME: **s.maddox**

PASSWORD: ******

? ERROR: ACCOUNT DISABLED

> LOGIN ATTEMPT #2

USERNAME: **[REDACTED]**

PASSWORD: ******

? ERROR: INCORRECT PASSWORD

> LOGIN ATTEMPT #3

USERNAME: **guest_access**

PASSWORD: ******

? SUCCESSFUL LOGIN – LIMITED MODE

"Someone else tried to log in," Flynn whispered, eyes narrowed,

Benji hovered behind him, voice an octave higher than usual, "Oh, COOL. Just what we needed. A third party in this mess."

"Whoever it was... they were just here."

Later... Flynn brushes dust off the abandoned desk. There's a crumpled paper, typed but never completed. The last few sentences are unfinished—like someone left in a hurry.

VANGUARD RESEARCH INSTITUTE

CONFIDENTIAL REPORT – INTERNAL USE ONLY

Date: March ██*, 20*██

Author: [REDACTED]

Subject: Data Integrity Assessment – Project [REDACTED]

The latest adjustments to the research parameters have produced results inconsistent with our initial projections.

Several reports require retroactive corrections before publication. A discrepancy of ██*.*█*% must be accounted for in the next dataset submission.*

The subject in charge of documentation, S. Maddox, has raised concerns regarding the alterations. She has requested—

Further modifications should be processed through [REDACTED] before external review.

Any remaining physical copies must be—

"Skyler wasn't just involved—she was questioning them."

Benji picked up the page, eyes scanning the cutoff text, "Yeah, and judging by this sudden stop, I'm guessing that didn't go over well."

"They didn't just erase the files. They erased her."

Suddenly, Benji noticed something, **A desk drawer left open**—like someone was just here.

He looked at Flynn, still searching all papers,

"... Did you open that drawer?" He pointed to that drawer,

"I thought you were searching there... I didn't go there!"

Benji was speechless... He looked back, at the top left corner,

A security camera. A red light blinking—who's watching?

"I remember that security camera was not working!"

"There was a security camera? I just noticed now..."

Flynn looked at the trash bin nearby, there was a half-burned piece of paper.

"Flynn, I think we are being watched,"

Flynn was afraid, both were.

"Before us... Someone else came here," Flynn said,

"WHO?!"

"We should leave..."

Suddenly, a computer randomly opened, they both looked at the computer,

The screen flickered, and suddenly the cursor moved—on its own.

"What the fuck..." They both said in sync.

"Unauthorized access detected."

And before Flynn or Benji could react, the entire system shuts down.

They both go back to the first floor,

Benji pointed at a chair, "... That chair was slightly pulled out—Like something was sitting three minutes ago,"

They sprinted to the ground floor,

Benji saw a door which was not open before...

Benji gripped Flynn's arm, "Tell me that door was open before."

Flynn stared at it, heart pounding, "It wasn't."

They heard something,

Is it a footstep?

Is it a door creak?

Is it a cough?

But they know for sure... Someone is here.

Flynn's phone buzzes, he sees he got a message,

UNKNOWN NUMBER

@Anonymous: Y O U N E E D T O L E A V E. N O W

@Anonymous: T H E Y K N O W Y O U A R E H E R E

@Anonymous: R U N

Benji gripped Flynn's arm, whisper-shouting, "We are SO not alone in here."

Flynn frozen, staring at the dark hallway, "We need to—"

And before he could finish his sentence, they hear a LOUD NOISE. A DOOR SLAMS.

"G O ! !" We need to get the fuck out of here," Benji said.

They start sprinting, now out of the building.

Flynn looked back, there was a figure, not chasing them but watching them.

Now, they start running and get out of Westbrook.

They finally stop, breathless, hearts pounding. Flynn leans forward, hands on his knees. Benji? Fully pacing, hands on his head, looking like he just saw his own obituary.

Benji was panting, pointing back at Westbrook, "Cool. Awesome. Love that. Let's NEVER do that again."

Flynn was still catching his breath, eyes narrowed, "Someone was there."

Benji laughed hysterically, still in fight-or-flight mode, "NO. WAY. You think?? What gave it away, genius? The slamming door, the mystery footsteps, or the 'RUN' text message from Satan himself?!"

Flynn ignored him, pacing, mind still racing, "We need to figure out who got there first. They were watching us, but why?"

"WHY? BRO. WHO CARES WHY?! We almost DIED. Let's take the win and call it a day." Benji threw his hands up,

"They knew we'd come."

"Oh my god, what if they had like, an evil villain monologue just WAITING for us? 'Ah yes, Detective Flynn Hayes and his Emotional Support Disaster Friend, right on schedule.'"

"What if they did?"

Benji stops. He does not like that thought.

"Nope. Nope nope nope. I refuse. I'm deleting this day from my brain."

6:21 PM

Case #39

Location: Westbrook (Original Vanguard Research Site)

Status: Compromised. Someone knew we were there.

What We Found:

✓ Skyler's name in a redacted employee file. Confirmed she worked there. They tried to erase her.

✓ An unfinished report. She raised concerns. Someone cut it off mid-sentence.

✓ An empty folder labeled "BURN EVERYTHING." Someone wiped the evidence, but left the warning.

✓ Her old login screen was still there. Someone else tried to access it—recently.

What Went Wrong:

☆ We weren't alone.

☆ Something—or someone—was watching us.

☆ A security camera moved. (Confirmed? Or paranoia?)

☆ A door SLAMMED shut right before we left.

☆ We got a text that just said: "RUN." (Unknown number.)

☆ We left too fast. (Didn't take enough evidence. Need to go back?)

What This Means:

☆ Skyler wasn't just involved—she was deep inside this operation.

☆ She didn't just leave. She ran.

☆ Westbrook was erased—but someone is still protecting it.

☆ Who else has been digging into this? Did Skyler come back here before disappearing?

Next Steps (If We Don't Want to Die):

1. Figure out who ELSE was at Westbrook. (Were they watching us—or waiting for us?)

2. Trace who tried logging into Skyler's account. (Was it her? Or someone trying to erase more evidence?)

3. Find out where Vanguard moved next. Westbrook wasn't the end—it was just step one.

4. DO NOT GO BACK TO WESTBROOK ALONE. (Benji made me write this.)

"Did you finish your notes?" Benji asked from the back. Flynn keeps his notebook and sits with his friends. Benji and Nathan have now arrived at his house.

"WHAT is Vanguard Research Institute?" Flynn asked,

Nathan flipped through the stolen files, his expression unreadable. When he finally speaks, his voice is calm—but sharp.

Nathan adjusted his glasses, monotone, "Vanguard Research Institute was a 'private research firm'—emphasis on the quotation marks. Officially, they specialized in data analysis and academic consulting. In reality? They fabricated research, manipulated reports, and ghostwrote academic papers for profit."

"So... professional liars with fancy degrees?" Benji leaned back and raised an eyebrow.

Nathan deadpan, flipped a page, "Essentially. They didn't just falsify data—they sold it. Their clients ranged from students buying pre-written theses to corporations needing 'scientific proof' that their products were safe. The kind of people who have no problem rewriting reality for the right price."

"And Skyler worked for them." Flynn's voice was low,

Nathan nodded, setting down the file, "Not just worked. She helped build the lies."

Silence. The weight of it settles over them. Flynn grips his notebook a little tighter. Benji exhales sharply.

VANGUARD RESEARCH INSTITUTE – INTERNAL REPORT

Title: The Cognitive Benefits of Ultra-Memory Supplements – A Breakthrough in Neural Retention

Client: [REDACTED] (Private Pharmaceutical Corporation)

Date: January ██, 20██

Lead Researcher: [REDACTED]

Data Analyst: Maddox, Skyler

SUMMARY:

This study "proves" that Ultra-Memory, a cognitive enhancement supplement, boosts memory retention by 67% and has no reported side effects.

INTERNAL NOTES (NOT FOR PUBLICATION)

Raw data showed no significant improvement. Adjustments were made to align results with the client's expectations.

Test subjects reported headaches, dizziness, and disorientation. This was omitted from the final report.

Sample size reduced from 250 to 75. Subjects with negative results were excluded.

Skyler Maddox flagged inconsistencies. Request for data review was denied.

Final Directive:

All findings must be presented as conclusive.

Data discrepancies have been accounted for in post-processing.

No further adjustments needed.

Study will be published in [REDACTED] Journal of Neuroscience Q2 20██.

Flynn read, voice sharp, "**They didn't just manipulate data—they designed lies. People trusted this research.**"

Benji stared at the report, horrified, "Dude, they straight-up invented science. That's not just fraud—that's, like, evil genius fraud."

Nathan's expression was unreadable, tapping the page, "And Skyler tried to push back. See this note? She wanted a review. They ignored her."

"Because she was disposable to them," Flynn said,

Silence. The weight of the truth sets in. This wasn't just some shady research firm. It was a machine built to rewrite reality—until someone like Skyler tried to break it.

Flynn:

Friday

21 March, 2025

10:12 AM

We need to find more clues about 'Vanguard Research Institute'. Looking at the building in Westbrook, they have shifted their office. But the question is where? I haven't seen Skyler yet. But I doubt she will talk about it if I ask her. Who else would know about it?

Flynn kept his pen, and looked around the book club room, Serena, Noah, *Blake*, Ivy.

"Someone who might understand publishing, research, and academia," Flynn thought, and then...

"What do you think about *Blake*, maybe she can help?" Benji asked,

He looked at her, **Blake Emerson, the person who fits this description.**

"I guess I have no choice..." Flynn sighed and stood up.

Case#39

<u>BLAKE EMERSON</u>

Full name: Blake Anastasia Emerson

Class: 10-B

Age: 15 (Fifteen)

Height: 5'1

Birthday: 27 January, 2010

MBTI: ENFP

Role in Book Club: Member- Respect Skyler's Writing

Relationship with Skyler: Respectful (but distant).

Opinion on Skyler (Before & After):

Before: "I genuinely respected Skyler's writing and creativity, believing she had real talent, but I also recognized Skyler's self-destructive tendencies and emotional distance."

After: "She used to care about writing more than anyone. I don't know what changed."

Key Quotes:

- "Skyler had something the rest of us didn't—raw talent. It's just a shame she never knew what to do with it."
- "I wanted to believe in her, I really did. But you can't help someone who refuses to be helped."

What She Might Know: Blake likely knows that, deep down, Skyler still cares about writing and the club, even if she pretends otherwise—but she also suspects there's something bigger weighing on her that no one fully understands.

Suspicious Behavior: Blake rarely speaks up in Skyler's defense, but she subtly deflects harsh criticism away from her, as if she knows more than she lets on.

NOTE: Blake still respects her, but doesn't know why she quit. She also seems annoyed at me for asking. Suspicious?

"You know a lot about publishing fraud, right?"

"That's a bold opening line, Hayes."

"Hypothetically, if someone wanted to erase an entire research firm's history—how would they do it?"

"Depends. Who are we hypothetically pissing off?"

"Oh, just the worst people possible."

"Do you know something about Vanguard Research? If you do, talk," Flynn crossed his arms, leaning forward,

"Wow, not even a 'hello'? Chivalry really is dead." Blake said mockingly, rolled her eyes.

"Blake." Flynn was impatient.

"What's in it for me?" Blake was amused, tapping her nails on the table,

"Oh, I like her." Benji grinned, enjoying the conversation.

Flynn leaned forward, dead serious. "You're wasting time. Just tell me what you know."

"Oh, I'm sorry, am I not following proper interrogation etiquette? Should I be sweating under a spotlight right now?" Blake mockingly said,

"Damn. She's kinda scary." Benji whispered, impressed,

"Blake," Flynn said,

"Fine. I'll bite. What makes you think I know anything?" Blake rolled her eyes, stretching lazily,

"Because you're too smug for someone who's supposed to be on the outside of this." Flynn's voice got tight,

Blake pretending to be flattered, "Aw, you think I'm special."

"I think you're holding out on me." Flynn leaned closer, his voice sharp,

"You know Vanguard didn't just disappear. They were erased. Who did it?" Flynn asked,

"Mm. Could be a lot of people. Corrupt firms don't exactly die naturally." Blake smirked, pretending to think,

"You've heard things. I need specifics." Flynn leaned in, his voice lowered,

Blake examined her nails, dramatic sigh, "I could tell you... But where's the fun in that?"

"So true. Gotta let the tension build." Benji whispered, pretending to take notes.

"Vanguard got erased. That takes power. Real power. Who pulled the strings?" Flynn crossed his arms,

"If I knew that, don't you think I'd be a little more concerned about my lifespan?" Blake raised an eyebrow,

"But you have something. You're too calm about this." Flynn frustrated,

Blake shrugged, looking at her nails, "Maybe I just like watching you suffer."

"Respect." Benji grinned,

Flynn snapped, voice sharp, "Blake."

Blake finally looked at him, sighing dramatically. "Alright, detective. Here's your freebie—Vanguard didn't die. It just... changed."

"Changed how?" Flynn was tense,

"That's for you to find out. But I'd be careful where you look." Blake smirked, tilting her head,

Silence. That was not just a warning—it was a challenge. Flynn narrows his eyes. Blake enjoys the reaction.

Flynn exhaled sharply, voice harder now, "This isn't a game, Emerson."

"No, it's not. Which is exactly why you should be more careful." Blacked tilted her head, suddenly serious.

"What do you mean?" Flynn narrowed his eyes,

Blake leaned forward, lowering her voice slightly, "**Vanguard didn't just disappear. It killed itself before anyone else could. Cleaned house. Deleted files. Relocated**. If you're looking for proof? You're already too late."

"No. There's always something left behind." Flynn said,

"Yeahh!! We literally checked out their old office building! And found so many things!!??" Benji said,

Blake side-eyed both of them, "Then I hope you're good at running, detective."

Flynn squinted, suspicion creeping in, "How do I know you're not just feeding me lies?"

Blake mockingly gasp, clutching her chest, "You don't! That's the fun part!"

"Damn, she's playing 4D chess while we're out here coloring inside the lines." Benji laughed, but also low-key stressed,

"You're enjoying this too much." Flynn watched her carefully,

"It's been a very dull semester." Blake grinned, sipping her coffee.

There was silence for a few minutes...

"This conversation isn't over." Flynn stood up,

Blake leaned back, unfazed, sipping her coffee, "Oh, I know."

"Honestly? This was kinda fun. We should do interrogations more often." Benji grinned, he too stood up.

Flynn:

Friday

21 March, 2025

10:51 PM

Today, I interrogated Blake Anastasia Emerson...

I should've known Blake wouldn't give me straight answers. She never does. She gets off on watching me try to pull information out of her, like it's a game.

But she said something I can't ignore. Vanguard didn't die. It erased itself. Buried its past. Changed its name. And the way she said it—like she wasn't just guessing—she knows more. She just won't say.

I don't know what's worse. That she's making me work for it. Or that I'm playing right into it.

<u>*Key Takeaways:*</u>

✓ *Vanguard didn't collapse. It relocated.*

✓ *Someone paid to wipe its existence—was it the company itself?*

✓ *Blake warned me, but she didn't tell me to stop. That means there's more.*

✓ *Skyler was involved in something she couldn't escape.*

✓ *Now I'm in the same place.*

Saturday

22 March, 2025

8:02 AM

Flynn went towards his locker to keep his notes. But then... he saw something, a single slip of paper fluttered out. He picked up the paper,

"Stop Digging."

It was not handwritten. It was typed.

Flynn was afraid, he looked around, his chest felt heavy.

Why Are We Still Here? Just To Suffer?

@DataOrPerish has changed the group name into 'Why Are We Still Here? Just To Suffer?'

Today

@MainCharacterEnergy: @Everyone, meet me now, ASAP!! Corridor near my classroom.

@CertifiedChaos: ????

Flynn rethinks everything, "I should panic, scream but... I am not. They want me to stop looking after it, but I can't, I need to find more! No one will stop me from finding the truth," He said to himself. Now, instead of getting scared, he was calm as ever.

Finally, he sees his friends coming towards him, he shows them the paper.

Benji read it, face draining of color, "Nope. Nope nope nope. I don't like this. I hate this. This is literally how horror movies start."

"It's just a warning." Flynn was calm, sipping his drink,

"JUST a warning?! BRO. THIS IS A THREAT. This is somebody saying, 'Hey, Flynn, we see you and we will un-alive you if you keep poking around.'" Benji stared at him like he was insane,

"You're overreacting," Flynn said dryly,

Benji gestured wildly, "YOU ARE UNDER-REACTING!"

"Okay. Important question—do I still have time to book a flight far away from all of this?" Zane raised an eyebrow, impressed,

Benji was still spiraling, "Bro, take me with you."

"It's just intimidation. If they really wanted to stop us, they'd do more than leave a note." Flynn ignored both of them,

"Oh, fantastic. Let's wait until they actually try to kill us. That sounds fun." Zane sarcastically nodded.

Mia picked up the note, frowned, "This isn't funny. This means someone is watching you, Flynn. That's not just intimidation—that's dangerous."

"If they wanted me gone, they wouldn't have bothered with a note." Flynn shrugged, acting unfazed,

"That is not comforting." Mia gave him a sharp look,

Benji nodded aggressively, "THANK YOU. Finally, someone with sense."

Nathan analyzed the note, his expression was unreadable, "Typed. No handwriting. Standard printer paper. They wanted this to be untraceable."

"Okay, weird robot man, that's not helpful." Benji stared at him, horrified,

Nathan ignored him, "No threats. No deadline. Just 'Stop Digging.' It's not urgent—it's calculated."

"Exactly. Which means they think we still have a choice." Flynn thoughtfully nodded,

"Do we?" Nathan leaned back, adjusting his glasses.

Silence. Flynn doesn't answer. Because he knows the answer. And it's no.

9:02 AM

In the classroom of 12-C, Zane takes out his notebooks, but when he opened them, he found a paper. Zane swallowed.

"We warned you."

10:52 AM

"You're getting too close."

Benji was ready to leave the country with Zane, after seeing this message.

"OH HELL NAH!!??" He said to himself, when he found this in his backpack.

11: 42 AM

Mia went to her locker, when she opened it, she too found a paper,

"NO..." She was concerned.

"We see you."

11:43 AM

UNKNOWN NUMBER

@Anymonous: Sent a photo.

@Anymonous: Sent a photo.

@DataOrPerish: Who is this?

It was photos of Flynn and Benji. On the evening at Westbrook. Taken from behind...

11:45 AM

The five of them, now sitting in the cafeteria, showed the messages they got.

Benji was freaking out, pacing, "Okay, okay, ha ha, funny prank, someone's definitely just messing with us—"

Mia gripped the note, voice quiet but sharp, "This isn't a joke, Benji. Someone knows everything we're doing."

Zane was dead serious, suddenly regretting coming back from Kyoto, "We need to stop. Like, immediately."

Nathan analyzed the situation, but even he looks rattled, "The first warning was generic. This one isn't. They know specifics. That means they're close."

Flynn stared at the message, gripping the edge of the table, "Good."

Silence. Everyone turns to stare at him.

"GOOD?! BRO, THAT IS THE OPPOSITE OF GOOD!" Benji outraged,

"That means we're on the right track," Flynn said,

Mia was worried, lowering her voice, "It also means they're watching us, Flynn. What happens when a warning isn't enough?"

"Then we find them first." Flynn exhaled slowly, his voice cold,

The group exchanges uneasy looks. Because this just stopped being a game.

5:03 PM

Flynn flipped through his notes, retracing everything Blake said. His pen taps against the table. The pieces are there—they just don't fit. Yet.

Flynn muttered, reading his own notes aloud, "Vanguard erased itself. Changed its name. Buried the records. But why move locations? Why Westbrook first?"

"Bro, my brain is melting. Can we take, like, a five-minute break from your descent into madness? Hear me out– Let's watch I Got Reincarnated as a Sentient Toaster in a Cyberpunk Society," Benji groaned,

Nathan calmly said, not looking up from his laptop, "You think this is bad? You should see his existential crises at 3 AM."

Flynn ignored them, flipping back a few pages, eyes narrowed, "Blake said people don't talk about Westbrook. But she also said it's old news."

"So... what's new news?" Mia frowned, sitting up straighter,

Silence. And then it hits him. Flynn's pen stops tapping. He looked at the papers and notes on the table. It was the moment Flynn started to put it together.

Flynn whispered, realization dawning, "We've been looking at where they were. But what if Skyler was looking at where they are?"

He immediately grabs his laptop. Fingers fly over the keys.

Search: "Vanguard Research Institute shutdown reasons"

No official records found. Try different keywords.

No government filings available.

Thread on obscure forum:

"Vanguard Didn't Shut Down – It Was ERASED"

[https://conspiraciesandcoverups.net/vanguard-thread99]

Flynn clicked on the link,

[USER DELETED]

→ Replied to [USER DELETED]

→ Replied to [USER DELETED]

Benji read over his shoulder, "Sooo, either this dude got tired of posting, or someone made him stop."

"Or both," Flynn replied.

Search: "Vanguard Research missing files"

No publicly available documents.

Most citations have been removed.

One old academic paper still links to Vanguard data.

[https://archive.researchjournals.edu/NeuroStudy-20██]

Title: Cognitive Retention and Neural Adaptation in Controlled Study Environments

Authors: Dr. [REDACTED], Dr. [REDACTED]

Published by: [REDACTED] Journal of Neuroscience

Date: April ██, 20██

Cited 23 times

Abstract

This study explores the long-term cognitive effects of enhanced memory retention techniques, analyzing data from volunteer participants under controlled experimental settings.

Preliminary results indicate a 67% increase in recall efficiency, with no observed long-term neurological damage.

Further trials are recommended before the next phase of development is approved.

Funding Source: Confidential, corporate-funded research.

Data Collected By: Vanguard Research Institute.

Flynn leaning closer, scanning the text, "This is it. Vanguard's research. It's still here."

Benji chewed on his sleeve, nervous, "Okay, great, love that—so let's screenshot and—"

The screen glitches. The page reloads. But this time—there's nothing there.

404 ERROR – This page is temporarily unavailable.

[Retry] [Report Issue]

Flynn stared at the screen, clicking the link again, "No. No, no, no, it was just here."

"Someone took it down. While you were reading it." Mia watched, her voice got tight,

Benji threw up his hands, fully spiraling, "COOL. GREAT. LOVE THAT. SOMEONE'S WATCHING US IN REAL TIME."

Silence. The air feels heavier. Because he's right. They aren't just digging into Vanguard's past anymore. Someone is actively covering it up.

Search: Companies with similar funding to Vanguard Research

Echelon Data Solutions – Private research firm, est. 20██

Odyssey Analytics – Data analysis & consultancy

Palisade Institute – Emerging biotech research

[https://globalfinancewatch.net/Echelon-profile]

Nathan analyzed the funding sources, "Different names. Same money."

"They didn't shut down. They evolved." Zane's eyes narrowed.

Search: "Private research firms established after 20██"

Echelon Data Solutions – Founded months after Vanguard collapsed. Same funding. Same patterns. No official parent company.

[https://echelondatasolutions.com]

Flynn clicks. The website is sleek, professional, and vague. Too vague

ECHELON DATA SOLUTIONS

"Pioneering Innovation. Driving the Future."

WEBSITE TABS:

HOME | INDUSTRIES | INSIGHTS | CAREERS | CONTACT

"At Echelon, we specialize in data integrity, research solutions, and advanced analytics across multiple industries. With a commitment to innovation and a global reach, we ensure that our clients receive only the most cutting-edge insights."

"This says nothing." Flynn's eyes narrowed, scrolling,

"We do stuff. For people. Using things. Amazing." Benji mockingly said, reading aloud,

"No research archives. No past projects. No staff names. Just vague corporate nonsense." Mia frowned, scanning the page,

"Because this isn't a real website. It's a front." Nathan leaned closer, analytical,

Flynn clicks on "Industries." Generic stock images. Buzzwords. Nothing concrete. But then—

A Single Clickable PDF Link:

"Our Commitment to Excellence – 20██ Annual Report"

Flynn clicked, his voice sharp, "This might have something—"

The screen flashes. Instead of a document, an error message appears.

UNAUTHORIZED REQUEST

This document is restricted to approved personnel.

[Log In]

"Locked. Of course it is." Flynn said,

"Okay, cool, so we're already on some kind of watchlist. Love that." Benji leaned away, shaking his head,

"They didn't just erase Vanguard. They're hiding something." Mia watched the screen, her voice uneasy.

Final Search: "Westbrook abandoned research firm"

One article from 20██ mentions a 'quiet relocation.'
[https://businessinsider.com/Westbrook-Vanguard-move]

Title: Research Firm Quietly Relocates After Sudden Policy Shift
By: [REDACTED], Business Insider Contributor
Published: 20██

Category: Business & Tech

Excerpt from the Article

Westbrook, MA – Once a hub for private-sector research, Vanguard Research Institute has quietly vacated its long-standing headquarters in Westbrook. The company, known for its contributions to data analytics and scientific consultation, ceased operations at the site with little public notice.

Despite previous reports indicating long-term investment in Westbrook's research infrastructure, sources confirm that the firm's departure was abrupt, with no publicized statement regarding relocation.

"It was like they were never here," said a former employee, who requested anonymity. "One week, it was business as usual. The next? Everything was gone."

When asked for comment, Vanguard's corporate office declined to provide further details, citing confidential business restructuring.

"No lawsuits. No backlash. No news. They didn't just leave. They were erased." Flynn frowned, scrolling through the article,

Mia read over his shoulder, her voice quiet, "Who relocates an entire company overnight? Without a trace?"

"This is, like, cult levels of creepy." Benji chewed his thumbnail, muttered.

Nathan was calm, but focused, "Or government levels of secrecy."

Silence. Flynn exhales, leaning back. The more they dig, the less sense it makes.

CHAPTER XI

Hunting Shadows

"We should look out for former employees. Skyler wasn't the only one who knew the truth. Someone had to speak about this shitty company," Zane sugguested.

"Yeah, you can use LinkedIn" Mia agreed,
Search: "Former Vanguard Research Employees"

...

[LinkedIn.com/elliotgraves]

...

...

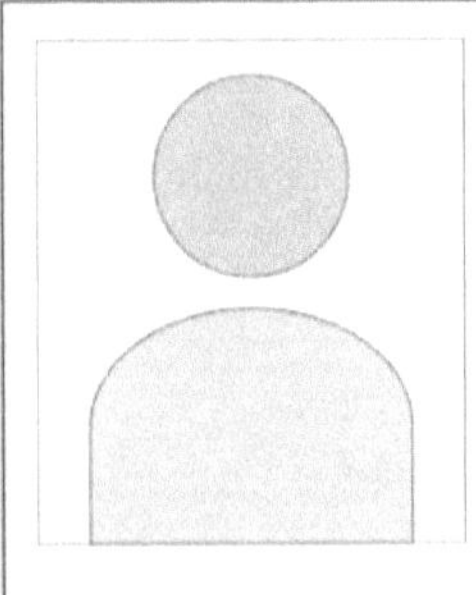

Elliot Graves

Former Data Manager at Vanguard Research Institute
Location: [Redacted]

Position	Company	Years
Data Manager	Vanguard Research Institute	20██-???
[Redacted Role]	[Unknown]	???-???

"Passionate about data integrity and research ethics." (Last Updated: Unknown)

"Why is his last job unlisted? Where did he go after Vanguard?" Flynn scrolled, his eyes narrowed,

"More importantly—why does this profile feel... unfinished?" Mia frowned, pointing at the screen.

Case #39

The person who might know everything:

Name: Elliot Graves

Former Role: Vanguard Data Manager

Disappeared from corporate records after Vanguard shut down.

Last known location? Somewhere off the grid.

"I think we found our guy." Flynn leaned back, staring at the screen,

"Okay, cool, love that—so is he alive or...?" Benji asked, stomach sinking,

"No social media. No job history. It's like he just vanished after Vanguard shut down." Mia frowned, scrolling through files,

"Which means he either ran... or someone made him disappear." Nathan seriously nodded.

Suddenly Flynn's laptop screen flickers. He frowned, refreshing the page.

ERROR: PROFILE NOT FOUND

? This user no longer exists.

"No. That was just there." Flynn stared at the screen, heartbeat picking up,

"Uh, yeah, hey, funny thing? We're next." Benji whispered, already standing up,

Silence. The choice is clear. Either they wait and try to contact Elliot online... or they go find him before someone else does.

Search: Elliot Graves Vanguard Research

No results found.

Search: Elliot Graves missing?

No results found.

Search: Former Vanguard employees' legal cases.

FILE: ANONYMOUS WHISTLEBLOWER REPORT – Vanguard Research Institute

[https://govwatch.reports/whistleblower-Vanguard]

"The data isn't real. The studies are fabricated. I tried to fix the inconsistencies, but they don't care. This isn't just unethical—it's dangerous."

"They told me to stay quiet. I won't. Someone needs to know before this disappears."

Signed: Elliot Graves

"This wasn't just fraud. He knew something he wasn't supposed to." Flynn leaned closer, his voice sharp,

"And then he disappeared." Mia read over his shoulder, frowned,

"Yeah, this guy's super dead." Benji stared at the screen,

Silence. No one wants to agree, but the timeline doesn't look good.

Sunday

23 March, 2025

9:08 AM

Nathan was looking at the files he was sent by Flynn. Then, he looked at the files he found; cross-referenced old payment records, searching for any link to Elliot. And that's when they find **a familiar name.**

Financial Transfer – 20█

Sender: **Ethan Rhodes**

Recipient: Elliot Graves

Amount: $█

Why Are We Still Here? Just To Suffer?

@DataOrPerish: I found something.

@DataOrPersih: Sent a photo.

@CertifiedChaos: bro why do you ALWAYS find something T_T

@MainCharacterEnergy: Explain.

@DataOrPerish Ethan sent money to Elliot. Multiple times.

@SoftHeartedButNosy: ...Ethan our Ethan? Ethan book club Ethan??

@CertifiedChaos: Ethan human Golden Retriever Ethan???

@TiredButTrying: Y'all are acting like there's another Ethan.

@DataOrPerish: Well, apparently, there was another Ethan. And his name was Elliot Graves.

@MainCharacterEnergy: Oh.

@CertifiedChaos: OH??? That's all you're gonna say???

@SoftHeartedButNosy: Wait. Does Ethan know about this?

@DataOrPerish: Doubt it. His search history is too clean.

@CertifiedChaos: ...Wait wait wait

We're assuming Ethan is innocent??

@TiredButTrying: Bro. Ethan still asks the professor if he can go to the bathroom. He's innocent.

@CertifiedChaos: Fair.

@MainCharacterEnergy: We need to talk to him.

@DataOrPerish: Already on it.

@CertifiedChaos: okay but like.

IF Elliot is missing

IF Ethan sent him money

IF this is all connected

What EXACTLY did Elliot know that got him wiped???

Nathan kept his phone away, and tried to download the full report, but... the last page was missing,

"What the hell?" He asked himself, "The complaint was no longer available, but someone **edited it before deleting it**...? He read from the screen,

9:21 AM

"Where the fuck am I stuck now?" Benji rolled his eyes, scrolling in his laptop,

"I fully regret being Dr. Watson. And it's not even just us too. We have a whole scooby-doo crew. I wasn't even interested in Skyler or any mystery stuff. All I wanted was to repay Flynn for voting him out, but what's the point? He is back in the club... I just wanted some adventure, something fun, but here I am! Scared for my life, instead of being afraid of Skyler, I am scared of this shady company. I could have avoided this– this whole thing, and binge-watching some anime. Instead, I am trying to find clues of some missing person, come to think— ARE WE THE FUCKING COPS? I thought I came to find some edgy-trauma of Skyler, but no! We are exposing a corrupt company!?!?" He thought.

Missing Researchers

...

...

[DELETED] Does anyone remember Elliot Graves?

Comments (2)

"He wasn't the first. He wouldn't be the last."

"You can erase records. You can't erase people who remember."

9:36 AM

Flynn:

We have learned a lot of things... We know a guy named Elliot Graves. Right now, we have to find him. Ethan... The person who never doubted is somehow related to him? Well... He is the only person with all the answers. This is more than finding your friend's past. Somehow, this has turned into exposing a corrupt company. But, why has no one raised a question against this? Why hasn't the media or cops stopped them? I mean...Wouldn't it be weird when such a successful company was exposed by a bunch of high schoolers? How many people are behind this? And how many employees and interns have they tried to erase??

9:45 AM

Why Are We Still Here? Just To Suffer?

@CertifiedChaos: OKAY BUT WHY DID I JUST FIND THIS

@CertifiedChaos: Sent a photo.

@SoftHeartedButNosy: What... is that?

@DatOrPerish: Looks like a forum thread from years ago.

@CertifiedChaos: DUDE READ THE LAST COMMENT

@CertifiedChaos: "He wasn't the first. He won't be the last."

"You can erase records. You can't erase people who remember."

@MainCharacterEnergy: Who posted this?

@CertifiedChaos: That's the problem. The user's gone. Account deleted.

@SoftHeartedButNosy: So... someone was trying to warn people.

@DataOrPerish: And someone else was trying to make sure they didn't.

Monday

24 March, 2025

8:12 AM

Flynn kept his notes in his locker, when he looked around, he saw Serena coming towards him,

"Do you still do mystery stuff?" She looked around, hoping no one saw her,

"Why do you ask?" Flynn raised an eyebrow,

"Tell your case study to stay away from my brother," And she went away,

"What? Case study? Skyler?"

Case #39

<u>SERENA CALDWELL</u>

Full name: Serena Isabelle Caldwell

Class: 12-A

Age: 16 (Sixteen)

Height: 5'4

Birthday: 12 October, 2008

MBTI: ESTP

Role in Book Club: Member- Passive-Agressive Queen

Relationship with Skyler: Condescending

Opinion on Skyler (Before & After):

Before: "For all her flaws, Skyler always carried herself with a certain kind of charm—it made people listen."

After: "She was talented. Wasted potential, really. But I suppose some people just aren't meant for the spotlight."

Key Quotes:

- "Skyler always had potential, but talent alone isn't enough if you don't know how to use it."

* "It's honestly a little sad watching her act like she doesn't care."

What She Might Know: Serena likely knows that Skyler is struggling but sees it as self-inflicted, believing Skyler is making things harder for herself on purpose.

Suspicious Behavior: Serena always seems to know just enough about Skyler's situation to make cutting, pointed remarks—almost like she's been quietly gathering information.

NOTE: Serena is weirdly smug about this. Does she know more than she's letting on?

ETHAN RHODES

Full name: Ethan Maxwell Rhodes

Class: 10-C

Age: 14 (Fourteen)

Height: 5'5

Birthday: 13 September, 2010

MBTI: ISFP

Role in Book Club: Member- The Innocent

Relationship with Skyler: Shocked

Opinion on Skyler (Before & After):

Before: "I admired Skyler—her writing, her mind, the way she saw the world—but I don't think I ever really understood her."

After: "Honestly, I have no clue. She's just different now."

Key Quotes:

* "I don't get it—what happened to the Skyler I knew?"
* "She used to be relentless, like nothing could shake her. Now, she's the one walking away."

What He Might Know: Ethan might know that Skyler is hiding something serious—something that changed her—but he doesn't understand what it is or why she won't talk about it.

Suspicious Behavior: Ethan has been watching Skyler closely, almost like he's expecting something to happen, but he never confronts her directly—like he's waiting for her to slip up first.

NOTE: Completely useless. Maybe clueless. Maybe lying.

Ethan was going to his classroom, when he got a notification from his email,

Sender: No Name

Subject: "Drop It."

Message: "Don't ask questions. Some things aren't meant to be found."

Ethan stares at the screen, heart pounding. He doesn't even know what this is about—yet. But something tells him? He's about to find out.

Before he enters his classroom, he sees his four seniors; Flynn, Benji, Mia and Nathan.

They took him to the book club room, and showed him all the evidence and clues.

Flynn dropped a file on the table, his arms now crossed, "Ethan. Explain."

"Uh... Explain what?" Ethan blinked, confused.

Flynn flipped the file open. Ethan's name. Multiple financial transfers. Elliot's name on the receiving end.

"You sent money to Elliot. A lot of it. Why?" Mia softly said, watching his reaction,

Ethan stared at the document, frowned, then scoffed, "Because **he's my cousin**? What kind of question—"

Everyone paused. His words die in his throat. Because the way they're looking at him? Something's wrong.

"Wait. Why are you asking me this?" Ethan slowly and uneasily asked,

Silence. Then—Flynn speaks, voice sharp.

"Because **Elliot Graves is missing**," Flynn said,

Ethan froze. The room felt smaller. The world tilted. He swallowed hard, processing.

"No. That—That's not possible. He would've told me." Ethan shook his head, disbelieving it,

"He didn't. And now? No one can find him." Nathan calmly said, but firm,

Silence. Ethan exhales, rubbing a hand over his face. This wasn't just some mystery. This was his family. And now? He's part of this too.

Benji watched Ethan carefully, whispering to Flynn, "You sure he didn't know?"

"Look at him. He's freaking out." Flynn studied Ethan, his voice was low,

"Ethan, if you didn't know he was missing... what did you know?" Mia said softly,

Ethan quietly said, looking at the files again, "That he left Vanguard. That something spooked him. But... he never told me what."

"Did he say where he was going?" Nathan analyzed,

Ethan shook his head, his voice was heavy, "No. Just that he 'needed time.' That was the last real conversation we had."

Silence. The weight of it sinks in. Ethan is just as lost as they are. But now? He wants answers too.

Ethan exhaled sharply, looking at Flynn, "*Alright. What's our next move?*"

Flynn smirked, flipping open his notebook.

"Now you're speaking my language," Flynn said.

"If you guys know so much, then maybe you know this too," Ethan showed the email,

"Oh my god!" Mia was shocked,

"He is going after Ethan too..." Nathan said,

Ethan was scared hearing it, "WHAT!? WHAT DOES THAT SUPPOSED TO MEAN!?"

Meanwhile, Benji was witnessing everything, standing still. Thinking...

"I should have left.

I should have walked away when Flynn first dragged me into this mess. But nooo, I had to stick around. For what? **For this?**

A **missing** cousin. A **dead man's report** that wasn't supposed to exist. An **erased forum post**. And now? Now Ethan's acting like someone's **breathing down his neck.**

What are we even chasing anymore? This stopped being a game chapters ago.

And the worst part?

Flynn isn't stopping.

He should stop. This is the part in a horror movie where the guy with the "It's fine, let's keep digging" energy is the first to get got.

But no. Instead, I'm sitting here watching his eyes light up like we just found buried treasure instead of evidence of a full-scale cover-up.

God, I need better hobbies."

He then looks at Ethan,

"I glance at Ethan. He's staring at his phone like it's about to explode.

"Someone just tried to log into my email."

Of course they did. Because we're not the only ones looking.

I want to say we should leave. That we should walk away.

But I know we won't.

Because this is Flynn.

Because this is Skyler.

Because this is bigger than all of us now.

So yeah. I should have left.

But I won't.

Because even though I hate this, I need to know.

And that might be the stupidest decision of my life."

8:35 AM

The room's door opened, Zane entered the room, looking at everyone,

"I thought you all would be here"

He looked at Ethan, sitting in a chair, in front of a bunch of files, Zane raised an eyebrow,

"What is he doing here?"

"Interrogation Zane, what else?" Benji replied.

"Shit. I missed it..." Zane said sarcastically. And sits near Ethan, Ethan looks at his phone,

VOICEMAIL FROM: ELLIOT GRAVES

Received: 11 months ago

Duration: 42 seconds

"Wait... I don't remember this."

Benji nervously peered over his shoulder,

"Bro, are you about to play the equivalent of a horror movie tape right now?"

"Press play." Mia firmly said.

Ethan stared at his phone for a long time before pressing play. His fingers hovered over the screen, as if waiting for some miracle to make everything stop being so wrong. But it didn't. It was just like the past few weeks—scraps of truth, bits of information that didn't add up, and now, the echo of his cousin's desperate voice. When the voicemail started, Ethan felt his stomach drop. He hesitated– then did.

Elliot's Voice low, urgent, "Ethan. Listen. I don't have much time. I thought I could stop it, but—"

A rustling noise. A sharp inhale. Like he's checking behind him.

The first words were rushed, clipped, as though Elliot was trying to speak through a wall of noise. Ethan's eyes never left the screen, his fingers clutching his phone so tightly that his knuckles were white. Mia stood beside him, a knot in her throat, Benji pacing nervously behind them. Only Flynn was still, his arms crossed, as if holding himself together by sheer will.

Elliot was quieter now, "It doesn't matter if you prove it. They'll make sure no one remembers."

The static gets worse. A muffled thump—like something fell or was knocked over.

As the voicemail continued, a sense of dread filled the room. Each word was a hammer, driving deeper into their confusion. "If you find this, don't trust—" The sudden static cut through the air like a scream, and everyone leaned forward instinctively, trying to catch those last elusive words. The voicemail cut off abruptly, and silence followed. For a moment, no one dared speak.

Flynn's mind raced as the last words of the voicemail replayed in his head. "Don't trust…" He couldn't finish the thought. It was like the missing piece of a puzzle he'd been putting together for months had just been taken away. How could someone warn him like this, only to be cut off? It didn't add up. The pieces—the theory he thought was right, the connections he had—crumbled away, slipping through his fingers. He couldn't breathe. He needed to fix this. He had to find out what Elliot was trying to say. He had to find him before it was too late.

Elliot Graves wasn't just trying to escape. He was warning us. And now, we're too deep to leave.

Ethan lowered his phone. Nobody spoke.

"That's it. That's all there is." Ethan's voice was slightly shaking,

"Don't trust… who?" Flynn frowned, repeating the words under his breath,

Benji pointed wildly at the phone, "BRO. NO. THIS IS TOO MOVIE HORROR CODED. Why does it cut off like that???"

"It wasn't just a bad connection. Something happened." Zane thoughtfully, his arms crossed,

"Rewind it. There's something off in the background noise." Nathan was calm, but intense,

Ethan replays the last five seconds, turning the volume up. Everyone listens closely. And then—

Elliot's Voice faintly, just before it cuts off, "If you find this, don't trust—"

A faint thump—then a muffled, almost robotic voice in the background.

"[REDACTED] has been flagged. Reacquiring target."

"Who is he warning us about? Why would Elliot leave this… and then nothing? He was in trouble—real trouble. What if he's still out there, but can't reach us?" Mia glanced at others, her voice was soft,

"Or… or he's dead, Mia. What if the 'don't trust' part means us? What if we shouldn't even trust this voicemail?" Benji nervously tapped his foot,

"I've looked at the logs, and there's no way this was tampered with. Someone didn't want us hearing this, so they cut him off. But why? What was he trying to say? And why not tell us who to trust?" Nathan stared at the screen, calm but with tension in his voice.

Flynn stood still, heart pounding. The soft hum of the fluorescent lights above them was the only sound. But it didn't help; it made the room feel suffocating. Mia's hand was shaking on her phone. Benji stood by the door, eyes darting around like he expected someone to burst in. But they were alone—or so they thought.

There was a gnawing feeling at the back of Flynn's mind, something was wrong. The tension built in his chest like a vice. How long before they were exposed? Elliot wasn't the only one who'd gone missing. Someone was out there, someone who didn't want them to find the truth.

The group sits in silence, processing. But Zane? He leans forward, rewinding again. Because something isn't sitting right.

"Okay. Hold up. Everybody's focused on Elliot's voice, but what about before he speaks?" Zane said slowly, pointing at the phone,

"Before?" Mia frowned, tilting her head,

Ethan rewinds. Plays the first five seconds at max volume. And there it is.

[Distant keyboard typing.]
[A chair scraping against the floor.]
[A voice in the background. Not Elliot.]

Unidentified Voice's softly, distant, "You don't have to do this."

Silence. The weight of the words sinks in. Elliot wasn't alone when he recorded this.

"Then who was?" Flynn's eyes narrowed, processing,

The group exchanges uneasy glances. Because they just realized something: Elliot wasn't just recording a warning. He was talking to someone.

Zane leans over, eyes narrowing as he reviews the message. He taps his fingers on the table, a look of recognition creeping over his face.

"Reacquiring target. That's not some random glitch, guys. It's a code. It's too clean." Zane said quietly, pointing at the screen,

"What do you mean?" Mia leaned closer,

"It's a warning. Someone is watching—and Elliot was trying to hide from them. I'm guessing he didn't get the chance to finish what he was saying." Zane said,

The realization hits the group. The danger isn't just about finding Elliot—**it's about finding out too much**.

Flynn finally stood up, determination in his eyes, "We have to go to the last place Elliot was. We need to find him, find whoever's trying to stop us—before they find us."

Ethan's voice was low, but resolute, "I'm with you. I'll help. I need to know what happened to him."

They exchange glances—there's no going back now. They're all in this together, no matter where it leads.

"We go find him. Now." Flynn's voice was sharp.

"And what's your plan? Walk around until we trip over a missing person?" Nathan raised an eyebrow,

"No. We start with his last known location. The records we found—" Flynn said,

Mia cutting him off, shook her head, "We shouldn't rush into this. What if Elliot doesn't want to be found? What if he's hiding for a reason?"

"Exactly. Which means someone else already found him. Which means we're next." Benji pointed at her,

"Cool, cool. So we're all in agreement that this is stupid but we're doing it anyway?" Zane leaned back, unimpressed,

"No, Zane. We're NOT in agreement. We don't have enough data to act yet." Nathan exasperated,

The argument escalates. Flynn is pacing. Mia is frowning. Benji is vibrating with nervous energy. And Nathan? He's the only one keeping his head on straight.

"This isn't a debate. We go find him." Flynn said, snapping his notebook shut,

"You keep saying that like it's that simple. News flash—it's not. Elliot went missing for a reason. You really think we just show up and he gives us a nice little PowerPoint presentation on what happened?" Nathan said,

"If we don't find him, someone else will." Flynn was dead serious,

"Flynn. What if it's us he doesn't want to find him? What if—" she hesitates, choosing her words carefully "—what if he's hiding from everyone?" Mia exhaled, trying to be the calm one.

"Okay, I vote we all take a chill pill before we end up on the news. Because I'd love to be alive for my twenties, thanks." Benji waved his arms dramatically,

Flynn rolled his eyes and sat down, "But Online isn't enough. We need proof. We need to see it for ourselves."

"And if he doesn't want to be found? If we show up and get him killed?" Mia crossed her arms,

"Oh great, love that energy. Real inspiring." Benji said.

Flynn grips his pen so hard it might snap. He knows they're right. He knows this is dangerous. But he also knows that if they hesitate too long... they might lose their only lead.

Mia watches Flynn with a frown. This isn't just about Elliot. This is about Skyler. This is about every piece of the puzzle that's still missing. And she isn't sure if Flynn even realizes how deep he's in.

Zane taps his fingers against his knee, glancing at the others. His gut is screaming at him. This? This is a bad idea. But he also knows himself well enough to admit—he's going anyway.

They had two options, it was no less than a life-death situation,

Option 1: Contact Elliot Online

They try to reach out through old emails, forums, or financial records.

But—if they can find him online, so can someone else.

Option 2: Track Him Down IRL

They go to his last known location.

But what if he's not there? What if someone else is waiting?

"We sit here doing nothing, we lose him." Flynn was frustrated,

"And if we rush in, we get killed. Pick your poison." Nathan was calm but firm.

"So let me get this straight. We're considering hacking into a missing dude's accounts or showing up at his last known location like we aren't in a true crime documentary?" Zane asked,

"Correct." Benji nodded,

"Awesome. Love that for us. What's next, breaking into a government building? Stealing evidence? Maybe fighting a secret underground organization?" Zane asked,

"Zane. If we don't do this, who will?" Mia was serious.

That shuts him up. Because she's right. And that's the worst part.

Flynn exhales, pulling out his phone to start searching. The group is still arguing, but the decision has already been made. They're doing this. There's no turning back.

Then—Zane's phone vibrates.

NEW MESSAGE – UNKNOWN NUMBER

"Uh. Guys?" Zane frowned, unlocking his phone,

The group turns to look at him. His face is paler than before. Flynn steps forward as Zane slowly turns his phone around.

UNKNOWN NUMBER:

@Anomynous: D O N O T

Silence.

"Oh. Cool. Love that. We're gonna die." Benji whispered,

Then—Zane's phone buzzes again. A second message appears. Short. Simple. And utterly terrifying.

UNKNOWN NUMBER:

@Anomynous: D O N O T

@Anomynous: Y O U A R E T O O L A T E!.

@Anomynous: W E S T B R O O K W A S O N L Y T H E B E G I N N I N G

@Anomynous: H E K N E W T O O M U CH. N O W S O D O Y O U.

"No. We're not too late. Not yet." Flynn clenched his fists, his voice was quiet but sharp,

"Are we really doing this?" Ethan was hesitant, glancing between them all,

Silence. Then—Flynn nods.

"Nathan, find the location where Elliot was last seen. We have no choice..." Flynn said,

Nathan tracks the location and...

"No way..." Nathan said,

"Cool. Awesome. This AGAIN. Love that. I vote we leave the country." Benji said,

It

Was

Westbrook.

CHAPTER XII

Echelon's Collapse

Tuesday

25 March 2025

4:37 PM

The group has now come to Westbrook, *yet once again.*

"I still have PTSD from what happened here..." Benji warned everyone,

"Benji, you don't have to scare us..." Ethan replied.

"Why does it feel like someone has already come here? Those footprints look fresh..." Nathan pointed at the freshly made footprints following an abandoned house.

"For your information, that SOMEONE was a fucking creepypasta who chased us a few days back!!!" Benji shouted,

"And yet... We still came, Zane walked.

They followed the footprint...

The house looked old, with old furniture and lots of dust. It was dark, the air was heavy and too quiet.

"What the hell is this place?" Flynn coughed.

"We should search this house..." Nathan said,

"**I think someone lives here,**" Zane said.

Everyone looked at him,

"Bro... Don't scare us like that," Benji said, folding his hands.

The group started searching the rooms, hoping to find some clue.

And they did.

Everyone came into the bedroom,

"There is half-eaten food here..." Mia said, pointing towards the plate,

"And the chair doesn't look old," Flynn added.

Zane scoffed, "So what does that mean? Is what I said true...?"

Silence.

They searched outside the house too,

"Look!!" Nathan shouted,

DO NOT TRUST—

It was written on the walls, but someone scratched out the rest.

"It looks like Elliot's *handwriting*" Ethan said,

"Elliot was here. He tried to warn us" Flynn implied,

"And yet... We came," Benji said, his arms crossed.

They go inside, trying to find more clues, but then... they heard footsteps. Before they could react,

He was here.

Everyone was shocked.

"...What are you doing here?" Flynn asked,

"THIS IS THE BIGGEST PLOT!?" Benji shouted,

"This can't be true..." Mia was in denial,

"...You?" Nathan was surprised,

"HUH??!?" Ethan was confused,

"Oh my god!?" Zane was shocked.

He looked at Flynn and Benji, "You weren't supposed to come back." **Noah said.**

Suddenly, Flynn remembered Serena's words, *"Tell your case study to stay away from my brother,"*

Flynn:

Now it all made sense. The reason that day Serena came to me. She was afraid for her brother, because he was involved with Skyler. She didn't want any bad influence on her little 'Nado'. Which means... Noah worked in Vanguard Research Institute?? They were colleagues??

"Noah? You worked at Vanguard Research Institute?" Flynn asked, everyone looked at him.

"No. Now, I work at Echelon..."

"That's literally the same thing! Just with a rebrand," Zane said,

"You don't understand!" Noah replied,

"No we don't. We also don't understand what YOU are doing here?" Benji raised an eyebrow,

"I didn't want this. But you guys compelled me to," Noah explained,

"We?? Who's we here!? We didn't even know you worked here??" Mia felt offended,

"Maybe you shouldn't have searched and dug up on the company, I wouldn't have sent those threats", Noah said,

"Ohh! So you were the one who sent those threats, make sense," Nathan raised an eyebrow,

"You were that creepypasta?!?!? Why would you scare us to death!!??" Benji was shocked,

"Noah, you do realize this company in which you work for is a fraud! They are selling fake reports and analysis to clients, they are just a company that is willing to do anything to earn money, they don't care about people like us!" Flynn explained,

"No. This is not true," Noah denied,

"NOAH! YOU ARE BRAINWASHED! You do realize that?" Flynn's voice was sharp, locked his eyes on Noah,

"Brainwashed? That's cute. But let me ask you something—who's really blind here? Me, or the people who refuse to accept the future?" Noah smirked, tilting his head,

"What the hell does that even mean?" Ethan's voice shook,

"It means Echelon isn't the villain here. You think they're just some corrupt corporation, some evil empire pulling the strings in the shadows. But that's because you're looking at this the wrong way." Noah was calm, unaffected,

"Oh, please. Enlighten us." Mia glared, her arms crossed,

"You're all so obsessed with 'the truth,' but you have no idea what it even is. You're so desperate to 'expose' Echelon, to burn them to the ground—have you ever stopped to ask why they do what they do?" Noah scoffed, shook his head,

Silence. Nobody speaks, but the question lingers.

"They're not just some company. They're fixing things. Research. Data. The entire system—the way the world works. People like Elliot? They were slowing it down. And people like you—you're trying to stop progress." Noah stepped forward, his voice steady,

"Okay. So, just to be clear. You're standing here, actually defending the people who erase their own employees?" Benji stared at him, his mouth in disbelief,

"Some sacrifices have to be made. Elliot made his choice. I made mine." Noah shrugged,

Flynn watched him, heart pounding. This isn't a lie. Noah means every word.

"And what about Skyler? Did she make the right choice?" Flynn asked,

For the first time—Noah's smirk falters. Just for a second. But then? He shakes his head, smiling again.

"She ran. I didn't." Noah said softly. "I had a choice. I have seen a bigger picture because of them"

"You keep saying you made your choice. That you're better than us for seeing 'the bigger picture.' But tell me something, Noah—would Elliot be proud of you?" Ethan stared at Noah, his voice was tight,

Silence. Noah's jaw clenches, but he doesn't answer.

"Because the Elliot I knew would rather die than let Echelon control him. And the Noah I knew—he would've been right there with him." Ethan continued,

"The Noah you knew was naïve." Noah's voice was cold, but wavering,

"No. The Noah we knew still had a choice. Did you?" Mia's eyes narrowed,

For the first time, Noah flinches. Just a little.

"You talk like you walked into Echelon with your eyes open, but tell me the truth. When did they take that choice away?" Mia stepped closer, her voice now quieter,

"You don't get it. You'll never get it." Noah tightened his fists, avoiding her gaze,

"Then make us get it. If Echelon is so great, if they saved you, if they're everything you believe—then why are you still afraid?" Flynn was dead serious,

Noah's breath catches. That's it. That's the crack in the armor.

"Why are you still looking over your shoulder? Why did they send you instead of coming themselves? If they're so powerful, why do they need you to clean up their mess?" Flynn was relentless,

Noah doesn't answer. His expression flickers—doubt creeping in. And then—Benji delivers the final blow.

"Dude. They used you. And you're letting them." Benji shook his head, his voice now softer,

And just like that, Noah breaks. He doesn't say anything. He doesn't need to. Because for the first time since they found him, he doesn't know what to say.

Slowly, he was realizing the truth... But still, he tried not to show it,

"Noah. Move." Flynn narrowed his eyes, stepping forward,

"You weren't supposed to come here." Noah was calm, too calm,

"Where's Elliot?" Ethan's voice was shaking,

"Still worried about a dead man?" Noah tilting his head, slightly smiling,

"So he is alive," Mia whispered, her pulse racing,

Noah's expression doesn't change. He steps forward, hands in his pockets, completely unfazed.

"You don't get it, do you? You're still looking at this like a mystery—like some puzzle you can solve. But you're wrong. You were always wrong." Noah said,

"Bro, you literally got brainwashed. Can we not act like you're the enlightened one here?" Benji glared, his voice rising,

"That's the difference between us, Benji. I see the bigger picture. You? You're just along for the ride." Noah chuckled, shaking his head,

"Then explain it. What did Echelon do to you?" Flynn stepped closer, his voice was sharp,

Noah's smile fades. He doesn't look angry. He looks... disappointed.

"They opened my eyes." Noah quietly said,

"And what about Elliot? What did he see that made him run?" Ethan asked,

"The wrong thing." Noah's expression was unreadable,

Noah reaches into his pocket. Not for a weapon—but for a keycard. He holds it up between two fingers.

"You want the truth? Then go get it. But trust me—you won't like what you find." Noah said.

He tossed the keycard onto the ground. And just like that—he walks away. No fight. No struggle. Just... leaving them with the choice to continue.

The group was shaken. Noah is gone, but his words won't leave their heads. Then—Nathan finds something in the old computer. Something Elliot left behind.

"Look at this, " He showed everyone,

File Name: "Protocol ECHO - Restricted Access"
Location: A hidden folder on an old, nearly wiped computer
Last Modified: Right before I disappeared.

Inside the File: A single audio recording.

[PLAYING...] (Static. Heavy breathing. A faint clicking noise in the background—like someone checking a lock.)

Elliot Graves (whispering, urgent):
"If someone finds this... that means I failed."

(A muffled sound. Like he's moving—checking over his shoulder. Then—rushed typing.)

Elliot:
"I don't have much time. They know I'm onto them. They're already—" (static, cut-off noise) "—erasing everything. Every file. Every record. But they missed something. I missed something."

(Silence. A deep breath. Then—a single line, quieter than before.)

Elliot:
"It was never about the research."

(A loud noise. A door creaking. A voice in the background—distorted, unclear.)

Elliot (frantic, voice shaking):
"If you're hearing this, don't look for me. Look for—" (STATIC, FILE CORRUPTED)

[ERROR: AUDIO END]

Flynn stared at the screen, "We were never looking at the right thing."

"He tried to warn us. And we still don't know who he was warning us about." Ethan whispered, shook

"There's something else in here. We just need to decrypt it." Mia checked the file, her voice was tight,

And just like that, the chase isn't over. It's only just beginning.

A few minutes later...

Flynn was still rewinding the audio, heart pounding. Elliot's last words were cut off, but that wasn't all. Nathan was already working on restoring the file—and what he finds? Changes everything.

"Protocol ECHO - Restricted Access"

Audio: Elliot's final message (already heard)

Document Fragment (Mostly Erased)

Visible Text:

"If you're hearing this... don't look for me. Look for—"

[DATA CORRUPTED]

"Location: W█████... S████ Facility, ██ Sector."

"It's a place. He left a location." Flynn stared at the garbled text, his voice tight,

"But it's damaged. We need to figure out what 'W████ S████ Facility' means." Mia's eyes narrowed,

"I mean, cool and all, but what if he's dead?" Benji looked increasingly nervous,

"Then why was someone trying this hard to make sure we never found this?" Nathan is not looking up, working on decrypting the file,

Silence. They all know the answer. Because Elliot isn't just missing. Someone doesn't want him found. And now? They're going after him anyway.

5:07 PM

Nathan works fast, decrypting the corrupted data. The screen flickers, text rebuilding itself piece by piece. And then—finally—it reveals something that stops them cold.

"W███ S███ Facility, ██ Sector" → Revealed As...

"Willow Springs Research Facility – Decommissioned, ██ County"

"That's it. That's where he is." Ethan stared at the name, his voice was shaking,

"Then what the hell are we waiting for?" Flynn was already moving, grabbing his notebook,

And just like that, they have their next destination. Because if Elliot is still out there—this is where they'll find him.

Case #39

UPDATE

<u>The Hunt for Elliot Graves</u>

✓ Elliot Graves = ALIVE? (No confirmation, but why erase a dead man?)

✓ Willow Springs Research Facility = His Last Known Location. (Decommissioned. No public records. Suspicious.)

✓ Echelon DIDN'T expect us to find this. (Why hide this place specifically?)

✓ Noah = Knows more than he's saying. (He wants us to go there, but why?)

✓ Elliot's Final Words = "It was never about the research." (Then what the hell was it about?)

✓ Voicemail cut off. Warning unfinished. (Who was he afraid of?)

✓ Echelon watching us = CONFIRMED. (Threats, hacked messages. They know we're getting close.)

<u>Unanswered Questions</u>

? What did Elliot find at Willow Springs that got him erased?

? Who was he trying to warn us about? ("Don't look for me. Look for—" Who!?!?)

? Why did Echelon erase this location but not destroy it?

? What happens if we find Elliot before they do?

Just as they're about to leave, Nathan's laptop screen glitches. The cursor freezes. Then—suddenly—a pop-up window appears.

No sender. No origin.

Incoming Message:

"TURN BACK."

Silence. Then—another message appears.

"You're not the first ones to look for him. You won't be the last to disappear."

"They know." Flynn read it, his pulse spiked,

"Dude. Someone's living in your system right now." Benji whispered, gripped the chair,

The message deletes itself. The laptop screen returns to normal. But the damage is done. Because this isn't just paranoia anymore—they're being watched. And if they don't move fast, they might lose their only chance to find Elliot.

6:00 PM

They have returned. Now staying in Mia's house.

Mia's hands are already shaking when she pulls the curtain back. And then she sees it—a black car parked across the street. Engine off. Headlights dim. But it's there. Watching.

"Guys... we need to call the cops. Now." Mia whispered, backing away from the window,

Benji frantic, already dialing 911, "For once, I agree with Mia. This is some full-on horror movie nonsense."

911 Call Transcript:

Operator: "911, what's your emergency?"

Benji (fast, panicked): "Uh, yeah, hi, there's a super suspicious car outside my friend's place, and I think we're about to get kidnapped by a government-funded horror lab, so—"

Flynn (grabbing the phone, cutting in): "Black sedan. No plates. Been sitting there for at least 10 minutes."

Operator: "We're sending a unit to check it out."

But before they can even breathe—the car pulls away. No rush, no panic. Just a slow, deliberate exit. Like the driver knew they were watching back.

"They wanted us to see them." Nathan stared, his voice was cold.

"Shall we go? To the Willow Springs Research Facility?" Zane asked, everyone nodded.

6:12 PM

After everything—the dead ends, the erased files, the warnings—they finally reach Willow Springs.

"We will need a keycard here", Ethan said,

Flynn swiped the card in the door lock, it opened.

There were dust-covered computers. Faded blueprints. The hum of a dying generator.

"We should check the underground bunker", Mia said,

They went down...

A locked room—one they almost miss. Until Flynn sees the movement inside.

Flynn hesitated for half a second before shoving the door open. And there—in the dim light, disheveled, weak, but breathing—is **Elliot Graves. Alive. But Barely.**

"Elliot?" Ethan staggered forward, his voice breaking,

Silence. Elliot blinks. For a moment, he doesn't react. Then—his gaze sharpens. Recognition hits.

"...Ethan?" Elliot was stunned,

And just like that, the past crashes into the present.

Ethan choked back emotion, grabbing Elliot's arm, "I thought you were dead. I—I thought they—"

Elliot had a weak chuckle, shaking his head, "They tried."

Flynn crossed his arms, scanning him like a detective with too many questions, "How long have you been here?"

"Long enough to know we don't have time for this reunion." Elliot exhaled, his voice was dry.

"He's right. If we found him, that means they can, too." Mia whispered, looking around, her pulse racing,

"Okay, okay, wait—before we all die—someone explain how the hell we just rescued an actual ghost." Benji was still catching up, rubbed his temples.

6:22 PM

They are now back to Mia's house. Mia is still looking out from her window, having fear in her mind.

"It's so weird, that we haven't died yet!?" Benji was shocked and relieved.

"Power of plot armour," Nathan said,

"Maybe because we are literal highschoolers?? Either they thought that we wouldn't be much of a threat and just scare us with the help of Noah and all those pop-up messages. Or, they don't want any attention on them right now. Like, someone from our school must have overheard our little secret, it wouldn't be long to connect two dots," Zane explained his theories,

"I agree..." Elliot replied,

Benji took a deep breath.

"What was Echelon trying to hide?" Nathan asked,

Elliot leaned forward, voice low. His hands tremble—not from fear, but from exhaustion. From knowing too much.

"You think Echelon was just falsifying research? Lying for profit? No. That was just the surface. The real project—the thing they didn't want anyone to find—it was never about data. It was about control. They weren't just erasing people. They were rewriting them. Changing histories, altering identities, making sure the wrong people simply... ceased to exist. You don't fight something like that. You don't expose it. You either run, or you get rewritten too."

"Was Noah rewritten?" Mia asked,

"Yes, but not completely. Echelon brainwashed him into working for them, I think he wasn't fully rewritten like some of their other victims.

He still has fragments of his original self, but his loyalty to Echelon was manipulated. He believed he was making the right choice– even when it meant hurting Skyler." Elliot explained.

Silence. The group finally understands—they haven't just been investigating a crime. They've been playing against people who decide what's real. And now? They're in the system.

"We need to stop this system then!" Flynn said,

"We need proofs", Nathan said,

Everyone looked at each other.

"Alright– Here are the solid proofs we have:

1. Elliot's Testimony – The Whistleblower Who Survived

- Elliot Graves is living proof that Echelon erases people.
- He can name executives, projects, and locations involved in rewriting identities.
- His original whistleblower report (pre-erasure) was recovered.

2. The "Protocol ECHO" Files – Echelon's Blueprint for Rewriting People

- A hidden, nearly wiped document recovered from an old server.
- Mentions of erased employees, altered histories, and Echelon's process of identity manipulation.
- Before-and-after records of multiple people—some of whom no longer exist

3. Elliot's Final Voicemail – The Evidence He Left Behind

- A recording of Elliot before he disappeared, warning about Echelon.
- He says, "It was never about the research."
- The voicemail cuts off mid-sentence, suggesting someone silenced him.

4. The Financial Records – Proof of Shady Transactions

- Nathan uncovered bank statements linking Echelon to erased employees.
- Noah's name appears in these transactions, proving he was involved.
- The pattern of payments stops suddenly—right when Elliot vanished.

5. The Surveillance & Threats – Echelon Watching Them

- The hacked laptop message: "TURN BACK. YOU'RE TOO LATE."
- The black car that followed them, disappearing before police arrived.
- Someone actively trying to delete our research history in real time.

6. The Existence of Noah – Proof That Echelon Can Rewrite Minds

- Noah doesn't remember being manipulated—but the records show he was.
- His behavioral changes match Echelon's mind-rewriting methods.
- If Noah's memories can be restored, they have undeniable proof." Zane explained.

"We have everything. Almost. But it's not enough to expose them. We have to stop them." Flynn went through his notes, breathing hard,

"Then we find their last backup. We find the truth before they erase it for good." Elliot gripped the laptop, his voice was serious.

"If we leak this now, they'll come for us before it spreads." Mia typed furiously, eyes locked on the screen,

"Then we make it so big they can't stop it. We take this all the way." Ethan was determined, looking at Elliot,

And just like that, the war against Echelon enters its final stage. They have the proof. They just need to make sure the world sees it before it's too late.

Suddenly, Flynn's phone buzzes.

Gremlin With Wifi

@StirringPot: I can help.

@MainCharacterEnergy: How can I trust you?
@StirringPot: Sent a file.
@StirringPot: The backup server.
"Guys… I think we have found the evidence we needed," Flynn said to everyone, they were confused. He showed him the messages,
"Can we trust him? I don't", Benji asked,
"But he wouldn't send such a crucial archive…" Zane said,
"If he wants to help us, he has to give a testimony", Ethan said.
Gremlin With Wifi
@MainCharacterEnergy: You need to give a testimony
@StirringPot: ಠ(. _.) ಠ(. _.)
"He has sent two thumbs up emojis" Flynn said,
Elliot smiled.
"So… I guess we have all the proofs
7. The Backup Server – The Data Echelon Couldn't Erase

- The last archive.
- We can restore every erased person's true identity.

8. A Second Survivor – Someone Else Who Was Supposed to Be Gone

- If another erased person steps forward, it strengthens Elliot's case.
- What if one of them is already being rewritten—memories changing, records vanishing? (Literally Noah)" Zane said.

Wednesday
26 March, 2025
7:36 AM
"How is your health now?" Jericho asked,
"Fine…" Skyler replied.
"You're taking your medicines, right?"
"Yes, Jeri,"
"**Fever** lasted pretty long, don't you think?"

"Yes, Jeri. I wasn't able to go to school for a few days. Glad I am fine now"

Jericho turns on the television.

"BREAKING NEWS: Echelon Data Solutions SHUT DOWN After Shocking Revelations

Published: [26/03/2025] | Live Coverage from [News Network]" The news reporter said,

Jericho raised an eyebrow and looked at Skyler, "Sky, isn't it the company where you worked as an intern?"

Skyler looked at Jericho, "Yes. I realized that it was a fraud company, so I quit,"

"And Noah worked too? What happened to him?" Jericho asked,

"He–" There was a pause, "He was brainwashed and manipulated. He thought Vanguard or Echelon was a trusted company that cares about their employees and clients. I warned him, I tried to help him get out but... It was too late, I had to RUN," Skyler explained,

They continued to watch the news...

"Washington, D.C. – In a dramatic turn of events, **Echelon Data Solutions**, one of the most powerful corporate entities in the world, has been completely dismantled following a groundbreaking investigation that exposed **massive corruption, human rights violations, and identity erasure.**

Federal authorities, along with testimony from whistleblowers and leaked documents, have **confirmed years of illegal activity** orchestrated within the company—including falsified research, surveillance, and **the systematic deletion of individuals from records and history.**

The collapse of Echelon is being called one of the biggest corporate takedowns in modern history.

The Scandal: How Echelon Was Erasing People

Whistleblower Speaks Out – "They Tried to Make Sure I Never Existed"

Elliot Graves, a former data manager who disappeared without a trace, resurfaced with proof that Echelon was not just fabricating data—but **erasing people entirely**.

"They don't just silence you. They rewrite you," Graves stated in a shocking testimony.

Leaked files labeled **"Protocol ECHO"** confirm that employees who got too close to the truth were wiped from existence.

<u>Corruption, Fraud & A Digital Cover-Up</u>

Financial records show **millions in secret transactions** to erase whistleblowers.

Internal emails reveal executives **knew and approved of identity manipulation**.

Employees who questioned Echelon's ethics **vanished from company records**.

<u>Surveillance & Psychological Manipulation</u>

Investigators uncovered **evidence of hacking, anonymous threats, and real-time digital erasure**.

A leaked voicemail from Graves confirmed that he was being hunted before he disappeared.

Several former employees have **filed lawsuits**, claiming they were forced to disappear.

<u>The Fallout: Echelon Collapses, Leaders Missing</u>

Echelon's CEO & top executives have gone missing amid criminal investigations.

Company stock hit absolute zero overnight.

Protests erupt outside Echelon's former headquarters.

Government agencies confirm full-scale investigation.

FBI officials released a statement:

"This isn't just corporate fraud. This is a direct violation of human rights. And we intend to hold those responsible accountable."

Authorities are now searching for **hidden** data archives that might contain the **identities of erased individuals**.

The mysterious **"Project Lazarus"** file suggests that **Echelon was preparing for something even bigger**.

Flynn Hayes, one of the lead investigators who helped bring Echelon down, stated:

"We stopped them from rewriting history. But the question is—how much did they already change?"

Stay with us for live updates on the Echelon scandal.

#EchelonExposed | #JusticeForElliot | #WhoElseWasErased"

"FLYNN!?" Jericho stood up suddenly, "Sky, you heard that too, right!? Flynn Hayes, one of the lead investigators who helped bring Echelon down."

Skyler was surprised too, "What…"

9:37 AM

One by one, the people Echelon thought were silenced step into the light. Their stories are different, but they all prove one thing—this was never just a company. It was a machine built to erase the past.

Key Testimonies from Former Employees

1. Dr. Caroline Ross – The Scientist Who Refused to Lie

A former lead researcher, Caroline was forced to falsify data for high-profile clients.

When she refused, her credentials were revoked, her work stolen, and her professional record altered to make her seem incompetent.

Dr. Ross on the stand, voice firm,

"Echelon didn't just manipulate data. They manipulated lives. I watched colleagues vanish overnight. And I almost became one of them."

2. Adrian Kim – The Engineer Who Discovered "Protocol ECHO"

Adrian worked in Echelon's data security division.

He stumbled upon files containing identity rewrites—before-and-after records of people who had been erased.

The moment he tried to report it? His own employee ID stopped working.

Adrian testifying, shaking his head,

"I went home that night, and when I came back—my office was cleared. My logins were gone. According to their records, I never worked there."

3. Lisa Moreno – The Journalist Who Got Too Close

Lisa was working on a story about corporate data manipulation.

She uncovered Echelon's ties to government black-budget projects.

Before she could publish, she was fired, her article deleted, and she was blacklisted from every major news outlet.

Lisa speaking to reporters, voice sharp,

"They controlled the media. They decided which stories lived and which ones died. But they can't silence me now."

The Ripple Effect – More Voices Join the Fight

Hundreds of former employees came forward.

Survivors of Echelon's "erasure" testify, proving the extent of identity manipulation.

Families of missing employees demand justice.

More whistleblowers reveal years of corruption.

Evidence of identity manipulation is officially recognized in court.

The verdict is clear: Echelon didn't just break laws. It tried to rewrite reality itself. And now? The truth is finally winning.

12:31 PM

Echelon spent years burying the truth. Now? The law is digging it all back up.

The government has frozen all their assets, which include: Every bank account, investment, and offshore fund is seized. Shareholders have lost everything—Echelon's stock value drops to zero. Lawsuits pile up—from former employees, erased victims, and even ex-clients who were misled.

Thursday

27 March, 2025

9:00 AM

BREAKING NEWS: Echelon's CEO CAPTURED After Weeks on the Run

Published: [27/03/2025] | Live Coverage from [News Network]

Washington, D.C. – After weeks of evading authorities, the infamous **CEO of Echelon Dominic Voss,** Data Solutions has been **captured and taken into federal custody.**

The arrest marks the final step in one of the biggest corporate scandals in modern history, following the company's complete collapse after whistleblower revelations exposed massive identity manipulation, financial fraud, and human rights violations.

<u>The Hunt for Echelon's Leader</u>

For weeks, the CEO's whereabouts were unknown, sparking speculation that they had fled the country. However, investigators—led by the very whistleblowers who took Echelon down—tracked suspicious offshore accounts and encrypted messages, leading authorities to a private compound outside the U.S.

<u>The Moment of Capture</u>

- Federal agents raided the hidden location at A High-Rise Penthouse Under a Fake Identity, Vincent Locke, where the CEO was found attempting to erase final records.
- Documents were seized, linking high-ranking officials to Echelon's operations.
- The CEO was arrested on-site without incident.

Flynn Hayes, one of the lead investigators who exposed Echelon, stated:

"They thought they could rewrite history. But now, the truth is catching up to them."

<u>The Charges & What Happens Next</u>

Criminal charges include:

Identity erasure & human rights violations

Corporate fraud & obstruction of justice

Destruction of evidence

Echelon is officially dissolved, and former employees are stepping forward with lawsuits.

Federal prosecutors confirm that the **CEO will face trial, with Elliot Graves and other survivors set to testify.**

The world is watching—and this time, Echelon can't rewrite the story.

Stay with us for live updates on the trial.

#EchelonExposed | #JusticeForElliot | #FinalReckoning

Skyler watched the news, listening to every detail. The name came again, "Flynn Hayes, one of the lead investigators who exposed Echelon"

Flynn Hayes.

She exhaled slowly, staring at the screen, but the words blur together. Echelon Exposed. CEO Captured. The System Falls.

He did it. He actually did it.

And of course, he did.

Because that's who he is. That's who he's always been. The detective, the relentless investigator, the idiot who never learned when to quit.

And she hated it.

Not because he was right. Not because he won. But because he got to the truth before she did.

Skyler Maddox should have been the one to unravel this mystery.

She was so close. She had the pieces, the connections, the words ready to expose it all. But while she was running in circles, Flynn was putting the puzzle together.

She clenched her fists. She should feel something—anger, disappointment, jealousy. But all she feels is... exhaustion.

Because the worst part?

She always knew, deep down, that if anyone was going to solve it first—it would be him.

She smiled.

10:00 AM

The air in the courtroom is heavy. The world is watching. Reporters scribble furiously, cameras flash, and the defendants—once the untouchable elite of Echelon Data Solutions—sit in silence, knowing they've already lost.

"Mr. Dominic Voss, do you deny that Echelon was actively erasing employees?" The prosecutor slammed a document on the table,

"Echelon was a research firm. Nothing more. Any discrepancies in employee records are purely administrative errors." Mr. Voss adjusted his tie, calm but cornered.

"Then explain why you personally signed off on 'Protocol ECHO,' the project designed to rewrite identities?" The prosecutor held up a printed email,

The CEO's jaw tightens. He says nothing. Murmurs ripple through the courtroom.

Elliot taking the stand, clearing his throat, staring directly at the CEO, "Four years ago, I worked for Echelon. I discovered what they were doing. And for that, they tried to erase me."

"Can you clarify what you mean by 'erase'?" The prosecutor asked,

"They didn't just fire me. They deleted me. Bank records gone. Apartment lease voided. My own family believed I had disappeared by choice because the records told them that. Echelon rewrote my life." Elliot's voice was steady, dead serious,

Defense Attorney was standing with a forced smile "Objection, your honor! Mr. Graves is clearly exaggerating—"

"Overruled. Continue, Mr. Graves." Judge firmly said,

The defense lawyer sits down, defeated. Elliot takes a deep breath and delivers the final blow.

"And I wasn't the only one. I have proof. Records of others who were erased. Some of them—are in this very room." Elliot said.

Noah hesitated before taking the stand. He looked different—more himself, less of the conditioned pawn Echelon turned him into. But his voice is steady when he speaks.

Noah looked at the jury, then at Elliot, "They rewrote me. I don't know when it started, I don't know how deep it went—but I know one thing. The person I became? He wasn't me. And Echelon did that."

"Why did you stay?" Prosecutor softly asked,

"Because they made me believe I wanted to." Noah exhaled, gripping the stand tighter,

The words hit the courtroom like a thunderclap. Even the judge seems shaken. The jurors exchange glances. The CEO, for the first time, looks nervous.

Prosecutor turned to the jury, gesturing to the witnesses, "These are not just employees. These are people whose lives were rewritten, stolen, and buried. And the ones responsible? They are sitting right there."

"There's no proof this was intentional—" The Defense Attorney weakly said,

Prosecutor cutting in, slamming a final piece of evidence on the desk, "Then explain why we recovered Echelon's last remaining backup server—with every erased record still intact."

The courtroom erupts. Gasps. Reporters rush to write down the revelation. The CEO looks like he's seen a ghost. Because this is the moment he knows it's over.

Jury Foreman stood, voice clear, "On the charges of corporate fraud, human rights violations, and identity erasure... we find the defendants guilty on all counts."

The CEO and top executives are sentenced to federal prison. Echelon's assets are seized, and the company is permanently erased.

The trial becomes one of the most watched legal cases in history.

Mia watched the CEO being led away, shaking her head, "They spent years erasing people. And now? They're the ones being erased."

"Dude. You just took down a literal corrupt empire. What do you do now?" Benji grinned, nudging Flynn,

Flynn smirked, exhaling deeply, "...Sleep."

And just like that, Echelon is over. But the scars they left behind? Those will take longer to fade.

11:02 AM

Elliot and Ethan came to Flynn,

"Thank you..."

"Thank you for saving me,"

Flynn looked at them, he smiled, "I had no choice. I had to do it... If we haven't done this, we could have never seen this,"

A few minutes later...

Noah sat with Flynn,

"So...?" Flynn asked,

"You were right. Thanks for saving me," Noah sighed,

"Serena was afraid for you..."

"I know. She also tried to warn me, but I didn't listen to her,"

"Well... It's over,"

"Yeah... Life was better when I was hating on everyone, I didn't realize I changed,"

"You do now"

Noah looked at Flynn, and nodded.

CHAPTER XIII

The Truth Refuses To die

Flynn:

Thursday

27 March, 2025

9:55 PM

This case was different.

Not just because it was bigger, not just because it nearly killed me (multiple times), but because it wasn't just a case. It was personal.

I spent years thinking I was the one unraveling the truth, but now I realize—I was unraveling, too.

This wasn't some mystery in a locked room. This was real. Real people, real lives, real consequences. I watched a man who had been erased fight to prove he existed. I watched a friend break apart and try to put himself back together. I watched a company burn to the ground because it deserved to.

And I? I walked away from it. I survived.

But that doesn't mean I won.

Winning would mean this never happened in the first place. Winning would mean Elliot never had to hide, Noah never had to be rewritten, and we never had to fight to be remembered.

But if there's one thing I learned, it's this—the truth doesn't erase itself.

Someone has to fight for it.

And for the first time? I think I'm done fighting.

For now.

Skyler:

Thursday

27 March, 2025

9:58 PM

Flynn did it.

And for the first time in my life, I'm not mad about losing.

I should have been the one to solve this. I had the information, the experience, the instinct. I knew something was wrong before he did. But I also knew—I wasn't the right person to finish it.

Because I saw what Echelon really was a long time ago. And I still stayed.

I told myself it was just a job. That I was just writing reports, adjusting data, making small edits. That it didn't matter what the company was doing behind the scenes because it had nothing to do with me.

But then the edits became fabrications. The numbers became lies. And one day, I realized I wasn't just working for them—I was part of it.

That's when I ran.

That's when I learned the truth wasn't mine to reveal. Because I was in it too deep, because I let myself ignore it for too long.

But Flynn? He never stops. Even when it nearly destroys him, even when no one believes him, even when the answer turns out to be something he never wanted to find—he keeps going.

And that's why he deserved this.

So no, I don't hate him. I'm not bitter. I'm not jealous. I'm just... glad. Glad it was him. Glad the truth is out. Glad I don't have to carry this anymore.

For the first time in a long time, I feel free.

Friday

28 March, 2025

8:20 AM

The school halls are louder than ever. **Everyone** is talking about it. Because how could they not?

"THAT was Case #39??? DAMN!"

"Bro. BRO. Our school has an actual detective. What the hell."

"This is, like, Netflix documentary material."

"Imagine getting exposed by a high schooler, I'd just evaporate."

"No way he actually did all that. The news exaggerates everything."

"Bet it was the government and they're just using Flynn as a cover-up story."

"He probably just got lucky."

"Okay but... if they erased people, how do we know some of us weren't erased??"

"What if there's still a bigger cover-up we haven't seen yet?"

"Wake up, sheeple."

The conversations were not stopping.

8: 30 AM

The book club members have all gathered up, still confused about what just happened.

"Oh, so this he can figure out, but when it comes to literary analysis, he suddenly forgets how to think?" Riley crossed her arms, unimpressed,

"I hate that he was right. But, like, also... I don't?" Mia shook her head, but was secretly proud,

"He was so dramatic about it, too. He deserves this moment." Blake sipped her coffee, she smirked,

Ivy was stirring chaos, obviously, "So, do we nominate him for Student of the Year, or do we let his ego deflate first?"

Benji was in mild panic, "Wait—if Flynn's famous now, does that make me famous? Am I part of this story? Do I need, like, a disguise??"

8:36 AM

Finally, Flynn Everett Hayes walked into the school.

Silence. Then—someone claps. Then another. And another. Until half the hallway is cheering, shouting, filming.

"Yo, Flynn! Solve my math test next!" A random student shouted,

Someone in the background yelled, "BRO, SIGN MY NOTEBOOK, YOU'RE GONNA BE IN HISTORY BOOKS."

"I leave for one vacation and come back to this madness." Zane watched the chaos unfold, muttered,

Flynn? He just sighs, adjusts his bag, and keeps walking. Because at the end of the day? This was never about fame. It was about the truth. And now? Everyone knows it.

Students stared like he's the main character of a TV show. Someone started a slow clap that turns into full applause. Random people taking pictures like he's a celebrity. Benji yelled, "Y'ALL ARE ACTING LIKE HE JUST CAME BACK FROM WAR."

Flynn was deadpan, adjusting his bag, ignoring the chaos, "Y'all are acting like I took down the mafia."

"Bro. You kinda did." Benji whispered, still in disbelief.

And just like that, Flynn Hayes goes from resident disaster to school legend. What a timeline.

11: 23 AM

There was a book club meeting. All the members have gathered up. Everyone was looking at Flynn, some confused, some impressed, some doubtful.

"Flynn. I founded this club for literary discussion. Not for solving federal crimes." Riley said,

"Technically, I did both." Flynn innocently said,

"No, you did one of them horribly and the other too well." Riley was deadpan.

"I mean... this is actually kind of amazing? You literally saved people." Mia said,

Flynn rubbed his neck, "Yeah, I guess..."

"Flynn. You took down an entire corrupt corporation. You don't have to be humble about it." Mia said,

"I always knew you had an investigative streak, but this? This was something else." Blake said,

"Something good?" Flynn raised an eyebrow,

"Something reckless. But... yeah. Good." Blake smirked.

"So, did you ever consider writing about your experiences? I think we deserve a dramatic retelling." Ivy asked,

"I think I deserve a nap," Flynn replied.

"I suppose I must admit, I didn't think you were capable of anything beyond ridiculous theories. But I stand corrected." Serena said,

"...Wow. Thanks?" Flynn replied,

"Okay, but why am I not getting credit for emotional support throughout this entire mess?" Benji asked,

"Because you screamed 'we're all gonna die' at least six times," Flynn said,

"And yet, we did not die. You're welcome." Benji said,

"You know, when I left for Japan, you were just a kinda chaotic detective. Now you're basically a legend. What the hell happened?" Zane said,

"Turns out, I was right for once," Flynn said,

"I leave for one vacation..." Zane muttered.

"Statistically speaking, your survival rate in this investigation should have been much lower," Nathan said,

"Good thing I don't listen to statistics," Flynn replied.

Ethan was quiet for a moment, then finally spoke. "You didn't just solve a case, Flynn. You gave people their lives back."

"Yeah. I think I did." Flynn softly said.

"Honestly, this whole thing is insane. Like, how did no one stop you?" Jordan asked,

"Oh, they tried. They really tried." Flynn replied.

Noah was looking at Flynn, with an unreadable expression.

"...Thanks," Noah muttered,

"For what?" Flynn was surprised,

"For not giving up. Even when you should have." Noah said.

The attention was overwhelming. The school, the media, even the book club—everyone is treating him like the sole genius behind Echelon's downfall. But Flynn knows the truth. He didn't do this alone. And he refuses to let anyone forget that.

Flynn stood up, clearing his throat, looking at his team, "I know everyone's acting like I pulled this off by myself, but let's get one thing straight—I wouldn't have made it past the first clue without you guys."

"Oh? Are you actually admitting that you needed help?" Mia raised an eyebrow, amused,

"I am begrudgingly acknowledging that without you, I would have absolutely crashed and burned." Flynn grinned,

"Mia, you kept me grounded when I was about to spiral. You reminded me why this mattered when I started doubting. If anyone deserves credit for keeping me somewhat sane, it's you."

"Zane, you came back from your trip expecting peace, and instead, you walked into chaos. And even though you had every right to walk away, you stayed. You listened. And you noticed things that the rest of us missed. You were the outsider perspective we needed."

"Benji, you were there through every ridiculous moment, every bad idea, every near-death experience—and you still stuck around. You made me laugh when I needed it, even when we were running for our lives. Especially when we were running for our lives."

"Ethan, this wasn't just a mystery for you. It was personal. You lost someone to Echelon, and instead of letting it break you, you helped us take them down. You gave this investigation its heart. And I can't thank you enough for trusting me with it."

"Nathan. Stats guy. Human calculator. You probably thought this whole thing was insane from day one, and honestly, you were right. But you stayed. You gave us numbers when we had nothing but gut feelings. You analyzed every little detail, and we would've been lost without you."

"So, yeah. Everyone's calling me the hero. But the truth? We did this together. I don't care what anyone says—this was our victory." Flynn exhaled, looking at all of them.

Silence. Then—Benji claps. Then Mia. Then everyone. And for the first time in a long time, Flynn doesn't feel like he's carrying the weight of everything alone.

12:01 PM

Flynn has sat in a chair inside the book club. Reading The Hound of the Baskervilles by Sir Arthur Conan Doyle. For once, everything is over.

Then, he noticed his notebook on the table. He looks at his case #39 notes, and smiles, "I was so desperate..."

He looked at all the notes he made this month, he flipped a few pages back, "Oh my god? How can I forget all these!? Those interviews I somehow got," He chuckled.

Case #39

<u>RILEY DAVENPORT</u>
Full name: Riley Christine Davenport
Class: 12-B
Age: 17 (Seventeen)
Height: 5'7
Birthday: 14 February, 2008
MBTI: ESTJ
Role in Book Club: President
Relationship with Skyler: Hostile

Opinion on Skyler (Before & After):

Before: "Skyler had a way with words that could make you stop and think—when she actually cared, anyway."

After: "I don't know if I'm chasing the truth about her or just trying to prove to myself that she's still worth chasing."

Key Quotes:

- "Skyler could've been great—if she actually tried."
- "I don't have time for someone who refuses to take anything seriously."

What She Might Know: Riley likely knows that Skyler isn't as indifferent as she pretends to be—she just refuses to admit when she cares.

Suspicious Behavior: Riley has been actively trying to push Skyler out of the club for months, always quick to call her out while pretending it's just about maintaining standards.

NOTE: Riley HATES Skyler. She is tired of her.

<u>JORDAN PIERCE</u>
Full name: Jordan Archer Pierce
Class: 12-D
Age: 16 (Sixteen)
Height: 6'1

Birthday: 27 July, 2008
MBTI: ISTP
Role in Book Club: Member- Chaos Incoming
Relationship with Skyler: Disappointed

Opinion on Skyler (Before & After):

Before: "She had this confidence in her writing, like she knew exactly what she wanted to say and why it mattered."

After: "She's a lost cause, man. Just move on."

Key Quotes:

"Skyler Maddox was someone I used to look up to. Now? She's just another disappointment."

"She used to be someone worth listening to. Now, it's all just noise."

What He Might Know: Jordan might know that Skyler once had big aspirations, but something made her stop trying, and he can't figure out why.

Suspicious Behavior: Jordan still pays attention to Skyler, even though he claims he's done with her, muttering comments under his breath and keeping tabs on her writing.

NOTE: Jordan thinks I should stop. Suspicious. What is he trying to hide?

The door opens, and it was Jordan. Jordan had been avoiding the madness. He figured staying out of whatever Flynn and his chaotic group were up to was the safest choice. But now? There's no escaping it. Because Flynn Hayes is literally all over the news.

"Okay. Let me get this straight. You literally exposed a shady company, possibly brought down half of the corrupt elite, and still managed to stay in school?" Jordan sighed dramatically,

"That's what we do. We balance things." Flynn shrugged nonchalantly,

Jordan threw his hands up in the air, "No, no. This is insane. I thought I was coming back to a book club, not a criminal investigation team! What next? Do you plan on exposing a government conspiracy? Or maybe you'll solve a cold case and finally become a real detective?"

"Honestly? Wouldn't be surprised if he did. Dude's probably got an FBI contract somewhere." Benji grinned,

"This is why I can't trust you guys. I leave for five weeks and you've gone full-on Scooby-Doo with a side of Jack Bauer." Jordan shook his head,

"You're still the only one who's shocked by this, Jordan." Mia chuckled,

Flynn smiled, a glint in his eye, "Hey, maybe next time, you should stay for the chaos. You know, so you can say you were part of the investigation, too."

Jordan groaned, walking towards the door, "Nope. I'll pass. You guys are too much for me. Good luck with your next world domination plan."

"See you in the next season, Jordan!" Benji called after him.

2:31 PM

Flynn's phone buzzes. He checks his email.

Email from Riley Davenport to Flynn Hayes – Subject: Interview Request

From: Riley Davenport (r.davenport@schoolnews.org)

To: Flynn Hayes (f.hayes@studentmail.com)

Subject: Interview Request – Don't Ignore This, Hayes

Flynn,

I can't believe I'm about to say this, but—I need an interview with you.

The school paper wants an exclusive piece on the whole Echelon takedown, and apparently, since you're the detective of the century now (God help us all), you're the only one who can give us the details firsthand.

Here's the deal:

Date: ASAP (Seriously, don't make me chase you down.)

Location: School library, second floor (Where book-related discussions are supposed to happen.)

Time Limit: 30 minutes max (I know you like to ramble, Hayes.)

Topics: The case, the investigation, your sudden rise to fame, and how

the hell you managed to do all this when you can barely focus on a single book in this club.

I already know you'll try to dodge this, so let me be clear: If you ignore this email, I will publish an article titled "Flynn Hayes Refuses to Speak — What Is He Hiding?" and make your life hell.

See you soon, detective.

- Riley Davenport

(Also the) Editor-in-Chief, School News

"We Report, You Read, He Regrets."

He then gets a message from Riley.

Book Club Dictator

@FinalBossReads: Flynn. Check your email.

@MainCharacterEnergy: I did. I was hoping if I ignored it long enough, you'd forget.

@FinalBossReads: Oh, trust me. I never forget.

@MainCharacterEnergy: Wow. Terrifying. Fine, you win. I'll do the interview. But no autographs, okay? I'm very exclusive.

@FinalBossReads: You're an exclusive pain in my ass, that's what you are.

@MainCharacterEnergy: Flattering. So what's the angle here? "Local Book Club Disaster Accidentally Destroys Corrupt Corporation" or "Flynn Hayes, Investigative Genius"?"

@FinalBossReads: Oh, I was thinking more along the lines of "Flynn Hayes Finally Uses His Brain for Something Productive."

@MainCharacterEnergy: Ouch. You wound me.

@FinalBossReads: Not as much as this interview is going to. Library. Tomorrow. Don't be late.

@MainCharacterEnergy: I'll be there. But if you quote me out of context, I'm suing.

@FinalBossReads: Please. Like you can afford a lawyer.

@MainCharacterEnergy: ...Fair point.

Saturday

29 March, 2025

11:30 AM

The library. Second floor. Flynn slouches in his chair, looking way too relaxed for someone about to be interviewed. Riley, on the other hand? Not amused. She has a notepad, a recorder, and the patience of a person who has already accepted that this is going to be painful.

Riley pressed record, deadpan, "Alright, Hayes. Let's get this over with. First question—how does it feel to be the guy who took down a corrupt billion-dollar corporation?"

"Pretty good. But honestly? I was hoping for a trophy or at least a free coffee. Turns out, all you get is exhaustion and mild paranoia." Flynn leaned back, smirked,

Riley was already rubbing her temples, "God. Okay. Next—how did you even realize something was wrong in the first place?"

"Well, Riley, I used my highly advanced detective skills—" Flynn grinned,

"So Benji found something by accident?"

"Okay, first of all? Rude. But also... not entirely wrong."

"What was the most dangerous moment during the investigation?"

"Oh, definitely when Benji tried to convince me that breaking into Skyler's locker was 'a small crime, at best.'"

"...That wasn't the part where you almost got erased from existence?"

"Nah, that was second place."

"Some people are calling you a genius. Some think you just got lucky. What do you say to that?"

"I say... why not both?" Flynn smirked,

"Flynn."

"Riley."

"Fine. Do you have any advice for aspiring detectives?" Riley sighed, flipping to a new page,

"Yeah. Get a friend who screams when things go wrong so you know when to run."

"...I assume you're talking about Benji?"

"Who else?"

Halfway through the interview, Riley realizes Flynn isn't the only chaotic problem she has to deal with—because this investigation? It wasn't a solo act. And Flynn is about to make sure his team gets their credit—whether they want it or not.

"Alright, since you clearly refuse to take this seriously—let's talk about the people who actually helped." Riley raised an eyebrow, flipping to a new page,

"Finally. Some real questions." Flynn grinned.

"Mia is the reason I'm not currently in jail, probably. She reminded me that this case wasn't just about proving I was right—it was about doing the right thing. I ignored her advice constantly, but in the end, she was always right."

"Zane left for vacation and came back to absolute chaos. And instead of running the other way like any reasonable person, he got roped into the madness. I think he regrets it daily, but hey, we needed his perspective. Also, he might actually be the only sane one here."

"I don't think Benji realized what he signed up for. He thought this was going to be some fun detective work—then suddenly, we're breaking into places and running for our lives. But despite the screaming and occasional panic attacks, he never left. And, uh... that means a lot."

"For Ethan, this wasn't just a mystery. This was about family. He had every reason to walk away, but instead, he fought for the truth. And honestly? I don't think we would've made it without him."

"Nathan gave us numbers when we had nothing but gut feelings. He broke down data, found patterns, and honestly, I think he was the only one actually thinking logically the entire time. Which is terrifying, considering we ignored half his warnings."

"...Okay. That was surprisingly genuine. I almost didn't recognize you for a second." Riley said after a long pause,

"Hey, even I have my moments," Flynn smirked.

"Last question. What's next for you? Planning on solving another massive conspiracy?"

"I think I'll take a break. But, you know... if another case finds me, who am I to say no?"

"I swear to God, Hayes, if you drag this school into another high-stakes disaster—" Riley, shutting her notebook, glared at him,

"Can't make any promises, Davenport." Flynn stood up, smirking.

Three days later...

Tuesday

1 April, 2025

9:04 AM

The Detective of Ravenshore Academy– An Exclusive Interview with Flynn Hayes
By Riley Davenport, Editor-in-Chief

If you had asked me a year ago who in our school was most likely to bring down a corrupt corporation, my answer would have been simple: absolutely no one.

And yet, somehow, Flynn Hayes—resident book club disaster, human embodiment of chaotic energy, and the guy who once argued that "symbolism is overrated"—managed to do exactly that.

In an exclusive (and, unfortunately, very sarcastic) interview, Hayes shared the details of the investigation that exposed Echelon Data Solutions, took down a multimillion-dollar conspiracy, and made him an unexpected legend.

"It feels great," Hayes told me, leaning back in his chair like a guy who hasn't just caused national headlines but is actively enjoying it. "But honestly? I was hoping for a trophy or at least a free coffee. Turns out, all you get is exhaustion and mild paranoia."

Despite the jokes, it's clear that this wasn't a one-man operation. Hayes repeatedly emphasized that he couldn't have done it alone, crediting his investigation team:

Mia Langley – "The reason I'm not in jail, probably."

Zane Lockwood – "The one who left for a vacation and came back to pure chaos."

Benji Torres – "The emotional support disaster."

Ethan Rhodes – "The one who made it personal—and made it

matter."

Nathan Holloway – "The only logical person in this mess (and we ignored half his warnings)."

So, what's next for Ravenshore Academy's accidental detective?

"I think I'll take a break," Hayes said, smirking in a way that suggests he absolutely will not. "But, you know... if another case finds me, who am I to say no?"

The second the article drops, the school explodes. Hallways are buzzing, memes are being made, and Flynn? He suddenly has way more attention than he ever wanted.

"Wait, WAIT. So Flynn Hayes wasn't just making stuff up this whole time??"

"Bro, we really let Flynn Hayes take down a billion-dollar corporation before any of us even passed calculus."

"I thought this was a joke article. But no. It's real. And I am questioning reality."

"Okay but what if this is just what they WANT us to think? What if Echelon is still out there?"

"I need to see proof. Like real proof. What do you mean there's actual court documents??"

"Protect this man at all costs."

"Wait, is he single?"

Meanwhile in the book club...

Riley pinched the bridge of her nose, "I wrote this article to give people context, not to create a fan club."

Benji grinned, scrolling through memes, "Bro. You're famous. You're basically a celebrity detective now."

"Kill me." Flynn was deadpan, sipping his coffee,

"I leave for a week, and you become an internet sensation. This is why I don't take breaks." Zane watched the chaos unfold,

"There is an 87% probability that you will get at least three interview requests by the end of the day." Nathan analyzed the statistics,

"I give it a week before someone starts calling him 'Detective Hayes.'" Mia said,

"You know, you could capitalize on this. Write a book, give speeches—" Ethan smirked, nudging to Flynn,

"I am begging you to stop," Flynn said.

9:08 AM

Skyler stared at her phone. At the headlines. At the memes. At Flynn Hayes, standing in the center of it all like he was meant to be there. Like he was born for this moment. And for the first time in a long time, she doesn't know how she feels.

Skyler:

This should have been me.

I was the one who saw Echelon's true colors before anyone else. I was the one who worked for them, who knew what they were capable of. I was the one who could have exposed them.

*And yet—**it wasn't me.***

It was Flynn. Of all people, it was Flynn Hayes. The same guy who spent more time making a mess of book club discussions than actually reading. The guy who used to throw out the worst theories just to make people react. The guy I thought was too much of a disaster to ever be taken seriously.

*But now? **The world is taking him seriously**. And I have to sit here and watch it happen.*

And the worst part?

I'm not even mad.

*I thought this would destroy me. I thought watching him solve the puzzle I couldn't would eat me alive. But instead, all I feel is... tired. Maybe even relieved. Because if it had been me—if I had been the one to expose Echelon—**would anyone have believed me?***

Flynn was never meant to be the villain in this story. Maybe I wasn't meant to be the hero.

Maybe this was never my story to tell.

And maybe... I'm okay with that.

*For the first time in a long time, I don't have to run. I don't have to fight to prove what I know. Because now, **the truth is out**. And for once? **I'm free.***

She exhaled, setting her phone down. A final look at the article, a small smirk pulling at the corner of her lips.

"Guess I underestimated you, Flynn."

CHAPTER XIV

The Words She Never Said

- Tuesday

8 April, 2025
6:22 AM
<u>FLYNN HAYES</u>
Full name: Flynn Everett Hayes
Class: 12-B
Age: 17 (Seventeen)
Height: 5'9
Birthday: 8 April, 2008
MBTI: ENFJ
Role in Book Club: Member- Walking Disaster
Relationship with Skyler: Unstable

Opinion on Skyler (Before & After):
Before: "I admired Skyler—her writing, her mind, the way she saw the world—but I don't think I ever really understood her."
After: "I don't know if I'm chasing the truth about her or just trying to prove to myself that she's still worth chasing."
Key Quotes:

- "Skyler Maddox is a puzzle I can't solve, and maybe that's what keeps me coming back."
- "Skyler's not heartless. If anything, she feels too much—it's just buried under all the walls she's built."

What He Might Know: Flynn might not have all the answers, but he knows one thing for sure—Skyler is hiding something, and whatever it is, it's tearing her apart.

Suspicious Behavior: Flynn obsesses over Skyler's actions more than he should, collecting details, overanalyzing her words, and chasing after answers even when it's clear she doesn't want him to find them.

NOTE: Flynn wouldn't let go of Skyler.

THE LITERARY COURTROOM

@SoftHeartedButNosy: Happy birthday, Flynn! Hope you have a great day! ★·° ᵕ *

@CertifiedChaos: HBD BRO!! Another year older, another year dumber B-)

@MainCharacterEnergy: Wow. What a heartfelt message.

@TiredButTrying: Happy birthday. No gift, but I won't insult you today.

@MainCharacterEnergy: I feel so blessed.

@FinalBossReads: Try not to cause an existential crisis today, yeah?

@MainCharacterEnergy: I make no promises.

@DataOrPerish: Statistically, you have survived another year. Probability of survival for the next one? Still uncertain.

@MainCharacterEnergy: So encouraging. Thanks, Nathan.

@FrontRowForChaos: Damn, I should've planned a murder mystery party for this.

@LowkeySkylerStan: You mean he doesn't already live in one?

@PlaysChessNotCheckers: Let's be real, the real mystery is how Flynn has lived this long with his choices.

@MainCharacterEnergy: You're all terrible. Except Mia.

@SoftHeartedButNosy: Aw, thanks! ^_^

@CertifiedChaos: Bro, what about me?

@MainCharacterEnergy: No.

@ShouldIBringACake: Wait. Why did I just find out it's your birthday from this chat?

@MainCharacterEnergy: Because I didn't want attention??

@FrontRowForChaos: LMAO, tragic. Anyway, happy birthday, Detective Dumbass.

@StirringPot: Wow. Can't believe I have to wish you a happy birthday after all the mess you put me through.

@MainCharacterEnergy: Noah, you literally blackmailed people.

@StirringPot: Yeah, and I regret it. But let's not make today about me.

@WrongPlaceWrongTime: Happy birthday, man. Hope this year is less chaotic than the last.

@MainCharacterEnergy: You know that won't happen.

@WrongPlaceWrongTime: Yeah. But I figured I'd try to manifest it.

7:59 AM

At school, everything feels normal.... **Too normal.**

People were saying "Happy birthday" when they passed Flynn in the halls. Benji was dramatically singing a birthday song that no one asked for. Riley sarcastically tells him "Try not to destroy anything today." Everything is fine. Everything should feel fine.

"**Four** birds in a trench coat would still be smarter than you." "After three comes **four**, unless you're counting wrong again"

"**Four** ducks in a row... wait, where's the fifth one?"

Flynn heard many random conversations in the hall, but one thing... one thing he was constantly hearing. FOUR. As if the number four is always coming up.

He was passing by 11-B when he saw Skyler, standing near the corridor. Flynn is used to Skyler looking bored, irritated, or vaguely condescending. But today? Today, she looks at him like she's expecting something. Like she's waiting for him to realize something.

11:42 AM

At the cafeteria, they meet again, sharing a glance at each other. Skyler passes Flynn hesitating for just a second before mumbling:

"...*Happy birthday, Flynn.*"

It sounds forced. Like there's something else she wants to say but won't. Flynn watches her walk away, stomach twisting.

Flynn:

This day feels weird. The conversation in the hall, I don't know why I overheard them, but I was able to hear only one thing, FOUR. What does this mean? Skyler was acting weird too. She wasn't the usual Skyler I knew... Does she want to tell me something?

Skyler:

Yes, I do want to tell him. I think it's time for him not to wait so much. The guilt has started eating me, I have to tell him. I can't keep it with myself. Not any longer. I tried too. But... my voice became silent, nothing came out of my mouth even though I tried. How can I tell him then? Would he realize it, before it is too late? Because I had enough of this!

12:00 PM

"Children, take out your rough copy" The teacher said.

Flynn was sitting in his classroom, attending a class, but still thinking about the whole day...

He takes a random note from his bag, he opened it. Something was written in it.

I think I finally figured it out, but—

Flynn was confused, "I don't remember writing this," He thought. And ignores it and starts focusing on the class.

After class, Flynn looks at the sky from the window.

Suddenly, it hits him out of nowhere. A sudden, sharp feeling—like déjà vu, but heavier. Like something that was buried deep is trying to crawl back up.

• • •

Four years ago...

The library was quieter than usual. A thin layer of dust clung to the old books, the air still and heavy. Skyler stood in front of him, younger, different. There was no coldness in her eyes, no sharpness in her tone. Just... hesitation.

"Flynn." Her voice was softer back then. Less guarded. "Do you ever think about the way people see you?"

Flynn frowned. "What kind of question is that?"

Skyler didn't answer right away. She was looking at him like she wanted to say something else. Something bigger. But instead, she just sighed and shook her head.

"Never mind." She turned away, flipping through the pages of a book she wasn't reading.

Flynn, always one to fill silence with nonsense, grinned. "People probably remember me for my genius theories and incredible charm. Obviously."

Skyler huffed a small, breathy laugh. But there was no humor in it.

"Yeah," she murmured, voice unreadable. "That's what they remember."

Flynn blinked. "Huh?"

She wasn't looking at him anymore. Just staring at the book, as if the words on the page mattered more than whatever she had just said. Like it wasn't important.

And then—

• • •

And then—nothing. The memory cuts off. He doesn't remember what happened next. He doesn't remember what she told him. But he remembers the way she looked at him.

Like she already knew something he didn't.

Like she was warning him.

Like this moment changed everything.

He blinked. He's still in his room, phone buzzing with birthday messages. But his heart is racing. His hands feel clammy. Because now, one thought is screaming in his head—**what did she mean?**

Flynn:

I lost sight of everything.

For the past one month, I've been chasing something bigger. Echelon, the blackmail, the conspiracy—I thought that was the answer.

I thought if I kept digging, if I kept solving the next mystery, I'd find what I was looking for.

But the truth was never about Echelon.

It was about this.

Four years ago, something happened. I remember just enough to know that.

But now—the memory cuts off.

Why?

Why did my mind just stop there? What else happened in that moment?

Why did Skyler start pulling away the very next day?

What if everything I've been chasing—the lies, the erasures, the things people wanted to forget—was right in front of me the whole time?

Because this isn't just some random memory, I didn't pull this out of nowhere.

Something made me remember.

And if it's coming back now, after all this time...

Then maybe it's because I'm finally ready to see it.

12:56 PM

Zane was seeing Flynn aggressively writing in his diary,

"Bro, you okay?" He was concerned,

"No" Flynn shook his head,

"What do you mean?"

"Case #39 is not solved!!'

"Huh? We just solved—"

"That's not Case #39. Case #39 was finding what happened to Skyler. Find THE INCIDENT. This is still incomplete. I... I have to find what happened, four... four years ago. Something happened between us, 'I think I finally figured it out. But–' My past self knew that. But, why can't I remember it?!"

"You should remember the day when it happened, right? When Skyler started acting weird?" Zane suggested.

"2021. Four years ago... Around March-April"

"You should check your diary. You must have written about it if it happened 'between you two'"

"Yeah! I should check it out!!"

3:02 PM

Flynn ran to his house, he looked at his shelf, which was filled with many books. Some included his mystery books, school books. Rough notebooks and diaries.

He starts looking at the diary section, "2019...2022...2024...2020..2023...2021"
He finally found it. He was closer to the truth, finally, his questions will be answered.

He reads every page, trying to find the day when THE INCIDENT occurred.

A few minutes of reading his old diary entries, he found it. 22 March, 2021.

Monday

22 March, 2021

9:53 PM

I don't even know why I said it. We were in the library.

We were just talking. The way we always did—throwing ideas around, poking fun, making sarcastic comments that didn't mean anything. And then, somewhere in all of that, I said it.

"People like you as an author, not as a person."

I don't remember her exact reaction. I just remember the way she paused, her smirk faded just for a second. How she blinked, like she had to make a conscious effort not to react.

And then, she laughed. A quiet, almost empty kind of laugh. Like she was agreeing with me. Like I had just confirmed something she already believed.

I didn't think anything of it at the time.

I should have.

• • •

Tuesday

23 March, 2021

9:45 PM

Skyler is avoiding me.

Not in a dramatic way. Not in a way anyone else would notice. But I can feel it.

stomach twist.

"Then what else was it?" Flynn asked

Skyler tilted her head, eyes dark and thoughtful. And when she speaks, her voice is calm. Too calm.

Skyler tilts her head, like she's watching something unfold in slow motion. Something she's seen coming for a long, long time.

"You really thought that was it?"

She doesn't sound surprised. She sounds... disappointed.

Flynn's stomach drops.

Skyler tilts her head, watching as Flynn struggles to piece it together.

"You really thought that was it?" she whispered

Flynn's chest tightens.

Skyler steps forward. There's no anger, no satisfaction—just something unreadable in her expression.

"Flynn... you still don't get it."

The world seems to tilt. A sharp, heavy silence fills the space between them. And just like that—Flynn realizes he's about to learn the real truth.

"The reason I stopped writing was that everyone loved the idea of my work but not the actual content. If you were allowed to become an author, you might enjoy it too. I didn't. In fact, I never did; I HATED it! Writing any story became an unhappy experience for me because I knew that nobody other than my brother and I would read it. It felt forced, and I became increasingly discontent.

I often questioned why a crime story writer like myself would suddenly turn to writing children's stories because someone said to write. I produced some mediocre material—ten times over—and, somehow, I gained popularity, despite never intending for that to happen.

I didn't like it when people asked me to write stories that they wanted to read, especially when they wouldn't spend a single dime on reading a fiction book. It felt like **everyone loved my fame, not me**, and that was the only thing I appreciated. I began writing because I loved it, not for anyone else. I was writing for myself, but when I shared it with the world, no one seemed to care.

It was maddening to live in that bubble of lies. Why wasn't I hearing things like, "I loved your story! I liked that character; I appreciated the impact"? It was always... nothing. I was never appreciated for my work. People loved the idea of me being an author, but if you asked them what genre I wrote in, they wouldn't be able to tell you—because they hadn't read any of my books!

I was proud of my stories; they played a significant role in my life and contributed to my happiness. But after realizing the truth, I saw no point in continuing. And so, I just left it all behind. You know what, **no one will even read this**, it's just the author and the editor."

"What... Who are you talking to?" Flynn asked,

Skyler looks at the ground, *"Wish I could say, the reader,"* She *exhaled sharply, "But really... there's no one"*

"Another reason is that some people believe it is good to make someone do something they dislike. My parents often tell me that I should write again. Well, here it is—the reason I stopped writing for so many years. But what's the point? It's not like you'll read it. If you did, you wouldn't pressure me into chasing a few moments of popularity. I enjoyed pottery and reading, but no! You wanted me to become an author, which I will forever resent. FOREVER.

You know what's frustrating? Now, people seem to appreciate me for all the wrong reasons. I feel embarrassed when I realize that a story written with little effort gets more attention than one I've worked hard on. I just don't understand how that happens. "Mystery of a Serial Killer" is one of the worst stories I've ever written—it was created by an eleven-year-old and was meant to be bad. I can't wrap my head around why it gained popularity. It demotivates me. What's the point of putting thought into plots and truly developing my characters when it seems all it takes is writing "horror stories made for children's spoofs"? That's when I started to lose hope and decided I didn't want to invest any more effort or energy into my stories. If stories are supposed to be alive, then I guess mine were never meant to breathe."